"I picked flowers for you..." Josie lifted them up for him to see.

Josie's daughter held out the jam jar for Heath to take.

"That's really nice. I'd invite you all in but the house is like an oven." He shook his head. "How about a seat on the porch?" He gestured to the white wicker chairs. "I made iced tea."

Her daughter grinned. "We don't have air conditioning either, but our house is really old with stone walls. Mom looks real hot, though. See? Her cheeks are all red."

"Lottie... I... We... I'm fine. It's a warm day, that's all." Josie gave her daughter a reproving look and sank onto another chair as her mouth went dry. Stopping for iced tea gave her the perfect opportunity to ask Heath about Bea's house, but she'd counted on being calm, cool and collected, not flustered, embarrassed and wrong-footed before she'd even started.

That tingle was definitely attraction. Now she had to steel herself not to react to it.

Dear Reader,

This story is first in my new Strawberry Pond miniseries for Harlequin Heartwarming. Set around a charming fictional small town in the beautiful White Mountains, Strawberry Pond is inspired by real places I've visited on happy New Hampshire vacations.

In *The Hero Next Door*, Josie Ryan, a single mom of two adorable daughters, lives with her grandparents and farms land that's been in her family for generations. Josie's content with her life until fish-out-of-water Boston financial analyst Heath Tremblay inherits the property next door—and upends her safe and predictable routine.

I was lucky to grow up in a loving multigenerational family, and some of my own experiences helped shape this story. It was also fun to write an opposites-attract book as, like my hero and heroine, when I first met my now husband, I thought we had nothing in common. How wrong I was!

I enjoy hearing from readers, so visit my website, jengilroy.com, and message me there, where you'll find my social media links and newsletter sign-up too.

Happy reading!

Jen

THE HERO NEXT DOOR

JEN GILROY

Harlequin
HEARTWARMING

If you purchased this book without a cover you should be aware that this book is stolen property. It was reported as "unsold and destroyed" to the publisher, and neither the author nor the publisher has received any payment for this "stripped book."

Harlequin®
HEARTWARMING™

Recycling programs for this product may not exist in your area.

ISBN-13: 978-1-335-46016-5

The Hero Next Door

Copyright © 2025 by Jen Gilroy

All rights reserved. No part of this book may be used or reproduced in any manner whatsoever without written permission.

Without limiting the author's and publisher's exclusive rights, any unauthorized use of this publication to train generative artificial intelligence (AI) technologies is expressly prohibited.

This is a work of fiction. Names, characters, places and incidents are either the product of the author's imagination or are used fictitiously. Any resemblance to actual persons, living or dead, businesses, companies, events or locales is entirely coincidental.

For questions and comments about the quality of this book, please contact us at CustomerService@Harlequin.com.

TM and ® are trademarks of Harlequin Enterprises ULC.

Harlequin Enterprises ULC
22 Adelaide St. West, 41st Floor
Toronto, Ontario M5H 4E3, Canada
www.Harlequin.com

Printed in U.S.A.

Jen Gilroy writes sweet romance and uplifting women's fiction—warm feel-good stories to bring readers' hearts home. A Romance Writers of America Golden Heart® Award finalist and short-listed for the Romantic Novelists' Association Joan Hessayon Award, she lives in small-town Ontario, Canada, with her husband, teenage daughter and floppy-eared rescue hound. She loves reading, ice cream, ballet and paddling her purple kayak. Visit her at jengilroy.com.

Books by Jen Gilroy

Harlequin Heartwarming

Montana Reunion
A Family for the Rodeo Cowboy
The Cowgirl Nanny
A Rancher's Return

Visit the Author Profile page at Harlequin.com.

For Heidi with love.

Cousin by birth, sister by choice and dear friend always
Thank you for everything.

CHAPTER ONE

DRIVING FIFI, HER trusty green tractor, Josie Ryan rattled along the hilly two-lane road and sang to a country song blasting from her phone. On this bright and breezy New Hampshire June afternoon, if she couldn't ignore her worries, she could at least do her best to forget about them for a few hours.

On the last hill before the flat stretch that led into the small town of Strawberry Pond, the tractor's engine labored. "You can do it, Fifi." She gave the steering wheel an encouraging pat. Between the cost of a vet's visit for a sick cow and leak in the barn roof at Snow Moon Hill Farm, she didn't have extra money for tractor parts.

"Atta girl." As they crested the hill where a red barn snuggled near a hayfield edged by forest and the rugged peaks of the White Mountains, she whooped in relief.

At a vehicle noise, she glanced over her shoulder as a sporty silver car she didn't recognize pulled out and passed. As it sped back into the lane in front, she glimpsed a Massachusetts license plate and lone driver. A tourist and likely from a city because they hadn't waved. Around here, waving was a way of life and used to greet everyone from folks Josie knew well to friends she hadn't met yet.

As she came into town, she turned off the music and navigated streets lined with nineteenth-century white-frame and brick buildings, many of them fronted by well-tended gardens. With the town's annual Strawberry Festival in full swing, parking was scarce, but she squeezed the tractor into a reserved space between the library and the town's historic green.

"Hey, Josie." Alana Hansen, a friend and Strawberry Pond's librarian, greeted her as she hopped down from Fifi's cab.

"Sorry I'm late." She smoothed her windblown hair. While Josie's grandmother called it strawberry blond, it was still red, Irish red, her grandfather countered with a fond smile. "Gramps and Grams came in earlier with the girls. Chores took longer on my own."

Josie was a single mom with two daughters.

"I understand. It's no problem. There's plenty of time." Like Josie, Alana understood agricultural life. While Josie managed the Ryan dairy farm, Alana and her family had a large orchard and Christmas tree operation. "Besides, you had a slower ride with Fifi."

"And a bumpier one." Josie laughed. "I still wouldn't trade in the old girl, though." The vintage tractor was a workhorse, and Josie couldn't manage the farm without it.

Alana, a petite brunette, gave Josie a dimpled smile. "If I haven't already said so, you volunteering to handle the kids' tractor rides is a lifesaver. Along with digging out the library's holiday lights, I made decorations for Fifi." She gestured to several boxes on the library's stone steps that overflowed with red, white and green bunting and a strawberry-themed wreath. "We can—oh no."

Brakes squealed, and Josie whirled around to see the silver car that had passed her earlier careen off Main Street on the other side of the green. *Her girls. Grams and Gramps.* Her family, her whole world, might be in the nearby refreshment tent. She broke into a run.

"It's okay." Alana kept pace with her. "Your girls and grandparents are in the library for the craft session. I was with them not more than five minutes ago." As if she'd read Josie's thoughts, Alana rushed to reassure her.

But Josie didn't slow her pace. Even though high school was twenty years ago, she'd been a county track and field champion and still ran, even if it was sometimes to try to escape from herself.

"It's okay, see?" Alana pointed to the car that had missed the white canvas tent by at least fifteen feet and had come to a halt at the edge of the pond that gave Strawberry Pond its name.

Josie pressed a hand to her chest to calm her racing heart. Panic over. Her family was safe. Everyone else was, as well. Although she'd been too young to remember the car accident that had killed her parents, losing them had marked her in other ways. Her ex-husband had called it her "savior complex," but she hadn't managed to save their marriage. Now her focus was looking after her small family and saving their farm.

A dark-haired man holding a phone got out of the car and stared around as if in a daze. People streamed out of the tent and from nearby streets. A medium-size black-and-white dog barked and jumped around the man like it wanted to play.

When Josie reached his side, the man rubbed a hand across his forehead. "That dog came out of nowhere and there's children and families nearby. I tried to stop but I couldn't. I thought I was going to hit the tent." He glanced at his car, then the gathered crowd, and his face reddened. "Sorry, everyone. I'll pay for any damage I caused."

Josie exhaled. She'd been set to tear into him for speeding, but maybe he hadn't been driving fast at all. Besides, the man, who looked around her age, seemed genuinely contrite as well as embarrassed.

"You'll need help getting out of there." She jerked her chin toward his car, its front tires partly submerged in mud, shallow water, reeds and white water lilies. "At least you didn't hit the strawberry patch." She forced a neutral smile. In dark jeans, a short-sleeved white linen shirt that showed muscular forearms, trendy sneakers and aviator sunglasses atop his head, the man had an air of suave sophistication both attractive and unsettling.

"The strawberry patch?" He blinked, and although he smiled back, his tone was uncertain.

Josie's heart sped up again. That smile softened his serious face and might once have charmed her. However, she wouldn't be charmed by him or any other man.

"We're known for our wild strawberries. Supposedly, in the early days there were so many strawberry plants bordering this pond, the town that grew up around it was called Strawberry Pond." She tried to keep her voice cool, almost disinterested. "The town still has a heritage strawberry patch." As she pointed to it, her arm brushed his. She took a quick step back as the skin beneath the sleeves of her white-and-pink "Just a Girl Who Loves Tractors" T-shirt tingled.

"That strawberry patch is a highlight of our town walking tours." Fred Sinclair, the local newspaper editor who played darts with Josie's gramps, elbowed his way to the front of the crowd. He had his phone and notebook in hand and signature pencil tucked behind one ear beneath his white hair. "Josie will get you out of there in no time."

"I will?"

"She will?"

Josie and the man spoke together.

Fred looked between them and then at Alana, who seemed to be trying to hold back a laugh. "Sure. Josie's got her tractor." He waved toward Fifi. "Josie and that tractor got me and my SUV out of a ditch in an ice storm last winter. I slid off the road near their farm driveway. Pulling you out of the pond should be easy by comparison. Like I said then, there's nobody better than Josie to get you out of a tricky spot."

The gathered crowd murmured agreement, and Alana gave Josie a gentle push toward the man.

"Thanks, but I'll call a tow truck." The man's face was now as pink as Josie's shirt, and he cleared his throat and crossed his arms in front of his broad chest.

Fred shook his head. "No need. Besides, Bob who runs the garage is on his own today and got called out to a breakdown over the mountain."

"You'd likely be waiting a few hours for anyone else." The town clerk, who'd held the job since before Josie was born, chipped in. "After all the rain lately that pond bank will be slippery, but Josie's your woman. She's been driving tractors since she was a kid. Worked part-time for Bob a few summers when she was in high school, too, so she knows lots about mechanics and towing vehicles."

Josie was outnumbered "Okay. I have a hitch and towing strap so I'll get my tractor and be back in a minute. I'm Josie Ryan." She nodded a greeting as her face heated. She didn't like being the center of attention, and now she was starring in what was likely to be the *Strawberry Pond Gazette*'s front-page story of the week.

"Heath Tremblay."

"Welcome to town, Heath." Fred stuck out a beefy hand for him to shake. "Are you planning on staying long?"

"I'm here for the summer." Heath looked around as if expecting the crowd to have moved on. "I'm from Boston, but I inherited Bea Thibeault's house, Tabby Cat Hollow, a few miles out of town. Bea was my great-aunt. My mom grew up near here and we lived in this area until I was seven, but I haven't been back since." They'd lived in several houses close to town although never in Strawberry Pond itself. Their last place, a split-level ranch in what had then been a new subdivision, had been Heath's favorite because he could ride his bike up and down the long driveway. He bent to pat the collarless dog. "I'm a financial analyst and I can work remotely for a few months."

The crowd's murmur rose in both volume and intensity.

Bea Thibeault. On her way to retrieve Fifi, Josie paused. Bea had died in a Boston nursing home several months ago at the age of 102. But before that, she'd been Josie's next-door neighbor, her small run-down house tucked into a hollow of maple trees near one of Snow Moon Hill Farm's original split rail fences. After Bea's death, the whole town had wondered whom her property would go to and what they'd do with it.

Josie made herself walk the rest of the way to the tractor, get into the driver's seat and start the engine. Given his car and wearing the kind of upscale and sophisticated casual clothes her ex had favored, she'd suspected Heath Tremblay was a city guy before he'd confirmed it. Bea had never mentioned any Boston family, but that must have been who she'd visited on her regular trips there.

She turned Fifi around, drove to the other side of the green and onto the grass where Heath stood at the rear of his car holding his key fob. As she drew to a stop, Josie drummed her fingers on the steering wheel. Was Heath here to sell Tabby Cat Hollow? If so, who might he sell it to?

Snow Moon Hill Farm had been in her family for generations. She'd reverted to her maiden name as soon as her divorce was final because being a Ryan, and running the farm under that name, were important to her. But the farm wasn't only a legacy she wanted to pass to her girls, it was their home. She was already struggling to keep it in profit, and somehow she had to get her gramps to see that to survive they needed to change *how* and maybe even *what* they farmed.

Except, in all her planning and late nights spent poring over income and expenditure spreadsheets, she hadn't considered someone like Heath and the kind of change he could bring. And what that change might mean for her.

WHY HAD HE thought coming back to Strawberry Pond was a good idea? Heath sat in a folding chair at a small table outside the refreshment tent and forced a smile. The motherly, gray-haired woman who'd introduced herself as Anne Sullivan slid a plate with a tall piece of strawberry shortcake in front of him.

"A bite to eat will fix you right up. You sure you don't want a ham or cheese sandwich?" Anne hovered at his side.

"No, thank you." He gestured to the cake and

a frosty glass of lemonade. "Everything's great." Although he'd literally crashed into the middle of the town's Strawberry Festival, everyone had been welcoming, more than he deserved.

"As far as looks go, you remind me of your grandfather. Gil Bergeron was older than me, but his family lived across the street from mine. The Sullivan and Bergeron families go way back. They intermarried a time or two, as well. You and I are likely what my mother would have called 'button-hole cousins.'" Anne gave him a friendly smile. "I still recall the time Gil was driving the fire truck in a town Christmas parade and slid right off Main Street into the side of the post office. It was icy, mind, but you're not the first to get the town talking and you won't be the last."

Heath winced as more embarrassment rolled over him. After getting the keys to Tabby Cat Hollow from the attorney's office, he'd planned to head out to Bea's property. Once he'd sized it up and done what the attorney called "necessary repairs," he'd contact a Realtor to put the place on the market and be out of here by the end of summer. Before if he was lucky. He hadn't planned to come here at all, let alone spend time in this small town, but since Bea had left him her house and small plot of land, he'd guessed he owed it to her to visit.

If only she'd left the place to his mom or older

sister instead. Or even the three of them together to share equally. However, after Bea's death when Heath had asked his mom about the inheritance, she said that while Bea had offered the property to her years ago, she'd turned her down. His sister and her family already had a house in Boston, and two years ago she'd inherited her godmother's oceanfront condo in Florida. Heath guessed Bea wanted to do something nice for him, but about now her bequest seemed more like a burden than a blessing.

He took a mouthful of lemonade and tried to pretend he wasn't bothered sitting here with what must be half the town strolling by to take a look at him.

"Come and join our guest." Anne was back again before he realized she'd left, this time with the redhead who'd been first on the scene after he'd driven across the town green and ended up in the pond.

The same woman who'd pulled him out of that pond with her tractor, and whose professionalism and brisk efficiency had made Heath feel even more inept.

Josie shook her head even as Anne, who carried a tray with another piece of cake and glass of lemonade, propelled her toward Heath's table.

"You must be right shook up so don't give decorating or those tractor rides another thought. Set yourself down and rest awhile." Anne patted the chair across from Heath's.

Josie sat. "Mrs. Sullivan, I'm fine and—"

"Your grams texted me. She'll be here as soon as the library's craft workshop finishes. She didn't want to disrupt the girls, or she and your gramps would have been here right away."

Josie frowned and pressed her lips together.

"Hi again." Heath suppressed a grin. Maybe he wasn't the only one feeling awkward and uncomfortable.

"Hi." Josie stared at the cake. "Sorry about Mrs. Sullivan. Our families are close, so she treats me like one of her grandchildren." She finally looked Heath in the eyes. "I live on the farm next door to Tabby Cat Hollow. Your great-aunt Bea was a good neighbor."

As her intense blue eyes studied him, they held a brief softness Heath hadn't expected. At that glimpse of what might be the real Josie, there was a flutter in Heath's chest and hair on his arms prickled. While she'd been polite and had done a great job helping with his car, her lack of warmth had seemed more than stereotypical New England reserve. Yet, despite her standoffishness, there was still something about Josie that drew him to her. While he was certain they hadn't met before, it was almost like he knew her, at least in some inner part of himself that until today he hadn't recognized.

"Bea was great." Heath dragged his thoughts back to why he was here. Although Strawberry Pond reminded him of when his dad left their family, he had happy memories of his great-aunt's trips to Boston to visit him, his mom and older sister. In between, he'd kept in touch with her through telephone calls and email, and when she'd moved into a care home in the city, he'd visited her most Sundays. "She lived to a great age, as well. She was bright and lively right up until the day she died."

"I heard she slipped away in her sleep." Josie took a forkful of cake as if, like Heath, she was conscious of Mrs. Sullivan watching them. "I'd have come to the funeral if there'd been one."

Heath swallowed an unexpected lump of emotion. "As you probably remember, Bea wasn't one for a fuss."

"No." Josie's throaty chuckle was sudden and engaging. "Bea never talked about you, but she was also one to keep to herself."

"Yeah, well, Bea didn't talk about Strawberry Pond, either." Was that because none of them wanted to be reminded of when all their lives had changed forever?

"I wonder why." Josie shook her head. "Bea always said this place was her little piece of heaven on earth."

Heath glanced around. As far as he could see, it was an ordinary small town. The place was pretty, but there was nothing special about it. However, there was nothing special about anywhere for him right now. He finished his cake without tasting it.

"Mom." A freckle-faced, blonde girl around eight or nine hurtled up to Josie and flung her arms around her. "Grams said there was a dog and a man who had an accident, but you helped."

Josie hugged the girl back and then turned to Heath. "Meet my daughters, Lottie and Bella." She gestured to a taller, dark-haired girl with an older couple. "And my grandparents, Tom and Martha Ryan."

Heath stood to greet the couple and shake their hands, aware of Tom's piercing blue eyes, the same color as Josie's, sizing him up. "Bea's place needs work and you won't be short of folks offering you advice. Make sure you listen and take the right kind." Tom's voice was gruff before he made a sound remarkably like a grunt.

"What happened to the dog?" Lottie's lower lip wobbled, and she frowned.

"I don't exactly know. It wasn't hurt, though. It was running around." Heath tried to reassure the kid, who looked to be about the same age as his youngest niece. He remembered patting the animal, but then Josie had returned with her tractor. When he'd next looked, the dog had disappeared, so he'd assumed the owner had claimed it.

"You didn't try to find the dog's family?" Lottie's blue eyes, a mirror of Josie's, accused him.

"I heard the animal control officer took the dog to the rescue. They'll try to find the owner." Josie drew Lottie into a hug and onto her lap. "You and Bella could make lost-dog posters to put up around town. I didn't recognize that hound so maybe it's a stray."

"We could adopt it, couldn't we?" Lottie's expression turned pleading.

"Mom said we can't afford any more pets, remember?" Bella, the dark-haired girl who might be around ten, elbowed her sister in the ribs. "We already have two dogs, a bunch of barn cats, rabbits and the guinea pig from school."

"Bella." Josie shook her head, and red patches bloomed on her cheeks. "We're doing okay."

"But when Dad's last money for Bella and me came, you said you had to take more pet grooming jobs because it—"

"Now, girls." Martha Ryan darted a glance at Heath and then gestured to Bella and Lottie. "You know we don't talk about our private business in public."

"It's not a secret." Lottie put her hands on her

hips like a pint-size politician prepared to stand her ground. "Everybody here knows Dad's—"

"That's enough, Lottie. Mr. Tremblay isn't from around here." Josie stood as well, and Lottie slid from her lap. "I'm sorry. You don't need to hear about issues with my former husband."

"It's fine." He'd already embarrassed himself enough today, and it was strangely reassuring he wasn't the only one with a messed-up, complicated family. In his marriage, though, kids hadn't been involved.

As Josie and her family said their goodbyes and left, a familiar pain shot through Heath's chest. He was the one who'd wanted a family, but it was his ex-wife who'd cheated on him and ended up having a baby with her new husband. Now Heath was on his own. Part of his reason for coming to New Hampshire for the summer was for a fresh start, far from reminders of his marriage. But, like Bea, he'd planned to "keep to himself" while he figured out a new way forward.

He drained his lemonade, declined a refill from Mrs. Sullivan and made his way across the busy green where a kids' sack race was now in progress.

Despite his family roots here, he didn't have to become part of life in Strawberry Pond. He'd focus on Bea's house, and if he bumped into his neighbors, he'd be polite as with any casual acquaintance.

Yet, as he reached the edge of the green, his gaze was drawn to the bright flash of Josie's hair on the other side. With Lottie holding one of her hands, and Bella the other, the three of them skipped toward that tractor now decked out in balloons, streamers and red, white and green lights.

Heath's breath quickened. They were a family. A *real* family.

Maybe it wouldn't be as easy to steer clear of Josie as he thought. *And maybe he didn't want to.* The thought ricocheted in his head like a ping-pong ball bouncing between his usual good sense and an attraction that was new.

He turned away to head to his car. Even if he hadn't sworn off dating, what would he have in common with a woman like Josie Ryan? Or a place like Strawberry Pond?

He'd be out of here as soon as possible. In the meantime, he wouldn't let himself be distracted.

CHAPTER TWO

THE NEXT AFTERNOON in the big farmhouse kitchen, Josie slid the cooled strawberry-rhubarb pie into a carrier and studied the crimped golden-brown crust without seeing it. She didn't want an outlet mall or condo vacation development on her doorstep. With its quaint small towns and rolling green fields and woodland, this part of New Hampshire, where she'd been born, raised and lived her whole life, was rural and unspoiled. Evoking a time when life was simpler, slower even, that was part of its charm for locals and tourists alike. Along with nature conservation, protecting agricultural land and built heritage was important around here.

But Heath Tremblay wasn't from around here, not really, and she had to find out what his plans were for Bea's property. Bringing him a home-baked pie wasn't the most original idea, but as she'd lain awake tossing and turning for most of the night, it was all she could think of.

"Mom?" Lottie's voice stopped her whirling

thoughts. "Aren't you gonna put the lid on the carrier?" Beneath the brim of a pink baseball cap, her eight-year-old daughter's trusting blue eyes stared up at her.

"Sure, sweetie. Here, you can help." Josie snapped one side of the pie carrier's lidded top into place while Lottie did the same on the other side. "Where's your sister?"

Lottie shrugged. "Bella's still in the barn with Grams and Gramps. The vet said Daffodil's doing better."

"Thank goodness." Daffodil wasn't only their best milker, the gentle black-and-white Holstein was also one of Josie's special pets, more like a dog than a cow. "Grab my straw hat from the hook, will you?" She smoothed her hair and then picked up the pie carrier before glancing around the kitchen. Like everywhere else in the comfortable farmhouse, it could do with a fresh coat of paint but any redecorating had to wait. Her priority had to be the farm itself.

Their livelihood. Her family's livelihood. She couldn't let the place go under on her watch. Ryans had farmed this land for almost two hundred years, ever since Patrick and Molly Ryan and their children had fled Ireland's potato famine for a new life in America.

"I picked flowers for Mr. Tremblay." In the small mudroom beyond the kitchen, Lottie collected a jam jar stuffed with daisies centered on a pink wild rose. "Bella said it was dumb because boys don't like flowers but I think some do. Gramps always likes the flowers I pick for him."

"He sure does. I do, too." Josie put on the hat Lottie had handed to her and shut the mudroom door behind them. "Bella?" She hollered her older daughter's name as Lottie ran ahead, her reddish-blond hair bouncing against the back of a T-shirt Bella had outgrown.

Although Josie didn't have the money to give them a lot of material things, her girls were happy and healthy and that was more important than having the latest electronic gadget or new clothes. But they were only eight and ten. What would happen when they hit their teenage years?

She gripped the pie carrier tighter and pushed the thought away. She wouldn't let herself look too far ahead. Drew, her ex-husband, whom she'd met one summer when he was here on vacation from New York City, paid child support. But since he hadn't mentioned wanting to visit the girls in over a year, apart from that monthly payment into her bank account he wasn't a real part of any of their lives.

Gramps was the only father figure Bella and Lottie needed, and Josie had long ago convinced herself she was fine on her own. Bella came out of the barn followed by Grams, who carried a metal bucket. Was her grandmother's posture more stooped than it used to be? Grams had turned eighty on her last birthday and Gramps was two years older. They should be enjoying a well-deserved retirement, not working around the farm from dawn to dusk. The ever-present guilt saddled Josie's heart. Yet, without her grandparents' help, how could she keep the farm going? Apart from spring seeding and fall harvest, there wasn't enough money to hire much extra help.

"We won't be long." She tried to smile for her grams. "The girls and I are taking this pie across to welcome our new neighbor."

Tabby Cat Hollow was only a five-minute walk across the fields so they'd be there and back in a jiffy. She'd often taken that route to visit Bea, bringing her a pie or, as the elderly lady became less mobile, a three-course meal. It wasn't Bea's fault she hadn't been able to keep up her house and land. Bea hadn't had family nearby and while Josie and other locals had done their best, Bea was independent and resisted help.

"Nice." A small smile played around Grams's mouth as she inspected the pie carrier. "Bea would have wanted us to welcome him. It's not right she passed in Boston so far away from home, but what else could her family do? Bea couldn't live here on her own." Grams sighed and smoothed Bella's flyaway long, brown hair.

"Your gramps says there's some kind of bugs in the potato field. I tried to dissuade him but he insisted on going out there on his own to take a closer look instead of waiting for you."

"That's Gramps." Like Bea Thibeault, Tom Ryan was independent and set on doing things his own way, even if that way no longer worked like it once had.

"He needs to remember he's not as young as he once was. He'd already done a day's work before sunup." Grams glanced around the farmyard dominated by the faded red barn with white trim, topped with a cow-and-calf copper weathervane.

"Try not to worry. The potato field isn't far and I'll see what's what as soon as I'm back." Josie had done a full day's work before sunrise, too, but she was thirty-seven, not eighty-two. "I'll also find a reason to send Gramps to the hardware store." She gave her grams a conspiratorial grin. "He'll chat with whoever happens to be around and that will give him a break. Come on, girls." She waved to Bella and Lottie, who played with one of the barn cats. "You helped make this pie so you should help me deliver it."

With the girls there, she wouldn't feel as awkward with Heath Tremblay as she was yesterday at the Strawberry Festival. Although she must have imagined any flicker of attraction to him, she'd resolved not to take any chances. While she was focused on her kids and the farm, she was also human and Heath was an attractive man. Still, she'd been drawn in by an attractive stranger once and she wouldn't go down that path again. If she was ever to date again, and it was a big *if*, it wouldn't be until the girls were older.

"What did you say, Lottie?" Josie turned to her younger daughter. "I didn't hear you." Was her inattention because she'd been thinking about their new neighbor? She slapped at a mosquito on her arm as much to brush away the pesky insect as to divert her thoughts.

"Can we make ice cream later? We still have lots of strawberries left."

With her reddish-blond hair and the freckles that marched across her cheeks and nose in tandem with the spring sun, Lottie was Josie's mini me as far as looks went. They were also similar in personality, both being homebodies. It was Bella with her dark hair and eyes, and restlessness and intensity, who was more like her dad. Still, both girls loved the farm and never complained about having to do chores and not going on vacations like some of their friends' families did.

"If you two help me weed the garden later, we can get the ice cream maker out before supper. What do you say?" The strawberries needed to be used and making ice cream would be fun for them to do together.

"I hate weeding." Bella made a face.

"But you like eating the vegetables we grow, don't you?" Lottie teased her sister, older by nineteen months.

"I guess." Bella laughed and ran one hand along the top of the wooden fence rail that enclosed the pasture where horses grazed. Two were their own and the other three they boarded for a family from South Carolina who spent summers in New Hampshire.

As they entered what Gramps called "the woods," a small grove of maple trees that separated their property from Bea's, Josie took off her hat and swung it in front of her face, the breeze cooling her hot cheeks.

"What's going to happen with Miss Thibeault's house?" Lottie pointed to the upstairs windows of Tabby Cat Hollow glinting in the sunshine at the bottom of a gentle hill.

"I don't know, honey. That's for Mr. Tremblay to decide." As the wooden door, with its round top painted in Bea's favorite lavender, came into view, Josie's worries roared back. The white porch that fronted the house sagged on one end, and it didn't take a masonry expert to see many of the bricks in the house and its chimney needed repointing. "Go ahead, knock on the door." Heath's car was parked at the side of the house by the sagging porch so he mustn't be far away.

"Me first. I'm oldest." Bella rapped on the door at the same time as Lottie so the two of them pounded on it together.

"Not so loud, girls. Along with the way you stamped up the steps, Mr. Tremblay is going to think there's a herd of elephants out here." Josie shook her head at them.

"There aren't any elephants around Strawberry Pond—"

"There might be if they escaped from a circus and—"

As Bella and Lottie argued, the door opened and Heath Tremblay appeared in navy blue shorts and a white T-shirt. He blinked in the bright sunlight and ran a hand through his tousled dark hair.

Josie's entire body tingled and she drew in a shaky breath as she tried to remember all the reasons why she couldn't be attracted to him. "I...we...brought you a pie." She held it out. "To say welcome to Strawberry Pond. It's strawberry rhubarb."

"My favorite." Heath's eyes crinkled when he smiled. "Thanks." He took the pie carrier and glanced between Josie and the girls.

Did she imagine his gaze lingered for an extra few seconds on her?

"It's homemade. We picked the strawberries, too," Bella said as she nudged Lottie, escaped circus elephants forgotten.

"I picked flowers for you." Lottie held out the jam jar for him to take.

"That's really nice. I'd invite you in but the house is like an oven." He shook his head. "Aunt Bea never saw a reason to get air-conditioning. However, take a seat on the porch." He gestured to the white wicker chairs where Josie had often sat with Bea. "I made iced tea."

Lottie grinned and took the nearest chair. "We don't have air-conditioning, either, but our house is really old with thick walls. Gramps says those walls keep us cool in summer and warm in winter. Mom looks real hot, though. See? Her cheeks are all red."

"Lottie... I...we... I'm fine. It's a warm day." Josie gave her daughter a reproving look and sank onto another chair as her mouth went dry. Stopping for iced tea gave her the perfect opportunity to ask Heath about Bea's house, but she'd counted on being calm, cool and collected, not flustered, embarrassed and wrong-footed before she'd even started.

That tingle was definitely attraction. Now she had to steel herself not to react to it.

HEATH TOOK THE jug of iced tea out of Bea's fridge and rummaged in a kitchen cupboard for glasses and a souvenir tray from a trip to Niagara Falls. What was he doing inviting Josie Ryan and her daughters to stay for a while? He should have thanked them for the pie and flowers and sent them on their way.

In Boston, the closest he'd come to speaking to his neighbors was saying hello when they happened to meet taking trash out to the curb. Depending on the season, they might occasionally have a brief conversation about baseball or hockey but nothing more.

He and his ex-wife had sold that house, its empty, echoing rooms a bitter reminder of the family he'd wanted but Danielle now had with someone else. He'd put his share into a one-bedroom condo in Back Bay close to his office and a practical choice for a newly single man who'd turned forty a few months before. But while the Realtor had waxed eloquent about the property's "elegance" and "style," and how it was ideal for a "working professional" and an "excellent investment," he'd nodded and forced a smile to hide the hurt in his heart.

He picked up the loaded tray and made his way from the kitchen along the narrow front hall to the porch. "Here you go." He set the tray on a white wicker table that matched the chairs and took the only empty seat, the one nearest to Josie. "Iced tea from a package I'm afraid so I hope it's okay. My aunt Bea didn't have much in her cupboards. I need to go into town and pick up groceries." Something he'd intended to do the day before if not for ending up on the town green thanks to that runaway hound.

"I'm sure the tea will be fine." Josie averted her face as she poured drinks for her girls. "If you need to stock up, there's a big grocery store on the highway on the west side of town near the arena and leisure center. Otherwise, you'll find several smaller stores and a bakery on Main Street."

"Good to know." Josie had pretty hair and how it curled around her face in soft waves softened her strong features. She also had pretty blue eyes and a sweet smile and those freckles that dotted the bridge of her nose...whoa. He reared back in his chair. *Stop right there.* "Would you like a piece of pie? I don't have cookies or other snacks yet."

"Grams always says pie should be shared." Lottie grinned and rubbed her stomach beneath a red-and-white-striped T-shirt and red shorts.

"Except Grams also says pie has to sit four hours before you cut into it." Bella, the brunette, who wore denim shorts and a pink T-shirt, gave him a solemn nod.

Heath put a hand to his mouth so he wouldn't

laugh. The girls reminded him of his nieces. The kind he'd once hoped for in daughters of his own.

"Girls." Josie made a shushing motion as she filled her own glass and then passed him the jug. "Mr. Tremblay can eat pie whenever and however he wants. But thank you," she added. "You keep the pie to enjoy. We've already had a snack and it will soon be time for supper. So, what are your plans for Bea's place?" She clasped her hands together.

"I...uh... I haven't fully decided." He couldn't fault her for being direct. She was only voicing what everyone in town must be thinking. He set the jug back on the table.

"You don't have any farming experience." Her eyes narrowed.

"Well, no, but Tabby Cat Hollow isn't exactly a farm, is it? And what's with the name? I don't remember Bea having cats." A brown rabbit scampered along the overgrown path beyond the porch, and at a nod from Josie, Bella and Lottie darted after it.

"It was once a farm and way back was owned by the Tabby family. It's in a hollow and at some point, 'cat' was tagged on. Likely one of those New England naming quirks." Josie's gaze drifted to an orange-and-black butterfly that hovered over the bushes below the porch. "Before Bea's time, much of the land was sold off. My great-grandparents bought some of it, as did the farmer on the other side. All those acres are still in agricultural use, and that's important here." Her gaze swung back to him. "There's also an orchard behind the house. Up until a few years ago, while she was physically able to, Bea kept it up. It would be a shame to see that orchard go to ruin. Bea also had wonderful gardens here."

Heath's face warmed and he drained his tea in two gulps. "As I said, I haven't made a final decision yet." Which was true because he hadn't called a Realtor. Still, he planned to, so maybe he was lying by omission. "To start, I'll need to do some work on the place."

He glanced at the porch. Although self-taught, he was a decent carpenter and could do part of the repairs himself. For bigger jobs, he'd get experts in. Apart from a week or so of vacation, his day job would keep him busy enough this summer without tackling major home renovations.

"Lots of us tried to help Bea with meals, visits and garden work, but she was independent and didn't like change much." Josie's half smile was wry. "My grandfather is the same but sometimes..." Her smile disappeared and she set her mouth in a firm line. "What I'm saying is there are good and bad changes. This part of New Hampshire is rural, and it makes sense to keep it that way. We also look out for our neighbors, for what's best for them and the town. It's important to us."

"I don't want to upset anyone. I'll only be here for the summer in any case." What other choice did he have but to sell Tabby Cat Hollow? His life was in Boston, and Strawberry Pond and Bea's property were a temporary hiatus.

"And after that?" Josie stood and waved to her daughters, half-hidden by tall grass.

An ordinary mower wouldn't make a dent in that growth. Heath would have to get someone in with a scythe. "That's my business." He stared at her, and she stared back, her gaze unflinching.

"It is but Bea was a big part of this community. You aren't." Josie's eyes narrowed. "I welcome and benefit from visitors like everyone else but people come here because it's charming. When you're dealing with that 'business' of yours, you might want to keep that in mind."

"I will but…" Heath stopped. With a muttered farewell, she'd turned away to join her daughters.

He jammed his hands into his pockets as he watched the trio make their way along the path toward a stand of trees. Although he'd been disarmed by both the pie and those adorable girls, when it came to Tabby Cat Hollow, Josie had an agenda, which meant dealing with Bea's property wouldn't be as straightforward as he'd expected. Starting with the strawberry-blonde next door.

CHAPTER THREE

"YOU LOOK DONE IN, JOSIE. Go on, sit." At suppertime, Martha Ryan patted Josie's chair at the dining room table. "Thanks, honey." She took the basket of rolls from Bella. "Lottie?"

"Coming, Grams." Her younger great-granddaughter skidded into the dining room with their two dogs, Buster, a black-and-white border collie, and Honey, a golden Labrador, in tow.

"What have I told you about dogs jumping around while we're eating?" Martha shook her head as she shooed Buster and Honey into the hall. "Go on and don't give me those sad puppy eyes. I already fed the pair of you."

"Tom?" She called to her husband. "Supper's ready." Although farmwork and school meant the family often ate lunch separately, Martha insisted they gather together for the evening meal.

"I could smell your fried chicken from the barn." With his thick white hair still damp from a shower, Tom smacked his laps and then gave

Martha a kiss on the cheek as he passed her on his way to his seat at the other end of the table.

"Oh, go on with you." She gave him a teasing grin. "I fried the chicken hours ago. In this heat we're having a cold supper."

Even after almost sixty years of marriage, Tom Ryan was still as handsome as the day she married him. Although she'd loved him then, she loved him more now. Back then, they'd thought they were grown up but they were still kids, setting off on married life thinking their happily-ever-after would be all sunshine and rainbows. Still, they'd faced the hard times together and it had brought them closer. It had also made them appreciate the easier years. She glanced around the oak table Tom's parents had passed down to them. Despite the agony of losing their only child, at least they still had Josie and her girls to take the family farm into the next generations.

If they could keep it going.

As Martha bowed her head for Tom to give thanks for their family and food, she tacked on a silent prayer of her own. *Bless this land and make us successful in tending it. And help Tom see he has to change his way of thinking and listen to Josie's ideas.* "Amen." She joined in with the others.

She wasn't being disloyal to her husband, Martha told herself as she served Lottie a cold chicken drumstick and helping of crisp tossed salad. Josie had good ideas and this farm was a family operation. They all had an equal say in running it, and Tom's stubbornness wasn't doing anyone any good, perhaps him most of all. She had to find a way to get through to him so they could enjoy retirement before it was too late.

And before Josie worked herself to the bone. Under the guise of passing her the plate of fried chicken, Martha scrutinized the dark circles under her granddaughter's eyes. "Have an early night. The milking's done, and the girls and I can shut up the poultry."

Josie shrugged and avoided Martha's gaze. "I've got a dog grooming booked for seven thirty. Have you finished your homework, Bella?"

Bella paused with a buttermilk roll partway to her mouth. "It's the last week of school. We hardly have any homework, but I did my reading and math problems after school on Friday."

"That's fine," Martha said, darting another glance at Josie. Her granddaughter was a good mom and a good farmer, but between caring for the girls, farming and extra jobs, she did too much. Yet, in her own way she was as stubborn as Tom. "Why don't I help Bella and Lottie get ready for bed and make their lunches for tomorrow. Give you a chance to relax after that grooming appointment."

"But—" Josie began.

"Do as your grams says," Tom interrupted, his gentle smile taking away any reproof. "Your eyes were closing during milking earlier. I caught you, twice, so don't try to deny it. Between the Strawberry Festival yesterday and catching up on work today you're tired."

"Okay." Josie smiled back. "Thanks, both of you."

"We can get ourselves ready for bed and help make lunches," Lottie added.

"I'll still check the back of your necks and behind your ears to make sure they're clean." Martha made the usual family joke and the girls rolled their eyes. "I saw our new neighbor driving to town when I came back from delivering the egg orders. He waved, friendly as could be. I knew taking him pie was a good idea. All he needs is a nudge in the right direction. It won't take him long to fit in around here."

"I wouldn't be so sure." Josie poured herself another glass of milk. "He liked the pie and Lottie's flowers all right, but I don't trust him to do the right thing with Bea's house. What if he sells the property to a developer?"

"You mean what *we* think is the right thing." Martha sighed as she finished her meal. "Bea left Heath Tremblay her house so it's not our business what he does with it. We have enough to concern ourselves with on our own farm." Her recent eightieth birthday had been a wake-up call. Even if inside she still felt like she was in her forties, she didn't have a lot of years left. All she wanted was to enjoy those years with her family, the people she loved in this place she loved.

"You don't want a waterslide next door, do you?" Josie put her elbows on the table and leaned forward.

"No, but—" Martha began. It wasn't surprising Josie was stirred up. This farm was her future and their family's legacy. When she came back from Tabby Cat Hollow, Martha had guessed Josie had had words with Heath Tremblay. From the way she walked to that spark in her eyes, she'd been in a fine temper but, like usual, she'd kept it all inside, brushing off Martha's attempts to get her to talk.

"A waterslide would be great. We could walk to it. Right now, there's nothing to do around here unless we get a ride somewhere." Bella's dark eyes sparkled.

"I guess it would be fun for you kids, but a waterslide or something like it could hurt our farm." Tom's voice was gruff. "That wouldn't be so great."

"Girls, if you've finished your supper, take your plates to the kitchen and you may be excused until dessert." Josie quelled any further discussion. "That ice cream we made needs longer to freeze."

After the girls left the dining room in a clatter of chairs, dishes and chatter about waterslides, Josie looked between Martha and Tom. "Mark my words, Heath Tremblay's trouble."

Martha straightened in her chair. Eighty or not, she'd been blessed with good health and still had abundant energy. Her work here wasn't done so she couldn't put her feet up yet. "Well, if he *is* trouble, we'll face it together. Tough times haven't broken us before and they won't now."

They were a family and come what may, they'd stick together and rely on each other. However, as she glanced at Tom's hunched shoulders and tight mouth, weariness etched in every fiber of his being, unease prickled. Although they'd always endured, would the cost this time be too high?

FROM EVERYTHING Heath had heard from his mom and remembered from his own early childhood, New Hampshire was quiet and laid-back. The perfect place to relax and forget your cares. But so far, after only a week in the Granite State, he hadn't experienced any of those things.

By Bea's still-sagging front porch, he took off his baseball cap and with the hem of his T-shirt, wiped away the sweat pouring down his face. Between trying to fix this porch, and long hours at his day job in a house with no air-conditioning, he'd never worked harder in his life.

At the sound of an engine, he turned toward the gate. A red pickup truck pulled up and parked by what must have once been a white picket fence but was now dingy gray. Fence painting was something else to add to his "to do" list. However, at least he could now see the fence and gate thanks to that college student he'd hired to tackle the overgrown lawn. Heath replaced his cap and peered into the fading sunlight to welcome this latest visitor.

The locals were sure friendly here. Since his arrival, he'd had a constant stream of people dropping by. Josie's strawberry-rhubarb pie had been followed by cakes, casseroles, bread and five different types of cookies, all of which were now in Bea's chest freezer. The few times he'd ventured beyond the property to go into town, he'd met even more folks. And directly or indirectly, after offering their condolences for Bea's death and talking about Heath's accident at the Strawberry Festival, like Josie they asked him what he planned to do with Tabby Cat Hollow.

And like with Josie, somehow he couldn't bring himself to tell all those well-wishers the truth.

"I expect you remember me. Tom Ryan from

next door?" The tall, white-haired man stopped in front of Heath.

"I do." Heath held out his hand, and Tom took it in a firm grip.

"I brought you maple syrup." Tom proffered the large can he'd tucked under his other arm. "Made it from my own trees. We've got a sugar bush out back." He gestured in the direction of the neighboring farm. "Used to be part of the Thibeaults' property way back until parts got sold off."

"Josie mentioned Bea's place was once much larger." Heath thanked Tom, took the maple syrup and set it on the porch. Tom must be in his late seventies or early eighties, but he was lean, muscular and evidently still worked harder than some much younger than him.

Tom nodded. "A few generations ago, Tabby Cat Hollow was over two hundred acres. Now it's down to what, about five acres?"

"Four and a half." Small hobby farm size is what the attorney had told Heath but also suitable for residential or commercial development.

Tom clicked his tongue against his teeth. "At least with Bea's place, the sold-off land was kept for farming or woods. Can't say the same about others around here. In New Hampshire, all across New England, we're losing agricultural land at a powerful fast rate." He grunted. "It's not right. If it weren't for farmers, folks wouldn't eat, would they?"

"No, I suppose not." Heath had never thought about where his food came from. In Boston, he usually ordered groceries online and had them delivered. However, even in the week he'd been here, seeing crops growing in nearby fields and hearing the Ryans' dairy cows bellow as they were herded for morning and evening milking had given him a new understanding of what "farm to table" meant. "I took a walk down the hill behind the house. It looks like there's a bunch of apple trees growing in Bea's old orchard." Tom didn't need to know Heath had used an app on his phone to reach that conclusion.

"Of course there are." Tom moved farther into the shade of the porch. "You've got Granite Beauties, Shaker Greenings and others."

"A...what?" By instinct, Heath reached for the phone tucked into the pocket of his shorts. Although Bea hadn't been able to maintain the house and gardens, she'd been keen on technology. She'd had internet installed early on, and as she'd become increasingly housebound, email and online communities had kept her connected to the outside world.

Tom's weathered face creased into an unexpected grin. "You can look them up online, sure, but anything you want to know about New

Hampshire heritage apple varieties ask me or Fred Sinclair. He's the newspaper fellow, you remember?"

"Yeah, sure." Heath's return smile was pained. How could he forget Fred? That "newspaper fellow" was the author of this week's lead story in the *Strawberry Pond Gazette*. It featured Heath's accident and included a half-page photo of Josie and her tractor pulling him and his car from the pond.

As if he'd guessed the direction of Heath's thoughts, Tom's expression became sheepish. "What's that saying about 'fifteen minutes of fame'? In Strawberry Pond, you get used to publicity. From growing the largest pumpkin to a prize for whoever guesses when the maple sap will start running in spring, life here is filled with what Fred deems 'newsworthy' moments." He chuckled and then sobered. "Josie can turn her hand to most anything. Right from a little thing, she was as smart and capable as they come. A real hard worker, too."

"You must be very proud of your granddaughter. Bella and Lottie, as well." What else could Heath say? Although he hardly knew them, he could see for himself that they were a fine family.

"I'm proud of all of them and that's why it pains me to see Josie fretting. As if she didn't have enough to worry about being a single mom and all." Neither Tom's intent stare nor his probing expression wavered.

"Fretting?" Heath swallowed and rested one hand on the porch railing. Perhaps he should have invited Tom to sit or offered him a drink. Yet, from the start there had been something about the man's demeanor that implied this visit wasn't a social call.

"Josie's losing sleep about what you're going to do with Bea's place. Not that she'd ever say so to me or my wife but it's a fact as sure as I'm standing here talking to you." Tom shook his head. "You're planning to sell, aren't you? The whole town's wondering what you'll do with the place, not only Josie. I suspect the attorney has put an idea in your head that you'll get a fast sale to some developer outfit."

Heath glanced at his sneakers. That was one of the options the attorney mentioned and at the time it seemed sensible. But maybe that was because Heath had also said he wasn't interested in farming even as a hobby.

So far, he'd brushed off everyone else's questions but Tom was different. He wasn't asking out of idle curiosity but because Tabby Cat Hollow was important to Josie and likely Tom and Martha, as well. He was here because he was looking out for his family. Tom also was what Heath's mother would call a "stand-up guy." Honest, reliable and loyal—all the things Heath's own dad wasn't.

"Although I haven't called a real estate agent yet, I have to sell this property, don't you see? I live in Boston for a start. My job...my life are there." His job, yes, but his life? That was debatable but he had family in Boston, his mom and sister and brother-in-law and their kids. He had friends and hobbies. And despite what happened with his ex-wife, his life was happy and full.

"Of course you have to sell. I'm not expecting any different. A fellow like you doesn't belong here." As Tom looked Heath up and down, Heath made himself withstand the older man's scrutiny without flinching. "It's *who* you sell to that's the issue. Some of the Johnny-come-lately types like that attorney fellow don't understand what losing good rural land to a housing development or tourist attraction means to this area as a whole."

Heath bit his lower lip. Cory Bailey, the attorney handling Bea's estate, seemed smart and capable. His great-aunt, who'd been independent and savvy to the end, wouldn't have chosen him to handle her affairs otherwise. "Cory's part of a long-standing local firm."

Tom sniffed. "That may be but he doesn't know farming, does he? He wasn't born to it. Comes from generations of paper pushers. People who've never hauled hay and don't know tomatoes don't ripen until August."

In other words, people like Heath. Ones who saw farmland as picturesque on a country drive, picnic or short vacation but, and even if they lived in a nearby small town, didn't know how rural life worked. "I'm sure Cory's doing his best." Had he only mentioned the possibility of a developer sale because Heath insisted he wanted to tie everything up quickly? Looking back, had there been a flicker of hesitation in Cory's eyes and doubt in his expression when Heath had asked about options for Bea's property?

"I'm sure Cory's doing his job just fine, but the point still stands. Same for Marie, his wife. Nice woman, but she's only first generation here." Tom frowned. "Her parents came from Vermont and no farming background there, either. Now Marie's dad is retired from teaching high school art, he makes pottery. Fair enough, but that won't help when the hay needs cutting, the price of milk all of a sudden drops, the barn roof springs a leak and potatoes need harvesting. You have to be real careful when you're handling potatoes. Don't want to bruise them."

Heath pressed his lips together so he wouldn't laugh at Tom's disapproving expression. Now wasn't the time to mention his sister. Jenna was an art teacher at a public elementary school in

Boston and, as a sculptor, she was part of a collective studio on the side. Her work was far from easy, but Tom Ryan's opinions seemed as fixed and hard as the granite rock that symbolized his home state. What must it be like for Josie? Was that what she'd meant when she'd likened Bea's resistance to change to her grandfather's? It couldn't be easy for a woman in farming anyway, but did Tom resist any new ideas Josie might propose?

Tom glanced toward the now-setting sun that painted the sky beyond the orchard in ribbons of pink, gold and orange. "I'd best be off. As they say, a farmer's work is never done. Martha will be wondering where I've got to. She's doing the books while Josie's fixing a fence in the horse pasture. Let's keep this chat between the two of us, shall we?"

"Of course." Heath's thoughts whirled. Tom hadn't offered to buy Tabby Cat Hollow, so was the Ryan family struggling financially? Maybe Josie had more keeping her awake at night than what Heath might do with Bea's place. If she did, it wasn't his problem, but as they said their farewells and Tom returned to the truck, Heath was left with a new problem: guilt. He'd only been thinking of himself and what he wanted. Not what was right for Strawberry Pond, his neighbors or even, his stomach knotted, Bea and what this place meant to her.

Tabby Cat Hollow was *his* legacy from her and his mother's family. Apart from his mom, sister and nieces, Bea was the only family Heath had. Like the pebbles he'd tossed into the pond as a child when Bea had taught him to skip stones, whom he sold this property to would cause ripples beyond his own life.

Especially for Josie, a woman who was still almost a stranger but nevertheless occupied his thoughts far more than she should.

CHAPTER FOUR

"I CAN'T BELIEVE you thought it was a good idea to go over there and talk to Heath Tremblay." On the last Saturday morning in June, Josie set an empty feed bucket on a shelf in the barn and turned back to her gramps. "I… I…" She swallowed tears of anger and frustration clogged at the back of her throat.

"I was trying to help. You weren't supposed to find out." He led one of the horses they boarded, a chestnut Morgan filly, out of the barn toward the horse pasture.

"Why?" She marched after him and lowered her voice, mindful of Bella and Lottie working in the nearby vegetable garden. "As for me finding out, Laura Sullivan saw you talking to him on her way to a house showing. She was running late so took a shortcut along the road by Bea's place."

As Josie did two Saturday mornings a month, she'd met Alana, the town's librarian, and another friend, Laura Sullivan, a Realtor and horse farm owner, for an early breakfast at the Strawberry

Spot, the town's diner. While it was a chance to spend time away from farm and family responsibilities, it also meant sharing ideas—and frustrations—with other women who worked in agriculture.

"So Laura saw me. It's not like she heard what I was talking to Heath about." Gramps patted the horse as he unlatched the pasture gate.

"No, but I can guess. You told him to mind who he sold Tabby Cat Hollow to." Josie sat atop the fence as Gramps settled the filly in the pasture with the other horses.

Along with turning away, his silence confirmed her initial suspicions.

"I don't need you trying to help. What if Heath guessed our farm is struggling?"

"How would he?" Her gramps shrugged. "Besides, there's nothing to worry about. Things will turn around come harvest time like always. You'll see."

"While I appreciate your confidence, nothing will change here unless we do." Josie gripped the top of the fence. "Don't you understand?" Although Gramps was patting the horse and had his back to her, she knew he was listening by the stiff set of his shoulders beneath his work shirt. "If we want this farm to survive, we have to do a lot of things differently. We need to adopt new and more sustainable strategies for crops, take new approaches to protect the soil and make it healthier and more resilient. Above all, we need to learn from and help others. Collective wisdom, you know?" She rubbed a hand across the back of her neck beneath her baseball cap and ponytail.

"Josie's right, Tom. I know it and underneath your bluster you do, too." Her grams joined Josie at the fence and gave Josie's back a reassuring pat. "Give the girl a fair chance."

"I think we should be cautious." When Gramps turned around from the horse, his face was red, but there was an expression in his faded blue eyes Josie had never seen there before. Could it be fear? "What if we invest in your newfangled ideas and they don't work? Then we'll lose the farm for sure." His voice shook and then he cleared his throat and looked at the sky and jagged mountain ridge.

Grams glanced at Josie and then back at Tom. "Josie's never been one to rush into things."

Except for her ill-fated marriage. A chill spread from Josie's stomach up to her windpipe. She'd rushed into it for sure. If she'd taken her time, she'd have realized all the ways she and Drew weren't right for each other. She'd been desperate to have her own family, though, so she'd convinced herself they could make things work. Still, without Drew she wouldn't have had her girls so despite the marriage being a mistake, it had also given her the biggest blessings of her life.

As Gramps marched back to the pasture gate, she took a deep breath. "I promise I won't invest in anything too risky, and you and Grams will be part of every decision." So many things would be different if her parents were still here. Josie's own life, of course, but this farm, as well. If her mom and dad had lived long enough to fully take over the farm, her grandparents would likely have retired by now. Her folks would also have introduced new ideas gradually so Josie wouldn't now have to make big changes all at once.

Gramps fiddled with the filly's lead rope. "What if Heath Tremblay sells to a developer?"

"We'll cross that bridge when we come to it." As always, her grams's gentle voice calmed not only her husband but Josie. Almost as far back as Josie could remember, Grams had been there for her, mother and grandmother, the two roles blurring into each other until they were indistinguishable in one steadfast love. "In the meantime, why don't you plant more trees along that property line?" Grams tweaked the bib of Gramps's hat. "I hear trees are good for soil protection and adding them isn't a big cost. We could even look at generating woodlot income in the future."

"I guess." Gramps gave her a slow smile and as

the two of them exchanged a loving look, Josie's heart pinched.

Her grandparents had a true and respectful partnership. The kind of relationship she'd once wanted for herself and hoped to model for her daughters.

"Mom, come quick." Bella skidded to a stop by the fence with Lottie behind her. "Clarabelle's loose. We saw her from the porch. She looked like she was heading for Mr. Tremblay's orchard."

"Little Ming's out, too. She's in the garden." Lottie clambered atop the fence as Josie jumped down.

"On my way," Josie shouted over her shoulder, already in pursuit of Clarabelle, while her gramps jumped into action to retrieve Ming the calf. "Stay with Grams, girls, and go back to the house."

Although Ming, Clarabelle's calf, was only two months old and gentle like her mom, she already weighed almost two hundred pounds. "Little" was now a misnomer, although with her clear black-and-white Holstein markings, she suited Ming, a name one of Lottie's school friends had chosen explaining it meant "bright" in Mandarin.

Running alongside the pasture fence, which still held several other cows and calves, Josie spotted the area of loose wire where Clarabelle and Little Ming had pushed their way through. "Don't get any bright ideas." As she pulled out her phone to text Gramps, she flung the words toward the cows in the field who, luckily, continued to graze. Clarabelle was more inquisitive—and independent—than most of the others in the herd and Little Ming was like her that way. Hopefully, when the time came, she'd be as good a milk producer, too.

Josie grabbed a half-full feed bucket and stopped by the farthest corner of the fence. She had to think like a cow and, whichever way she went, keep her movements slow and deliberate. Given what Bella had said, Josie would start by working her way downhill to Heath's property. If Clarabelle had indeed headed in the direction of the orchard, hopefully, Josie could herd her back without being visible from the house. Although it had grown wild, along with old apple trees there was a strawberry patch at the rear of the orchard. Since Clarabelle loved strawberries, and if she hadn't found the patch herself first, Josie might be able to entice her with some of the sweet, ripe treats.

"Coboss." She raised her voice so it would carry. Cows weren't pets but they were still smart and trainable. While each farmer called their cows in a particular way, Josie stuck with what Gramps used, "coboss," short for "come boss" or "a call to cows."

She made her way along a rough grassy and stone-ridged track looking from left to right. Clarabelle couldn't have gone far, but if she'd made it into the woods behind the farm, it could take Josie several hours to get her out again. Loose livestock were one of the many unpredictable realities of farm life and she had to be flexible for what the day might bring.

Josie rattled the food bucket and called Clarabelle again. With bright green foliage, a duck-egg-blue sky, clear, fresh air and the White Mountains all around, it was a perfect summer day. Despite the inconvenience, she had to enjoy the moment and not let herself think about all the other chores waiting for her.

When Heath appeared around a curve lower down on the path, Josie took an instinctive step back. In black tailored shorts, a white polo shirt and trendy gray sneakers, he could have been a spectator at one of the big tennis tournaments Josie and Grams liked to watch on TV. Someone like him didn't belong in the backwoods of rural New Hampshire, so why did Josie's heart beat faster and her mouth go dry? He hadn't seen her yet and if she—

"Josie? I heard a voice and thought it sounded like you. What are you doing out here?" He stopped in the middle of the path. "I was on my way to Bea's orchard."

"I'm looking for a cow. She got out." As Josie reached the narrow place where Heath stood, she stopped in front of him. "That orchard's where I'm headed. It borders the property line near here. Bea's...your property. As soon as I find Clarabelle, I'll herd her home. I'm not trespassing." She put her free hand to one cheek and pretended to swat away a fly. She was what her Gramps would call "running off at the mouth." She only talked too much when she was nervous, but there was no reason for her to be uncomfortable around Heath.

"I didn't think you were. Trespassing, I mean." Heath gave her a half smile and stepped aside so she could move by him on the path. "If you need any help I could...not that I know anything about cows...but as another person I could give you a hand." His voice trailed away.

"Here." Before Josie knew what she was doing, she handed him the feed bucket. "Shake it and follow me. Like all cattle, Clarabelle's food motivated."

She didn't need his help or even welcome it, but she didn't want him going off on his own, either. Even a gentle cow like Clarabelle could be unpredictable, especially if she'd gotten into a tight spot. Josie owed it to Bea—and herself as a responsible farmer—to keep Heath safe.

In addition, the best way to overcome that foolish attraction he seemed to spark in her was to get to know him better. If she made a friend of him, he'd also be more inclined to understand and take account of her concerns when it came to whoever bought Tabby Cat Hollow.

At least that's what she told herself as she led the way to the orchard with Heath rattling the feed bucket a few steps behind. She'd fallen for someone like him once and had the wounded heart to prove it. And she'd learned from that mistake to be sure never to repeat it.

HEATH SWUNG THE bucket of livestock food back and forth, and in front of him Josie called out something that sounded like "co boss." Maybe a cow-calling language? He didn't want to show his ignorance by asking so he'd look it up online later.

He glanced at the clothes he'd put on when he'd planned to drive to a bigger town over the mountain. After stopping at a store to pick up home office supplies, he'd intended to be a tourist for the day. He'd also wanted to get away from Strawberry Pond, where there were too many reminders of his fractured family—and too many questions about his plans for Bea's property.

Instead, though, something had pulled him toward the orchard first. The same something that had made him speak before he thought and offer to help Josie track down that cow. So, here he was, dressed in weekend city-casual clothes supposedly "helping" a woman capable of handling whatever life tossed her way all on her own.

That wasn't even the worst of it. His only experience with cattle was to spot them from the safety of a car, driving by at speed. Since he had no idea what he was doing, any "help" he could offer Josie would likely be more of a hindrance. He should have made his excuses, gone back to the house and now he'd be in his car on his way in the opposite direction. Still, he'd never been a quitter and now he'd gotten himself into this situation, he'd make the best of it and try to learn something.

As the path widened and the orchard came into view, Heath straightened his shoulders and moved to walk at Josie's side. In denim overalls, work boots and a short-sleeved blue-checked shirt, all she needed was a red and white polka dot bandanna covering her hair and she'd be a match for Rosie the Riveter. Last Halloween, one of Heath's nieces had dressed up as Rosie, a symbol of American women who'd worked in factories during the Second World War.

Yet, unlike Rosie, a composite of many

women, Josie was real. Beneath her battered baseball cap, her strawberry blond hair gleamed in the sun. And there was something about the way she walked, each step firm and determined, that caught at Heath's heart. Instead of stepping around rocks on the path, she either hopped over them or kicked smaller ones aside, never breaking stride. It was the walk of a woman who forged her own path. But, in the slight hesitation when she encountered a wider, taller rock, there was also a hint of vulnerability and maybe even hidden softness. It was those complexities that, despite his reservations, made Heath want to get to know Josie better.

"There you are, Clarabelle. What do you think you're doing?" Josie's voice was gentle, almost cajoling. "Come here, girl."

Half-hidden by tall grass in the middle of Heath's orchard, a large black-and-white cow raised her head and studied them.

Heath drew in a breath. Seeing a cow from a car or in pictures or in movies was one thing but this up-close view was something else entirely. "She's magnificent."

"She sure is but most people don't understand how special cows are. They only see them as useful livestock." Josie paused. "*Magnificent* is a good word. I also think cows are beautiful." Her cheeks pinkened. "It's their big eyes and how they vocalize to express themselves." She gave a light laugh. "Cows are social animals and smart. I like looking at them, and it's not surprising that in some cultures they're sacred."

Heath stopped under a tall tree with wide, spreading branches where a wooden gate rested drunkenly between two posts, which must once have marked the orchard's entrance. "Your grandfather told me about the apple trees in here."

Josie nodded. "There's also a strawberry patch. Along with that delicious green grass, it's the strawberries Clarabelle's going for. She's in cow heaven. Lots of treats and no competition for them." She glanced around and then back at Heath. "She's fine where she is for now. It's pretty, isn't it?"

"Yeah." Heath breathed out the word. "Pretty" was an understatement. Sunlight filtered through the leaves and gnarled gray branches and tree trunks to cast a patchwork pattern onto the ground. Nearby, a bee buzzed and a light breeze waved the tall grass. When he'd been here before, he'd only taken a cursory look around and as soon as he'd spotted fallen blossoms he'd gone on his phone to try to identify the trees. Now, in the stillness, it was like he was seeing the place for the first time and everything about it was magical.

"Behind the orchard is your hayfield." Josie

pointed through a mist of green beyond Clarabelle.

"I didn't know." He took a deep breath. He needn't be embarrassed by his ignorance. He likely knew lots of things Josie didn't and now was his chance to learn from her. "I don't know what owning a hayfield means or what I should do with it." There, the words were out and he didn't feel as awkward as he'd expected.

"Why would you?" Josie gave him a sideways glance but it was without malice or, seemingly, any agenda, either. "I could give you a spiel about what to do with an old hayfield, including the environmental benefits of rejuvenating it, but there's lots of good information online. If you want, I can send you links."

"I'd appreciate that. Here." He unlocked his phone and handed it to her so she could input her contact details. "If it's not too much trouble, some basic information about what to do with an old orchard would also be helpful." Heath gestured to the apple trees. "Your gramps said to ask him or Fred Sinclair, the newspaper editor, but…" He stopped.

"Both of them are pretty set on doing things their own way, which they also think is the *only* way." Josie laughed and perhaps the first genuine smile she'd ever given Heath spread across her face.

"I didn't want to speak out of turn but, yeah, that's the impression I got." Heath laughed, too.

"It's not because Gramps and Fred are from an older generation, either. My grandmother is a similar age and she's open-minded." Josie let out a heavy breath. "With his attitude, a lot of the time Gramps drives me around the bend and we bump heads. He never used to be so stubborn and grumpy. I'm sorry he came to see you. He needs to mind his own business. I shouldn't have gotten on your case, either." She dipped her head and dug the toe of one of her boots into a hillock of grass.

"It's no problem. It's forgotten, but in Tom's case, he didn't want anyone to know about that visit. He asked me to keep it to myself." Heath's suspicions about Josie's difficulties with her grandfather had been right.

"He would have." This time her laugh was forced. "It is what it is and yes I'd be upset if you sold Bea's place to a developer but I'd cope. It wouldn't be the end of the world."

Her tone implied that like him, she'd already experienced an "end" of her world and had come through it. "I expect I'll have to sell, but I can see how selling it to someone who'd bulldoze the orchard and that hayfield might not be right." Heath knew it would be outright wrong but that only made the situation more complicated.

"You've got good land here and I know it's none of my business but…" Josie brushed a hand across her eyes. "If you have questions, ask me, please? If you decide to do anything with the orchard, I'll introduce you to my friend Alana Hansen. Her day job is town librarian but she also works at her family's orchard. It's a commercial operation so much bigger than what you've got here but Alana could give you pointers." She hesitated for several seconds. "You may be what Grams calls a 'fish out of water' but your family's from here so your roots are and Strawberry Pond's home, I guess."

It was but it also wasn't that simple. Heath had done his best to pretend those roots never existed. As for home, Danielle had put an end to what he'd thought was his home, their home, when she'd cheated on him.

"Forget it, I'm not making any sense." She moved forward and tripped over an exposed tree root.

"No, you're—" Heath grabbed her arm to keep her from falling and as his hand connected with the warmth of her bare skin, his palm tingled with a jolt of awareness.

"Give me the feed bucket and stay here." For an instant, Josie stared at his hand on her arm as if she'd experienced that same jolt. Then, with murmured thanks, she stumbled away, this time keeping her gaze fixed on her boots, avoiding the root and any other possible trip hazards. "Clarabelle isn't generally aggressive so she's likely to move away when someone approaches her, but she's cornered back in there. That's why she could become defensive."

"I understand." At least he did when it came to Clarabelle. What he couldn't grasp was what had just happened between him and Josie. That moment of connection and the undercurrent of attraction between them.

"Once I get Clarabelle out of the orchard, I'll herd her back uphill and be out of your way." This time her smile was guarded and the same polite mask she'd worn the day she'd towed his car out of the pond and brought him the pie was back in place.

As she continued toward Clarabelle, all the while speaking softly to the animal, Heath gripped the top of the broken gate.

Josie had gotten under his skin. And now, having seen the real woman behind the mask, he was even more intrigued and wanted to see more of her. Which meant that no matter how he looked at it, he had a bigger problem than Bea's property.

CHAPTER FIVE

"SEE YOU NEXT WEEK." Late on Saturday afternoon, Josie grabbed her bag and waved goodbye to the high school caretaker waiting to lock up.

"Great class, Jojo." Alana fell into step beside her. "I never enjoyed working out before taking fitness classes with you."

"Me, neither, although I'm sure going to feel it tomorrow." Laura, a willowy blonde, rolled her shoulders and gave Josie a mock glare. "Actually, I can feel it now, but I burned off the pancakes and whipped cream you encouraged me to order at breakfast."

"What else are friends for?" Josie grinned. Seeing her two closest friends twice in less than six hours was rare. Between that leisurely breakfast and the class she'd taught, it had been a good Saturday.

But spending that time with Heath while rounding up Clarabelle had also brightened her day. He'd been surprisingly easy to talk to, and she'd opened up to him about Gramps in a way she never did, not even to Alana and Laura. For a city guy who didn't know anything about his orchard or hayfield, he seemed keen to learn. And when he'd stopped her from falling over that tree root, his touch hadn't unsettled her so much as given her a sense of rightness and maybe even kismet. Which was ridiculous because even if he hadn't only been here for the summer, Heath wasn't her destiny. How could he be?

She dismissed the thought and focused on her friends. "I need to drop by Stella's Jewelers for Grams so I'll leave my car here and walk over. I'll catch Stella before she closes and still get home in time for milking and to watch a movie with the girls before bed."

"I'm going to muck out stables, update a house listing and then take a long, relaxing bath." Laura dug in her tote for her car keys.

"As if launching the children's summer reading program at the library wasn't enough excitement for today, I'm going to bake pies for our farm stand." Alana chuckled. "Sounds like a typical Saturday night for all of us, then?"

"I wouldn't have it any other way." Josie's marriage had given her enough excitement, if she could call it that, to last a lifetime. Now her busy life was a simple but predictable routine that both grounded her and made her feel safe.

After saying goodbye to her friends, Josie

jogged across the high school football field to a narrow lane behind the bowling alley. The route brought her out on Strawberry Pond's main street three doors down from Stella's Jewelers. Dodging clusters of pedestrians, she darted along the street and into the store twenty minutes before closing time.

"Hey, Stel." Behind one of the glass display counters, the fifty-something owner, whose miniature schnauzer was one of Josie's dog grooming clients, greeted her with a smile. "I'm here to pick up my grandmother's bracelet."

"Of course." As Josie handed her the claim ticket and then tucked her windblown hair, which had fallen out of its ponytail, behind her ears, Stella disappeared into the back.

"What's happening, Alf?" Josie bent and scratched the big black-and-white cat in his favorite place behind his ears as Alf wound himself around her legs.

"Josie? We meet again."

There was no mistaking Heath's voice, as smooth, delicious and heart-melting as Josie's favorite amber maple syrup atop homemade vanilla ice cream. "Oh, hi." The cat forgotten, she stood up quickly and banged an elbow on the counter. "Oops. No worries, I'm fine. I didn't see you over there."

She rubbed her elbow. She'd never been accident prone, but from tripping over that tree root earlier to now, Heath must think she was a complete klutz. Under his intent gaze, her face heated. It shouldn't matter she probably looked a mess but yet, somehow it did.

Alf gave a loud meow as if reminding Josie that *he*, not Heath, should be the center of her attention.

"I was behind the mirror." He gestured to an ornate standing Victorian looking glass that sat at one end of the narrow store. "You should probably put ice on that elbow as soon as you can." He introduced himself to Alf, then crouched at the cat's side and gave Josie a lopsided grin. "I played hockey from when I was a kid all the way through college and am still in a rec league. When it comes to bruises, I'm your guy."

"I'll keep that in mind." Josie cleared her throat. He was joking. He wasn't *her* guy in any sense of the term so why, for a second there, did it feel like the reference fit? "My dad was a hockey player. Not professionally but in a few minor leagues. He was good."

She bit her lower lip to stop herself from making any more personal revelations. She never talked about her dad because apart from a few hazy memories, in any real sense he'd never been part of her life. Still, each June when Father's Day came around and she and the girls celebrated

Gramps, she never quite suppressed the ache of not having her own dad.

"Alf! You rascal." Stella was back and gave the cat, now purring with a smug expression as Heath petted him, a mock glare. "I hope he wasn't making a nuisance of himself. He must have slipped in here when I opened the workroom door."

"Not at all. There you go, big guy." With a final pat and fond smile, Heath stood again.

Josie's heart flipped. Heath was a "big guy," too, a good few inches taller than her, even though at nudging five feet nine she'd never considered herself short. And there with Alf, if anything he'd looked even more "manly" than usual. His gentle affection for the cat, and Alf's evident trust in him, was sweet. It spoke of an innate kindness and a man who was a strong, confident protector but never a bully. If he earned it, the kind of man even she might be able to trust.

"Here, all fixed." Stella handed Josie the bracelet Grams had brought in to have the clasp repaired. "Have you decided between the pendants, Heath?" As Josie found her wallet to pay, Stella turned back to him.

"The silver heart with the July birthstone. I left all three on the counter back there." He pointed toward the mirror. "Gift wrapped, please, in pink or purple if possible."

He had a wife or girlfriend. Josie lowered her

head as she passed Stella her credit card. While it wasn't surprising he was paired up, she'd assumed he wasn't because he was living here alone and hadn't mentioned anyone. Yet, why would he? She was an acquaintance and Heath's relationship status didn't matter to her. Except, somehow it did.

She muttered her thanks to Stella and stuffed the jeweler's envelope with the bracelet into her bag. Gramps had given Grams that bracelet for their twenty-fifth wedding anniversary, and apart from her engagement and wedding rings, it was the piece of jewelry Grams cherished most. "Forever love" was engraved inside it along with her grandparents' initials and wedding and anniversary dates. What would it be like to be someone's "forever love"? Since she'd never known it, she couldn't let herself imagine it.

"What do you think? The pink or dark purple?" Heath's voice pulled her away from dwelling on what might have been.

"For what?" Josie stared at him, bemused.

"Which color of paper should I choose to wrap my niece's birthday present in?" He gestured to Stella, who now held a white jewelry box in one hand and two rolls of paper in the other. "Ava's turning thirteen in a few weeks and her favorite colors are pink and purple. You have girls so what do you suggest?"

His niece. The tightness in Josie's chest eased. "I'd say go for the pink with the sparkles. It also has purple in it, see?"

"You're right." Heath shook his head. "I didn't even notice but Ava will. The sparkly pink it is. As a single guy, I'm not up on these kinds of details. Thanks."

"You're welcome." Their gazes held for a few seconds before Josie looked away. The last thing she wanted was for Stella or anyone else to get the wrong idea. Josie loved Strawberry Pond, but it didn't take much for people to start talking and make something out of nothing.

And this *was* nothing. She was merely helping a neighbor who'd asked for her advice. Even if it felt like a whole lot more.

Whenever he left Tabby Cat Hollow, Heath bumped into at least one person he'd met before and usually more. However, the town's small size didn't explain how often he seemed to bump into Josie Ryan. He'd now been here over two weeks, and the days he hadn't seen Josie stood out from ones he had. And the latter were the days when the sky seemed bluer, the sun brighter and he had a new spring in his step.

After Josie had texted him information about maintaining a hayfield and introduced him to Alana, they'd exchanged other texts. Heath had asked about Clarabelle and from there they'd gotten chatting about the rest of the herd. Josie had asked him for Bea's chicken and dumplings recipe so Heath had found it in a wooden recipe box, taken a picture and emailed it to her. They were all small, ordinary things but somehow not.

Now leaving the town's library, Heath waved at Alana ushering the Strawberry Pond Stitchers, a knitting group, into the activity room and tucked the books she'd suggested he borrow into his small backpack. They were all about caring for fruit trees and growing an orchard. Along with several dusty hardcovers he'd found on a shelf in Bea's bedroom, he could at least learn about what was in the orchard while he decided what to do with it.

At the bottom of the library steps, he stopped by one of the town's bulletin boards, his attention drawn to a colorful poster with "Lost Dog" in meandering orange capital letters. The accompanying stick drawing, evidently done by a child, was nevertheless a good approximation of the sad-eyed black-and-white hound he'd swerved to avoid his first day in town.

Josie had suggested her girls make lost-dog posters so this one must be the result. She was a good mom, one who followed through with her kids. Like his own mother, even though Heath had long been an adult. While he hadn't appreciated it at the time, it must have been hard for his mom to raise him and his sister on her own. Yet, and while she'd always made their lives fun and like a great adventure, he'd missed his dad.

His parents were getting divorced, and his dad had left town for work, but why hadn't he kept in touch with his kids more often or visited them? All his mom ever said was Heath's dad was a "rolling stone" and "needed to find himself," whatever that meant. But then, only a few years later, his dad had died and since then, Heath tried not to think of him.

"That poor dog is still at the animal rescue." Anne Sullivan, one of those people he kept bumping into, made a clucking sound as she stopped beside him. "Such a shame they haven't managed to find her owner."

"I guess so, yeah." Heath glanced at Anne before turning back to the poster.

"The rescue's on the side street around the corner from the post office." Anne spoke softly. "It's only on the other side of the green. You could walk there in a few minutes." Behind tortoiseshell glasses, Anne's brown eyes were clear and guileless.

Heath swallowed and adjusted his backpack. "I could but I'm on my lunch break and need to get back."

"Can't you set your own schedule? Advising

companies all around the world, you must work all hours because of the time difference." A small smile played around her mouth. "Between rebuilding that porch and everything else you're doing around Bea's place, you're keeping real busy. Maybe too busy." His gaze drilled into him.

He gave a casual shrug. "I like working on lots of different projects." That newspaper article had mentioned Heath's job and it wasn't surprising people around here had looked him up online. He was also new in town and he supposed people were curious.

Anne chuckled. "You can either say we're nosy parkers or we care about our neighbors. Take your pick. My brother lives on the farm across and up the road from yours. His wife's recovering from hip replacement surgery so when he's up with her in the night, he sees your house lit up like a Christmas tree and sometimes, depending on where you're sitting, you hunched over your computer or on the phone." Anne's smile widened. "The first night, he brought the dogs and came across to check on you while Marcy—that's my sister-in-law—watched from their kitchen window ready to call the police in case you were being burgled."

"I didn't know." Heath wasn't sure whether to be annoyed or touched but he tended to the latter. In a way, it was comforting that people cared about his well-being, but from now on, and despite the heat and wanting a breeze from open windows, he'd close the drapes at night.

"No, you wouldn't have had any inkling. Mike, my brother, walked around, saw you were busy working and went back home." Anne shook her head. "He says you're making good progress on the porch. Except for Mike's bad back and Marcy needing him, he'd have offered to lend a hand, but they've got a son in construction. Pat's coming home from Boston in a few weeks and would be happy to help. It's too big a job for you on your own."

"I... Yes, that would be great," Heath stammered, the words at first stuck in his throat.

He'd always been independent but maybe there were times when he didn't have to be. Along with his full-time job, the amount of work that porch needed *was* too much for him, and if he sold the place to someone who'd only tear it down, what was the point? But he'd kept going, determined to finish what he'd started.

Was that what he'd done in his marriage? He and Danielle had drifted apart, and while she was the one who'd cheated, maybe the two of them hadn't been suited from the start. While marriage had seemed the next logical step in their relationship, perhaps it would have been better for both of them if they'd each gone their separate ways back then.

"I'll let Mike know right now before I forget. I tell you, my mind's like a sieve these days. My husband says I need to wind down but that's not for me. I'll keep winding up and having fun as long as I'm able." Anne opened her purse and took out her phone. "You should drop by Mike and Marcy's place. No need to wait for an invitation around here. They'd have called on you except Marcy only came out of hospital last week and isn't so mobile yet."

Given the traffic by his front door, Heath had already experienced Strawberry Pond's informality, but for him, dropping by other people's homes uninvited was more than a little uncomfortable. "Sure, I guess."

"That's where a dog can be handy." Anne paused with her hand around her phone. "Walking it gets you out and about and part of things. We all tried but Bea, God rest her soul, spent too much time on her own those last few years. It's not healthy, is it?"

"I…no." He was sixty-odd years younger than Bea and, unlike her, had plenty of social connections and interests. But most of those were work-related and perhaps he'd used keeping busy to distract himself from moving on in his life and stayed stuck. Strawberry Pond was supposed to be a fresh start so maybe he should make more of an effort to be part of the community. Temporarily, of course.

As Anne bustled away, tapping on her phone as she walked, Heath didn't head for his car parked in the library lot. Instead, he went in the opposite direction and across the town green, over to the post office and around the corner. He didn't have to return to work right away, and he had his phone with him in case of an emergency. It would only take a few minutes to stop by the rescue and check on the dog—to make sure she was doing okay.

The place was marked by a small wooden sign on a metal gate in the alley across from the rear of the post office. An arrow pointed to the main entrance by a sidewalk outside a grassed-in yard surrounded by a chain-link fence. Why had Anne sent him this way? Heath could have avoided the narrow alley lined with delivery vehicles and continued on into the next intersecting street.

As he turned to retrace his steps, a bark stopped him and then a black nose nudged its way between the links in the fence. Two limpid dark brown eyes looked at him from a furry white face, with a black patch over one eye like a mischievous bandit.

"Cookie?" a girl's voice called followed by a whistle.

"Hey, girl." Heath knelt to her level. It was the same dog who'd been running loose, he was sure of it. "How are you doing, sweetheart?"

The dog nudged his hand with her wet nose and her steady gaze never left his.

"Come on, Cookie." The girl's voice now came from the other side of the fence. "I'm sorry, sir, the main entrance is at the front door but we're closed for visits and adoptions on Tuesdays. I've had the dogs out to play and Cookie here got left behind."

Heath finally raised his head. The brown-haired girl looked to be around sixteen, perhaps a high school student working here for the summer. "Cookie?"

The dog wagged her tail and barked again. While the first bark had been like a greeting, this one was higher-pitched, almost a yip, as if Cookie wanted to come out of the yard and play with him.

"That's what we called her when she was brought in. She's been here a few weeks now." The girl ruffled the fur on the back of the dog's neck. "My boss, the rescue's manager, found her running loose the day of the Strawberry Festival. Cookie didn't have a microchip and we haven't had any luck tracing an owner so she'll be available for adoption from tomorrow. She's about a year old and such a sweetie-pie I expect she'll go fast."

Still crouched at Cookie's level, all of a sudden Heath knew what he wanted to do, what he had to do.

"I want to adopt her. Cookie." Whenever he'd pictured himself with a dog it was one with a name like Max, Duke or Sheba. Strong, noble names for a man's loyal companion. Cookie was a silly name but this poor dog had had enough change. Cookie she was and Cookie she'd stay. "I'll come back as soon as you open tomorrow. Don't give her to anyone else, please?"

"Well, we have to do a background check and then there's an adoption fee and…" The girl stopped and stared at him. "You're him, aren't you? The guy in the newspaper with his car on the green. I recognize you from the photo. The article's on the bulletin board in our staff room."

"Yeah, that's me." Heath got to his feet. Until now, he'd been embarrassed about that article but if it gave him an advantage in adopting this dog, he'd take it.

"I'll get my manager. Come around to the front and I'll see what we can do. No promises but we're a small rescue so for the right person my boss might be willing to start the adoption paperwork for Cookie today. At least that's what I heard her tell her mom earlier."

"Her mom?" The hair on the back of Heath's neck prickled.

"Mrs. Sullivan. She dropped off a pet store donation not more than half an hour ago." The girl's expression was puzzled. "She's here a couple of times a week. My boss calls her the rescue's 'Granny Annie.'"

"I see." He grinned at Cookie. Why hadn't he recognized it before? He needed this dog, and she needed him. Anne Sullivan was a wonder.

Cookie's gaze met his again, and she seemed to smile back as she wagged her tail in circles like a miniature windmill.

In his heart and where it counted most, this dog was already his and he was hers. The paperwork and everything else were only a formality.

CHAPTER SIX

ON A HOT Thursday afternoon in early July, Josie tugged her wide-brimmed straw hat farther down over her forehead and grabbed another berry pail.

"I wish we could pick strawberries all year round." In the patch of bushes nestled into a shady hollow in the woods below their farm, Lottie's face was stained pink with strawberry juice.

"Then strawberry season wouldn't be as special, would it? We're lucky it's lasted longer than usual this year." Josie grinned and cradled her daughter's pointed chin. "You look like you're eating more than you're picking."

"No I'm not. See?" Lottie held out her tin pail for Josie's inspection. "I'm fast, that's all."

"And I'm bored." Bella was sitting cross-legged beneath a tree, and her voice held a plaintive whine. "I filled my pail ages ago."

"Why not fill another one, then?" Josie gestured to the red wagon that had been hers as a child and then the girls had used, transporting everything from barn cats to their dolls and play construction tools. Now it had been brought into service to bring empty and full pails to and from the berry patch.

Bella shrugged, and Josie felt her forehead prickle into a worried frown. Bella was only ten, surely too young for a teenager's "attitude," but she was also getting to the age where she needed more than farm life.

"Tell you what. Why don't you invite a friend and we can all go to the baseball game in town on Friday night. With cotton candy, hot dogs, ice cream and all the rest. You, too, Lottie."

She'd gotten a few extra pet grooming jobs recently, including a visitor from Philadelphia whose Maltese had been sprayed by a skunk. The owner had been so grateful for Josie's help in restoring the dog's white, floor-length hair to its pristine glory, he'd given her an amazing tip. She'd use that money to treat her family.

"Really?" Bella's expression mixed wariness with hope.

"Sure, the time to have fun is now."

Because who knew what tomorrow might bring? Josie dismissed the morbid thought. The farm business would get better. Like Gramps said, it always did. She'd likely sign a big new milk supply contract soon and the crops were doing well. As long as they could hold off for a few months on machinery repairs, they'd be fine. The bank's loan officer had been encouraging about Josie's loan application, too. One way or another, they'd get through the fall and winter and these strawberries, either frozen or made into jelly, jam and syrup, would help.

"Yay." Lottie gave her a sticky hug, and Josie inhaled the scent of strawberries, sun lotion and hay and horses.

The seasons and years went by so fast and the girls were getting older. With her grandparents also growing older, sooner than Josie wanted to imagine she could be alone here. She couldn't wake up one day and decide she wasn't suited to solitude. Maybe, if the right man came along, she should at least be open to a relationship. Had she gotten too closed off and focused on the farm and her family?

She concentrated on plucking red berries from the low, creeping plant, the methodical, repetitive movement steadying her. Josie didn't have to think about the future today. The girls would be at home with her for years yet, and Grams and Gramps weren't going anywhere anytime soon, either.

"Thanks, Mom." Bella joined the hug, her expression once again open and childlike. "Can I use your phone to call Peyton?"

"We don't have much of a signal out here but you can try." Josie dug in the pocket of her shorts, unlocked her phone and scrolled to the number for Peyton, Bella's best friend, who lived in town.

"And then can I call Emily?" Lottie tugged on Josie's arm.

"Sure."

"If I had my own phone, I wouldn't have to borrow yours." As Bella held out her hand, she gave Josie a teasing smile. Her lack of a phone was currently grievance number one. "Everyone else my age has one and—"

"Who's a good girl, Cookie? That's right, you are." Heath's voice echoed from the woods, higher than usual and with an almost singsong intonation.

"Cookie?" Lottie giggled.

"Shush." Josie gestured to the girls while trying to suppress her own laughter.

"Cookie, cookie, cookie." The voice came closer. He made sloppy kissing noises.

"Grown-ups are weird." Bella rolled her eyes and began to mimic Heath.

"Bella, no. He's coming this way." Josie shook her head.

"So, it's funny, isn't it?" Bella's dark eyes twinkled.

It was but Heath had no reason to suspect he wasn't alone. As for Josie, while the serious, urbane man was attractive, this unexpected playful, almost goofy side of him was even more compelling. She pressed a hand against her stomach to hold back more laughter.

A black-and-white dog darted into the hollow, and Heath careened after it. Wide-eyed, he gripped the end of the dog's leash like an inexperienced water skier being towed behind a speedboat. "Cookie want a cookie? Oh." As he caught sight of Josie and the girls, his face flushed brick red. "I can explain. Cookie's my new dog and she, we…"

"No need." Josie glanced at Lottie and Bella who, small shoulders shaking, had their backs turned as the dog tumbled around their legs. "Sorry, I…" Her voice shook before she started to laugh.

Heath joined in, all four of them roaring with laughter as Cookie bounced between them.

"I'm trying to teach her to come when she's called." Heath spoke between gasps as he caught his breath. "The rescue staff named her Cookie, not me. I get how it must sound. How I must have sounded talking to her."

Josie couldn't remember the last time she'd laughed so hard or with such unabashed joy. "Cookie isn't an unusual name for a pet. It's cute and it suits her." She gestured to the girls now playing with the dog. "She's sweet like a cookie." While Heath could have changed the dog's name, he hadn't and that said something important about his character. He was more concerned with making Cookie comfortable than what anyone else thought.

"Even though our lost-dog posters didn't work, Cookie still found her forever home." Lottie came over and nestled into Josie's side.

"She did." Heath's voice was gruff as he wound the dog's leash around his hand to bring her closer to them. "And it was seeing one of your posters and then talking to Mrs. Sullivan that made me think I should go to the rescue and see how Cookie was doing. From there, as soon as I saw her again I knew I had to adopt her. Maybe it was fate I came around that corner when she ran out. We were meant to be together."

As he bent to rub the dog's ears, the love and happiness in his face made something in Josie's frozen heart crack. Warmth flooded through her and she took a step back.

The strawberry patch looked exactly the same as it had seconds before with its mix of sunshine and shady nooks. Her tin pail was still where she'd set it when she'd been overcome by that oh-so-unexpected laughter that had released a tight knot inside—one she hadn't realized she'd been carrying. And now she was somehow lighter in mind, body and spirit, as if Heath's playfulness had sparked an answering response in her and forged a new and more meaningful connection between them.

"I know." Lottie tugged on Josie's arm. "Heath and Cookie can come to the baseball game with us. You said we could invite friends." In Lottie's happy and excited expression, Josie glimpsed her own childhood self.

"Oh, I couldn't," he said.

"I expect Heath already has plans." Josie spoke at the same time as Heath. She kept her gaze on the girls and Cookie while she tried to manage a neutral expression.

"But you're the only one who hasn't invited a friend. Heath's a friend, isn't he?" Lottie looked up at her, innocent and trusting.

"Yes, well…" Ordinarily, Josie would have invited Alana, Laura or both of them. However, her friends were out of town, Laura for a horse show and Alana a family wedding. "You're welcome to join us. It's this Friday night. The game starts at seven at the ballpark south of town."

"If Bella and me go with Grams and Gramps, you can drive with Heath and Cookie to show them where." Lottie hugged the dog. "Dogs are allowed." She turned to Heath. "Please say yes?"

"It sounds fun. I'd be happy to join you." Over Lottie's head, and as Bella studied them with an inscrutable expression, Heath's gaze caught Josie's and held. "What time should I pick you up?"

"Around six would be fine." What had she gotten herself into? Or rather, what had Lottie gotten her into? Now Josie was the inexperienced water skier being pulled along by a speedboat, one half of her excited and the other scared at being yanked out of her comfort zone.

"Good." Heath smiled. Softer, more intimate and, for the first time, a smile that reached his eyes and seemed to come from deep in his soul.

"We can also help you train Cookie," Lottie said.

Bella turned away and picked up an empty berry pail.

"Mommy knows lots about dogs. Here." Before Josie realized what Lottie intended, her daughter took Josie's hand and placed it atop of Heath's on the fluorescent pink handle of Cookie's leash. "Show him walking manners, Mommy."

Still, Josie stared at him, and her hand, as good as holding his, tingled at the connection. A new kind of warmth shot through her. Maybe Heath wasn't her opposite at all. And maybe she wanted to get to know him better to find out what they did have in common.

"As you saw, Cookie and I need some pointers." There was a slight hitch in Heath's voice. Was he as affected by her touch as she was by his? "I've never had a dog before, and since it's summer, there aren't any group obedience classes offered here until September."

When he'd be back in Boston. Josie pulled her gaze away and then, more reluctantly, her hand. "Sure."

"I'd pay you, of course. If it works, we could start now?"

"Great." She had to think of this situation as a business transaction. Extra money was always welcome. As for the baseball game, it would be friendly. Neighborly.

Even if it felt like a lot more and despite her better judgment, part of her wanted to embrace those feelings. No matter the consequences.

"Park anywhere between the orange traffic cones." From the passenger seat of Heath's car, Josie directed him to a space in the middle of a grassy field.

Since he'd picked her up, and apart from some stilted conversation about the weather, they'd had a mostly silent ride into town and out here to the baseball diamond. However, Heath had been keenly aware of Josie's nearness.

Her crisp fragrance, floral mixed with a fruity tang, infused his senses and made him think of a summer day by the ocean. And with her hair pulled up in a high ponytail beneath a white ball cap, and wearing a denim skirt paired with white sneakers, a green tank top and a sweatshirt tied around her shoulders, all her natural beauty shone through.

"Here we are." He shut off the car and got out of the vehicle to go around to Josie's side. However, before he reached her door, she'd already hopped out and was waving to a group exiting a wheelchair-accessible van several spaces over.

"Sorry." Pink tinged her cheeks. "I'm used to doing things on my own so I didn't think to wait." She fiddled with the handle of her purse.

"It's fine. I know you can get out of a car by yourself." Although his mom had raised him to be considerate, Josie was smart, strong and capable and didn't need him or any other guy to jump in to try to handle things for her, big or small. He opened the rear door and unbuckled Cookie from her pet restraint.

"Still, you wanting to open my door was kind of nice." Was that a hint of vulnerability in her face? "I'm not used to… Never mind, it's not important." She gave him a bright smile and patted Cookie. "We'd better find our seats. My grandparents and the girls will have saved space for us. It's a good time to practice getting Cookie used to walking on her leash around other people."

"Let's walk, Cookie." Heath put his key fob in his pocket and tried to focus on the dog.

Yet, as they made their way to the ballpark's

entrance, he kept stealing quick glances at the woman by his side. Josie didn't need a man, but she also wasn't used to being cared for, cherished, protected and supported in all the ways a loving and respectful man should treat the women in his life, a wife or girlfriend especially. A memory sparked of the day they'd met. Lottie's comment, before Martha had hushed her, about her dad and what was evidently child support money. Was it not enough?

"Will you let me pay for your game ticket? In exchange for that fantastic pie?"

"Sure, thanks." Josie's smile and brief words of appreciation were almost shy, and as they reached the booth, she stood back as Heath got their tickets.

"Where to now?"

"I'll show you." She grinned and when the sun caught her hair and turned it red like fire, his heart about stopped.

He turned and followed as she led them around the edge of the field to the bleachers near home plate.

It was a perfect summer evening, warm with high clouds and hazy sunshine, and rich with the scents of popcorn, hot dogs and cotton candy. Heath often attended games at Fenway, and this small-town ballpark, home of the Strawberry Pond Strikers, was far from being in the same league. Yet, it had its own appeal and, he had to admit, a lot of that was because of the woman he was with.

"There they are." Josie called to her girls. "See? Gramps always comes early to get great seats."

"Yeah." Heath led a surprisingly obedient Cookie up the bleacher steps to join the Ryan family.

When he'd picked Josie up, the others had already left. While he'd appreciated not having a group meet him at the farmhouse's front door, it wasn't a date so he'd have had no reason to feel awkward. Since his divorce, he'd only had a couple of casual dates, but tonight felt different. It was the first time in a few months that he'd gone out with a woman he wasn't related to, which was a little momentous in itself. It was part of moving forward, though, despite the unexpected butterflies in his stomach when Josie had greeted him and still seemed to have no intention of subsiding.

"Hey, everyone." He exchanged hellos with Tom, Martha and the girls before taking the empty seat at the end of the row, beside Josie who had Tom on her other side. She was even closer than she'd been in the car and as she put her purse on her lap, her bare forearm brushed his, making Heath's awareness of her even more pointed.

"Oops." She gave him a half smile as she settled herself and gave Cookie a treat.

"No problem." He'd expected she'd sit with Bella and Lottie but they were on the opposite side of Tom and Martha with other girls their age.

"My dad was one of the founders of the Strawberry Pond Strikers after the Second World War." Tom, in jeans and wearing a cap and shirt emblazoned with the team's logo, leaned across Josie toward Heath as if about to tell a story he'd recounted many times before. "When Dad came back from overseas, he and a bunch of other boys from around here who helped liberate Paris in 1944 had a notion they'd put together a team."

"Gramps." Josie touched her grandfather's arm. "Heath might not be interested in your stories."

As she sat back, Heath drew in a breath as the breeze caught a strand of Josie's hair and it brushed his cheek. It was soft, silky, and that brief touch was almost like a kiss. "It's okay, I'd like to hear about local history." Maybe it would stop him from thinking about Josie and kissing her. He mustered an interested smile for Tom.

"Of course you would." Tom grunted. "It's your family history, too. A lot of Bergerons, Thibeaults and Tremblays have played on this team over the years. Back in the day, Bert Tremblay was the best pitcher in five counties. In the 1950s, he and a few others put this town on New Hampshire's baseball map. Strawberry Pond was known as a hotbed of talent. We might be small but we're mighty."

Anne Sullivan had mentioned Heath was related to a Gil Bergeron and when he'd asked his mom, she'd said that like the Thibeaults it was through her mother's side of the family. The Tremblays were related to Heath's dad, a family he knew nothing about and had nobody before now to ask.

"Who was Bert Tremblay?" Heath clenched his hands together in his lap, the crowd noise and vintage ball game organ music coming over the speaker system fading into the background.

"He'd have been... Let me see." Tom squinted. "I don't know exactly but one of your great-grandfather's brothers or cousins, I expect. The Tremblays all had big families and got scattered around. Your dad's branch lived over the mountain. Of course, they're all either dead or gone away now but a lot of them had what my mother called 'itchy feet.' Couldn't stick in one place. Like your dad, I guess. There's a bad apple in every crop but it doesn't mean the rottenness gets passed down." Tom's steady gaze studied Heath. "Your mom did right by you and that's all that matters. You don't want to go digging into the past, now, do you?" He took off his cap and they all stood as a man with a microphone announced they were about to sing the national anthem. As the crowd turned to face the flag, Tom glanced at Cookie, who stood quietly between Heath and Josie.

Heath joined the others in putting his right hand over his heart as a teenage girl led them in "The Star-Spangled Banner." As he sang the familiar words, his heartbeat slowed. He didn't want to go digging into the past whether it was with his marriage or his dad. However, maybe if the time was ever right, he should ask his mom some more questions about why his dad had left. Still, all that was over and it was this fresh start he had to focus on.

As the anthem ended, and the Strawberry Pond players in their red-and-white uniforms ran onto the field below, Cookie tugged on her leash and barked.

"You're a baseball fan, too?" He rubbed her ears, and the dog nuzzled his hand.

"Once she has better recall, I bet Cookie would like to chase a ball." Josie laughed and patted the dog, as well. "What do you think, sweetie? Should Heath get you a ball the next time he's at the pet store?"

Heath blinked. For a second, he'd thought Josie

had spoken to him rather than Cookie. While he was a practical guy who'd never been big on endearments, the affection in Josie's voice made him wonder what it would be like if he was her sweetie.

He glanced at Bella and Lottie, eating pink cotton candy and talking and laughing with their friends.

Which also made him wonder what it would be like if he and Josie were at this game on a real date, as a couple with *their* family.

CHAPTER SEVEN

"STAND BACK, GIRLS, over by the trees." Three days after the baseball game, and from her seat in the tractor parked in the middle of their hayfield, Josie waved Bella and Lottie out of the way. "Grams is meeting you, and if you go through the woods you'll be back at the barn before me. Take the dogs." She waved to Buster and Honey, and the black-and-white border collie and yellow Lab ran to join the girls.

"But we want to ride with you." Bella put one hand on her hip as Buster, the collie, tried to herd her nearer the trees as if she were an obstinate cow or sheep.

"Not this time. I'm going around by the highway and have a heavy load." She gestured to the baled hay piled high on the wagon hitched to the back of the green tractor. While she sometimes let the girls ride in the hay wagon, it was only when the wagon was empty, they were crossing a field and she could keep her eyes on them. None of those things applied today. "Go on, scoot. I already texted Grams. She'll be here any second." She grinned as she glimpsed the pink of her grams's T-shirt in the trees beyond where her daughters stood.

Bella made a sulky face as she followed Lottie and the dogs into the woods. If only the girls knew they were the lucky ones. Josie rubbed a hand across her sweaty forehead. Unlike the blazing sun beating down on the hayfield, the woodland path was shaded by tall maple trees and crisscrossed by a small stream. It was a shady, tranquil oasis and Josie would have exchanged places with her daughters in a heartbeat.

"Come on, Fifi." Josie patted the tractor's wheel and pressed the accelerator pedal. Only a few more hours and they'd be done haying. Then she could take a break. With a sputter, the vehicle jerked forward and then they were off across the newly cut field to the county road. While this route was a few miles farther, it was flat and with a loaded wagon that was more important.

Stopping and looking both ways, she drove Fifi onto the road, the heavy wagon bumping along behind. Although the sky behind her was still blue and the sun shone bright, gray storm clouds hovered up ahead over the ridge. "Faster, Fifi." While more modern tractors could reach twenty-five miles per hour or even higher, Fifi's top speed was about fifteen—and that was on a good day. "Come on, girl." Rain on hay was bad for lots of reasons, but the biggest was because the hay lost nutrients and wasn't as good for animals, like their dairy cows, who relied on it for feed.

Glancing over her shoulder, she chewed her lower lip. It might not look like it to the ordinary person, but there was a lot of money in that wagon. Money she couldn't afford to lose. Through the open window, a cold wind swept into the cab and dust and bits of loose hay swirled across the road in her wake.

As Josie fumbled for her phone to call Gramps, a red pickup truck came toward her in the opposite direction, slowing as it approached. *Their* farm truck. She let out a breath. Gramps was already here with a tarp.

Several fat raindrops plopped onto the windshield, and she eased the tractor as far onto the shoulder of the road as possible and turned off the engine. Meanwhile, the pickup made a U-turn and parked behind her.

She jumped out of the cab and ran along the side of the hay wagon by a field of corn, mentally berating herself for not thinking to bring a tarp with her in the first place. She'd grown up in the White Mountains so there was no excuse for not knowing how fast the weather could change here. Still, if Gramps would only see sense and agree to wrapping the hay in plastic when it was in the field, they wouldn't be in this situation. Josie had lost count of how many times she'd explained the plastic would protect the hay and could then be recycled, increasing their farm's sustainability.

"Gramps, thank goodness..." She stopped as a much younger man got out of the truck's cab. "Heath? What are you doing here?" Since the baseball game, and although she'd been busy on the farm and hadn't seen him, he'd never been far from her thoughts. It wasn't only they'd had a fun evening. It was also that connection she'd first sensed between them seemed to deepen the more time they spent together. She couldn't pretend it didn't exist, but she didn't know whether she could—or should—act on it, either.

"I was going into town and dropped by your farm to see if you needed anything. Your gramps was worried about you with the hay and a storm blowing up." Heath brushed a hand through his thick hair, momentarily distracting Josie. "He was all set to drive out here himself but..." He hesitated. "He pulled a muscle in his back so your grams and the college student you hired are moving the earlier load of hay in. The girls are helping with the lighter stuff."

"Oh no." Josie's thoughts spun as panic gripped her. Bella and Josie weren't big enough to manage full-size hay bales. As for Grams, at Josie's insistence she'd given up heavy work several years ago.

"I may not know hay from wheat but I have some muscle." Heath gave her a tight smile. "Only from working out at a gym so not like yours, but I expect it's better than nothing. Tell me what to do and I'll do it." He pulled a white tarp from the bed of the pickup. "Here. Your gramps sent it. I've got two."

"Take one end and I'll show you." The rain hadn't started full force yet and with luck they'd get the bulk of the hay covered before it did.

Working as fast as she could, Josie maneuvered one end of the billowing piece of plastic over the top of the hay. "That's right. Pull it as tight as you can. We don't want water to pool or a gust of wind to catch it." She demonstrated.

Two more vehicles drew up, one towing a horse trailer.

"Need help?" Fred Sinclair, the newspaper editor, got out of his car and rolled up his shirtsleeves.

"Grab the other tarp." Josie gestured toward the pickup truck's bed as two of the Sullivan boys, Anne's grandsons, sprang from the truck with the horse trailer.

"It's starting to rain harder." Atop the hay, Heath's frown was worried.

"I know." She wrestled with a rope to tie a corner of the tarp down.

"If you want, Fred and I can toss some of the bales from the back into our horse box. It's empty." Connor Sullivan, one of Josie's former high school classmates, shouted to her above the rising wind.

She gave him a thumbs-up as Colm, Connor's twin, showed Heath how to fix a rope to secure the other side of the tarp.

In silence, Josie worked her way around one side of a tarp as Colm and Heath did the same across from her. Dull thuds echoed as Connor and Fred flung hay bales, ones that couldn't fit under the tarps, into the trailer.

Thunder rumbled and lightning lit up the darkening fields. *One more corner.* Josie slid down the side of the wagon and grabbed the final rope. "Almost there." With wet fingers, she fumbled to make a knot.

"I've got it." Heath's hands covered hers and they made the tie together.

"We did it." She gasped, her heart pounding with relief and excitement. Heath had pitched in with the others and she'd almost forgotten he was a city guy. *Her* city guy. No, that was ridiculous. She pushed wet hair away from her face and slid down the side of the tarp to the ground.

"Hay's all in, Jojo." Colm whooped. "We'll drive

our load home for you." He and Connor got back into their truck to escape the now-pouring rain.

"You should get back in the cab." Heath's voice was low as he joined her by the side of the wagon. "I'll follow you to the farm and pitch in with whatever else is needed. I already took this afternoon off work."

"That would be great." Her teeth chattered and her body shook as Heath took her arm and guided her around the wagon and back into the tractor's seat.

"You've got this." His voice was matter-of-fact, and he gently squeezed her arm before taking his hand away. "I had no idea, but Colm told me how much this hay crop is likely to be worth. Here." He found Josie's phone where she'd dropped it on the floor. "You probably want to call your gramps and tell him we're on our way." He gave her a teasing smile. "Clarabelle, Little Ming, Daffodil and the others will have their feed this winter."

They were only three miles, tops, from the barn but it had been three miles too many. She tried to smile back. Heath's hair was plastered to his forehead, he had a piece of hay stuck to his chin and his blue polo shirt and previously crisp jeans were now sodden and streaked with mud. Josie didn't want to think what she must look like. Having been in the field all day, likely even worse than him.

"For a city guy, you almost look like a real farmer." She plucked the hay off his chin, teasing him back. He'd never looked better was what she'd almost said because that's what she'd first thought.

"Maybe there's hope for me yet." Heath leaned nearer and his warm breath brushed her cheek.

"Say, can you two give me a smile?" With a camera around his neck, Fred poked his head into the tractor's cab. "Everyone pitching in to save the hay is a crackerjack of a story. That's it. Stay right where you are, Heath, nice and close to Josie. Heads together." He took a few shots before Josie could stop him. "Saving the hay, saving the day! What do you think?" He chortled at his joke. "Right there on the front page in next week's edition."

Heath made a noise that sounded like something between a snort and a groan while Josie sat rigid with a fixed smile. It was pointless to try to stop Fred. In his pursuit of what passed for Strawberry Pond news, he was relentless, albeit cloaked in folksy humor and down-home charm.

"There, all done." Fred beamed. "I'll email you copies, shall I? Your folks would be real proud of you, Josie. You know, you remind me a lot of your mother. Not that she ever looked at me, but I was real sweet on her back in middle school. My missus and I've had thirty-five happy years together but you never forget your first unrequited crush, do you?" Shirt buttons straining, he squeezed out of Fifi's narrow cab. "Coming, Heath?"

"Yeah." Now Heath looked as if he was trying not to laugh. "See you back at the farm?"

"Of course." As she started Fifi again, Josie's own laughter bubbled up. Fred was part of her small-town life and despite its occasional embarrassing moments, she wouldn't change it or him.

But what might have happened if he hadn't interrupted her and Heath? The way Heath had leaned in close and she'd moved toward him, instinct taking over.

She shivered and yanked on the sweatshirt she kept in the cab. Like thinking of him as her city guy, it was another foolish thought she'd never have considered if not for being shaken up.

So why was the thought of kissing Heath also so appealing?

"You promised you'd stay in bed until at least eight." At seven the next morning, Martha shook her head at her husband as he entered the farmhouse kitchen.

"The doctor said exercise is good for back pain. Keeps me mobile." Tom took a chocolate chip cookie from the cooling rack and gave her the smile Martha had never been able to resist.

"But the doctor also said you need your rest." Martha swatted his hand away from the cookies. "It won't do you any harm to sleep in now and again."

"I've always been an early riser and you can't teach this old dog new tricks." Tom shrugged and sat at the table. "Is Josie in the barn?"

"Yes, and she was already out there when I came downstairs over an hour ago." Martha glanced out the kitchen window where the garden was still wet with dew. "The girls are asleep. Poor things, they can sleep as long as they want. The way they pitched in yesterday. Like little troopers they were."

"They're farm kids, all right." Tom made as if to rise from his chair.

"Now that you're sitting, stay sitting." Martha waved him back and poured two cups of coffee from the pot on the stove. "They may be farm kids but it was too much for them. Too much for all of us. We need to hire steady help. A college student for a day here and there isn't enough."

"Martha—"

"No, I need to say my piece." Putting the rest of her cookie dough back in the fridge, she took the coffees over to the table and sat across from Tom. "If yesterday wasn't a wake-up call, I don't know what will be. Back pain or not, you can't work like you once did. If Heath and then the

Sullivan boys and Fred Sinclair hadn't come along when they did, we'd have been in a fine fix. How would we ever have gotten all that hay into the barn yesterday?" Although Martha tried not to let herself imagine "what-ifs," they nevertheless preyed on the edges of her mind like the itch from midge bites.

"We were lucky." Tom swirled a spoon in his coffee cup.

Martha reached for Tom's hand and held it. "I know it's not easy growing older, but we both have to face facts." She stroked the sinews and knots as familiar to her as those on her own hands, a map of their lives together. "If we can't afford to hire help, maybe we should think about selling up. Who knows if Bella and Lottie will want to take on this farm, and Josie can't manage it alone."

"She thinks she can." Tom's voice was gruff. "Let's give it another year. If the weather holds, we're on track for a good crop and we're still managing with the dairy business."

"Only just and our costs keep going up. Feed, fertilizer and fuel are all expensive." From doing the books, Martha knew their profit and loss margins to the last penny and there wasn't any more room to cut. "We need a miracle."

"I have to believe we'll get one." Tom gave her hand a reassuring squeeze.

"We might if you'd only take that next step. Listening to Josie isn't enough. You've got to let Josie implement some of her ideas and support her." She took a deep breath. "You, me and Josie all have an equal say about what happens on this farm. Up until now, I've always been on your side and haven't gone against you but…oh, Tom. What is it? Tell me." His expression wasn't so much angry as despairing and it tugged at her heart.

"Nothing. Stop fussing over me." He shoved his chair away from the table and stumbled to his feet.

"But I love you, and I'm worried about you." If only they could have had more children, that big family they'd wanted, but it wasn't to be. Long ago they'd had to make the best of it when it came to the farm.

"Can you see me living in town? In one of those houses they're building for retired folks?" He grimaced. "They look like shoeboxes."

"I didn't mention moving to town, but as for those houses, you've never been inside one of them. They might be real nice and cozy. They'd sure be new and more convenient than this old place. Besides, if the farm improved with Josie's ideas, we wouldn't have to move." Martha followed him as he limped to the kitchen door. "Come back here and I'll fix you some breakfast. You can't take one of your pain pills on an empty stomach."

"I'm not hungry, and I don't need a pill." Tom half turned to her. "I'll go out to the barn and see how Josie's getting on. If only she had a husband, a partner in this, I could rest easier."

Martha gave him a one-armed hug. "No husband is better than the one she had. She's happy on her own and does the work of two men around here."

Tom's tight shoulders relaxed under Martha's gentle touch. "I want her to have what we do. All these years, I couldn't have managed this place without you by my side."

"We're a partnership in farming *and* life. We complement one another." But that partnership meant talking to each other and really listening. "You're my best friend, Tom, and I need you to be honest with me about this farm and everything else."

"Of course I'm honest with you." He grabbed his work boots from the tray by the mudroom door. "It's been too long since we had a date night. What do you say we go to the Strawberry Spot for dinner on Friday? Leave Josie and the girls to fend for themselves. You could wear that blue dress that matches your eyes. It's the same color as the one you wore to your senior prom. Remember?"

"How could I forget?" Martha suppressed a sigh. Inside, she still felt a lot like that eighteen-year-old with her whole life ahead of her, but the wrinkles reflected back at her in her dressing table mirror told a different story. She was in the last part of her life but that didn't mean it had to be any less fulfilling or fun. "Dinner on Friday sounds good. Now, go on with you and bring Josie in. Tell her I'll have breakfast ready in twenty minutes for both of you." She wagged her forefinger at him. "Don't overdo."

As Tom walked along the path to the barn more slowly than usual, Martha stood at the kitchen window and watched. Some might think age had made Tom cantankerous. Although she hadn't said it in so many words, Josie did. But Martha knew better. Tom was afraid. She also suspected what he feared. While at their age they both worried about growing older and becoming infirm, that was something they shared. If Martha was right, Tom was afraid of something that was for him even bigger. Losing control of the farm and, with it, the only way of life he knew.

When he went into the barn, she turned to the fridge and opened it to get out eggs and the other ingredients to make her husband's favorite Western omelet. Somehow, she had to help him see that instead of being frightening, the unknown could be both joyful and exciting.

She cracked eggs into a bowl and considered her next steps. Then, she picked up her phone and found Anne Sullivan's number. If anyone might have some good advice in this situation, it would be Anne, her best friend since their schooldays. But she'd have to make her swear to not breathe a word to anyone, Josie and Tom especially.

CHAPTER EIGHT

"Good girl, Cookie. Great walking manners." With the dog's leash in one hand and a wicker picnic basket he'd found on a shelf in Bea's pantry in the other, Heath made his way across the town green greeting people as he went. Cory Bailey, his great-aunt's attorney, was here with his wife and kids along with Anne Sullivan and her family, the teenage girl from the animal rescue and many more. "What about here under this tree? Is it a good spot?"

Cookie wagged her tail, which he took as a "yes," so he set the basket on the grass and pulled out a tartan blanket. The last time he'd picnicked was with his ex, Danielle, at a concert in a Boston park a few weeks before they split up, but he was a different person now. And tonight, listening to Strawberry Pond's brass band, even by himself, was another part of his fresh start and new life.

He rubbed Cookie's ears and poured water into a dish for her. "There you go." He set the dish in front of her, laughing as she slopped water on the grass.

"Heath." Lottie ran across the green toward him, and Cookie tugged on her leash to greet the girl.

"Hang on, Cookie. Don't jump. Sit." Clearly, the two of them needed more obedience lessons with Josie. "Sorry about that." He pulled Cookie back, although after she'd already given Lottie a slobbery kiss.

"It's okay." Lottie giggled. "Mom and Bella are coming with our picnic." She glanced at his basket. "If you're not with anyone, can we sit here, too?"

"Sure, I'm here by myself." Since he'd come to this park concert on his own, he'd assumed he'd stay that way. But, and as if he'd needed another reminder, Strawberry Pond wasn't like any other community he'd known. He was grateful to have neighbors with whom he enjoyed spending time.

An almost-forgotten memory surfaced of his own childhood, running around this same green with a bunch of other kids. It must have been a community event because half the town and lots from the surrounding area were here and a barbecue had been set up over by the pond. It was also one of the few times Heath remembered all four of them, his parents, sister and him, had been together as a family.

Lottie sat on the edge of Heath's picnic blanket and kicked off her sandals. "What did you make to eat?"

"I didn't, actually. I ordered food to take out from a store and picked it up." At Lottie's raised eyebrows, a mirror image of Josie, Heath's face heated.

"You must be rich."

"Lottie." Josie's voice came from behind Heath. "What have I told you about making personal comments?"

"That it's rude?" Lottie grinned.

"She's fine." Heath tried not to laugh as he greeted Josie and Bella. "I told Lottie you were welcome to join me."

"Knowing Lottie, I expect she invited herself." Josie shook her head at her daughter. "If you'd rather listen to band music on your own, we won't be offended, Heath. It would be quieter, that's for sure, without these two chattering away." She gave the girls a fond smile.

"I'd enjoy your company, all of you." He turned to Bella, who stood behind Josie. She was quieter than her younger sister and seemed to approach life with more caution. He patted the blanket and Bella sat by Lottie although she kept her sneakers on.

Josie set a cooler and reusable grocery bag filled with food containers on the grass and then spread out her blue-and-green-striped blanket next to his. "Who's hungry?"

Cookie barked and nosed Heath's picnic basket.

As Josie and the girls laughed, Heath joined in. He'd laughed more in the past few weeks than he had in months, years maybe. "You want your supper, too, do you?" He unpacked the basket and set out Cookie's food. Then he gestured to the take-out containers of deli salads, sandwiches, fruit, chocolate brownies and a cheese, cracker and olive plate. "Help yourselves. I've got plenty."

"You sure do." Lottie's eyes went wide as she took in the feast.

"Girls, we have our own picnic." Josie took out plates, cups and a thermos followed by thick-cut cheese sandwiches, a bag of potato chips and smaller containers holding carrot and celery sticks. "Thank you, Heath, but…" She swallowed and looked away.

Studying her stiff profile, Heath's stomach knotted. He'd wanted to be hospitable but this lavish picnic, which he'd ordered from a specialty food store catering to tourists, had embarrassed her. He wanted to make things right, but how?

"I want—"

"Not now, Lottie. Bella, please pour your sister some lemonade." Josie's voice hitched as she rummaged in the cooler for a tub of raspberries.

"I ordered way too much food for one person. You guys would be doing me a favor by helping out." He glanced at Lottie and Bella. "What do you say I trade you chocolate brownies for one of your sandwiches? I love homemade cheese sandwiches. Yours look like ones my mom used to make for my birthday parties when I was your age."

Those parties didn't cost a lot of money but they'd been fun and filled with love. And as Heath looked at Josie's simple picnic beside his gourmet spread, the knot in his stomach tightened. He liked good food, sure, but more than what he ate, what he'd remember most was whom he shared this meal with and the memories they made.

"Can we, Mom?" Bella tugged Josie's arm.

"Please?" Lottie wrapped her arms around Josie's neck and planted a noisy kiss on her cheek.

"I guess so. It's very kind of Heath to offer to share." Josie's face was still pink and, when she turned back to him, her eyes glistened. "Sorry." She glanced at the girls, who, after giving Heath his choice of sandwich, filled their plates with food from both picnics. "I overreacted." She spoke in a low voice and gave him an awkward smile. "I know you meant well. I have kind of a thing about expensive treats and not only because I don't have the budget for them. How you spend your money is your business but my ex-husband, he…" She grimaced and almost whispered. "While he likes the finer things in life, that doesn't always extend to providing enough for his children. Or making time to see them."

"That must be hard." Heath clenched his hands. The guy didn't know how lucky he was. Even if his relationship with their mother didn't work out, what kind of man didn't support his kids in every way they needed him?

"Yeah, it is." Josie took a piece of creamy brie, two crackers and several olives. She wore her wavy hair loose and it tumbled across the front of the casual white embroidered blouse she'd paired with faded jeans and green sandals. "I've gotten used to it and between the farm, dog grooming and teaching fitness classes, I manage. My grandparents are a big help. Grams and Gramps raised me after my parents were killed in a car accident by a drunk driver when I was three. They'd gone out for dinner to celebrate their anniversary and on the way back, a guy in a pickup truck crossed the center line and hit them. He killed himself and Mom and Dad."

"I'm so sorry." Heath unclenched his fingers and his mouth went dry. Josie was strong and more capable than most, but she also had a delicate femininity and grace that made for a potent—and appealing—combination.

"Thanks." She nibbled an olive, and Heath made himself focus on his sandwich rather than the gentle curve of her rosy lips. "It was a long time ago but I still miss them. Even though I hardly remember them. Is that weird?"

"Not at all." Bella and Lottie were absorbed in their food and watching several girls turn cartwheels, and Cookie lay quiet at Heath's side. "It's not the same but my dad left my mom and my sister and me when I was seven. I still miss him, although I'm also still mad at him. I guess that's weird."

"No." Josie's eyes were two blue pools of sympathy. "Families are complicated. I know that sounds trite but it's true. I'm still in touch with my mom's older sister, but after her parents, my grandparents on that side of the family passed, she moved to Colorado. There's nobody else from my mom's family left here. Did you ever hear from your dad again?"

"A couple of notes scrawled on the back of postcards. They were sent from all over. Alaska, New Mexico, Florida, Texas. Then someone he worked with got in touch with my mom." Heath set aside his sandwich. "Dad was working on an oil rig in the Gulf of Mexico and there was an accident. He was killed instantly." Heath frowned. "I was ten and even though by that time Mom and Dad were divorced, a part of me had still hoped Dad would come back, say he'd made a big mistake and want us to be a family again."

"I'm sorry for you, too." Josie's warm hand reached for Heath's cold one and although she only gave it a brief pat, warmth slid through him, comforting, right and reassuring.

"So, where are your grandparents tonight?" Heath coughed and cleared the unexpected emotion from his throat.

"On a dinner date at the Strawberry Spot." Josie smiled and exhaled as if grateful for the change of subject. "They'll be along soon. Gramps loves what he calls 'toe-tapping' music. He used to play the trumpet with that band." She waved her cup of lemonade in the direction of the bandstand where the musicians, including Fred Sinclair, were setting up. "He was good but with things being so busy on the farm he didn't have time for rehearsals so he gave it up." Her smile slid away.

"That's too bad." *But what had Josie given up?* As she turned to speak to Bella and Lottie, Heath couldn't shake the sense Josie might have sacrificed even more than her grandfather. Between the farm, girls and those other jobs, she must hardly have time to sleep, let alone for hobbies. *Or dating.* Would she have time for a man in her life? Did she even want one?

Heath hadn't thought he wanted a woman in

his life, but together with this town, something about Josie was also changing him. While he was attracted to her, it was more than that of a man being drawn to a pretty and interesting woman. They had more in common than he expected, having both come through a divorce and losing parents in childhood. Both those things left scars, invisible but deep, that only someone who'd experienced them could understand.

"Mr. Tremblay?" Without him noticing, Bella had scooted over beside him. "Want a brownie?" She held out the container. "You better have one before Lottie eats them all." Her soft giggle made it seem they were sharing a joke.

"Yeah, sure. Thanks, and please call me Heath." Mr. Tremblay was his dad and he didn't need that reminder, especially from these sweet girls. He took one of the rich chocolate treats as the band started playing a marching song he vaguely recognized.

He'd never considered keeping Bea's property, but what if he did? With some repairs and modern upgrades like air-conditioning and a power shower, Tabby Cat Hollow would make a fine summer home. Josie was the perfect person to give him advice about tending the surrounding land.

But what if she was also the perfect person for him?

A WEEK LATER, Josie pulled open the diner door and rushed through it, heading for a booth at the back. She was running late but with Gramps still having back problems, even more of the farmwork fell to her. Still, meeting her friends for their regular breakfast was a priority. She took the empty seat across from Laura and beside Alana. "I had to drive around the block three times before I found a place to park. I need coffee."

The Strawberry Spot Diner had been a fixture in Strawberry Pond since Josie's grandparents were young. On the town's main street, nestled between the hardware store and pharmacy, its red vinyl booths, white Formica-topped tables, red-and-black-tiled floor and restored vintage jukebox had a timeless retro vibe.

"That's tourist season for you." Alana waved down a waitress who'd been a few years ahead of Josie in school. "We'd have understood if you'd had to cancel." Her friend's smile was both concerned and sympathetic. "You look tired."

"I am but you know I can't miss the FarmHers." She smiled at her friends. While the name "FarmHers" had started as a joke to describe their bond as women working in agriculture, it now symbolized a close friendship that extended far beyond farming. "These breakfasts keep me going."

Josie thanked the waitress for the coffee and ordered her usual "Farmhouse special," eggs over easy with a side of pancakes, home fried potatoes, grilled ham, cottage cheese and a fruit bowl. She'd been up since before sunrise. And after morning milking, feeding the animals and other barn chores, watering the garden and putting in a load of laundry, she was ravenous.

"They keep *all* of us going." Laura raised her coffee mug in a toast.

"Hear, hear." Alana drained her glass of orange juice. "The wedding was fun, but between the library and orchard, I'm still trying to catch up. Don't get me started on working at our farm stand. A man yesterday complained the raspberries weren't red enough. I was tempted to say we'd run out of red food coloring except he might have believed me."

After their laughter subsided, Laura sobered. "He sounds like the woman who came to my barn and only wanted to buy a horse in what she called a 'pretty color.' It was like she wanted to coordinate the animal with her clothes. I didn't sell to her but can you believe some people? She didn't even mention the horse's temperament and what might fit with her as a rider."

As Josie joined in with more laughter and joking, her thoughts drifted to Heath. Why did she feel so comfortable with him? And why was she thinking of him when she was with her friends, the women she was closest to but yet still hadn't told anything about him?

"So, what's new with you?" Alana turned to Josie as if she'd plucked the thoughts out of Josie's head.

"Nothing much. The usual. Work. Except for Gramps and his back, everything's fine." As the waitress brought their breakfasts, Josie took a paper napkin from the metal holder and focused on her plate.

"No, what's really happening? With *you*?" After the waitress left, Alana elbowed Josie's arm. "At least five people have told me about your gramps and his back but that *fine* sounds like what you say when a checkout cashier asks if you're having a good day."

"Alana's right." Laura poured maple syrup onto a stack of fluffy buttermilk pancakes. "We've both known you too long to be put off with the same old, same old. The guy at the gas station where I filled up my truck yesterday told me all about your gramps right down to him refusing to take his pain pills. We want details about *you*."

"There's nothing to tell." Josie speared one of her eggs, and sunny-yellow yolk slid across the plate into a thick slice of maple-glazed ham. "You know I don't have an exciting life."

"We don't either, but from what I heard your

life has been picking up lately." Behind her bowl of oatmeal, Alana gave Josie a teasing, sideways look. "The word is you're spending a lot of time with Heath Tremblay."

"He lives next door." Josie kept her expression neutral. "I'd be friendly with anyone who'd moved in. I've seen him around town a few times. So what?"

"A baseball game, the band concert and he helped you get the hay in." Laura counted each instance on her fingers. "With another picture of you both in the newspaper and looking very cozy indeed."

"Only because that tractor cab is small, and Fred Sinclair made us squeeze close together." Still, Josie hadn't minded Heath's nearness and if she hadn't known better, she might have thought they were a couple in that second front-page picture.

"You were seen in the jewelry store with him as well, although that was likely a coincidence." Alana grinned. "I'm surprised you haven't said anything to us."

"That's because there's nothing to say." At least not about her feelings, which Josie wasn't ready to share with anyone, not even her dearest friends. "It's not as if we've gone on a date. My grandparents or the girls have always been around. As for getting the hay in, Heath happened to drop by and offered to help. Connor and Colm Sullivan pitched in, too." Except if she and Heath had been alone, the baseball game and band concert would have felt like dates.

"Yes, but the Sullivan boys are married. Heath's not," Laura said. "He's also not bad-looking."

Josie paused. "Not bad-looking" was an understatement and along with his good looks, Heath's single status made him way too appealing.

"He's also smart and has a great job," Alana added. "He's kind as well and all the older ladies in town haven't stopped talking about him. You should have heard them at the last knitting club meeting. When we were short-staffed in the library, he helped a visually impaired patron look up a book in the online catalog and then found it on the shelf for her."

"If he's so great, why don't either of you date him?" Josie ate some egg and fried potato without tasting it.

"Gotcha!" Laura gave Alana a high five and they both laughed.

"What?" Josie glanced around the busy diner hoping nobody had overheard their conversation.

Heath was free to go out with whomever he wanted and so were her friends. Yet, she didn't want him to date anyone but her. Awareness hit her full force, like that rogue ocean wave had knocked her flat when she'd gone to Maine with a high school friend and her parents. She had feelings for Heath that went beyond being friendly, and how he sometimes looked at her suggested he might feel the same. Like in that picture of them in Fifi's cab.

"If you like Heath and he likes you back, why not? All that 'togetherness' you two have going on can't only be coincidence." Having finished her oatmeal, Alana buttered a strawberry muffin.

Laura nodded. "If Heath could make you happy, go for it. Life's short and so's summer. Have some fun."

Laura and Alana had been there for Josie when her marriage broke up, and since then they'd all been single together, focused on work and, in Josie's case, her daughters. But sometimes good friends knew you better than you knew yourself. The best friends pushed you out of your comfort zone when you were stuck in it.

At the front of the diner, several women in their seventies and eighties clustered around the jukebox as Anne Sullivan put coins in the slot. Then the sound of ABBA's "Take a Chance on Me" swirled around the room, the upbeat tune rising above the buzz of conversation and clatter of dishes.

Sometimes, you also got a sign exactly when you needed it. Josie laughed as Laura and Alana sang along like they'd done last summer when the three of them had dressed up in 1970s flares, ponchos and glittery platform shoes for an ABBA tribute concert Laura had won tickets for. As the song went, Josie could take a chance on Heath because if she didn't, she might always regret it.

Because no matter what, she could always count on her friends to be by her side, along with her family.

CHAPTER NINE

"Oh no." Late on Saturday afternoon, Heath jumped up from behind the wooden table he used as a desk and waved his arms in front of the half-open living room window. "Go on, shoo."

The massive black-and-white cow stared at him and then continued grazing.

Were any of the plants out there poisonous to cattle? On his way to the front porch, he stopped inside the screen door, grabbed his phone and scrolled to Josie's number. He was putting in a few hours of weekend work to meet a deadline and help a client. He'd been less productive than usual, though, distracted by thoughts of Josie.

The band concert had been fun and now, a week later and without having seen her, he wondered what she was up to. Between trying to come up with a reason to drop by her farm and remembering how Josie's pretty hair had curled around her shoulders and the sparkle in her gorgeous blue eyes, he'd spent more time daydreaming than working.

More time thinking about the past, too, as other childhood memories surfaced. His mom and sister teaching him to skate on a frozen pond and coming home to hot cocoa in front of a log fire. Shoveling snow after a big storm with his dad and feeling like the two of them were "guys" together. A day at the beach, eating ice cream cones and laughing at his dad's knock-knock jokes.

His dad had made bad choices but now, from an adult perspective, Heath tried to consider what had really been going on in the guy's head. He remembered his dad losing his job and not finding a new one, which must have been devastating. However, that alone didn't explain why he left his family behind. Whenever Heath had asked his mom, she'd always been evasive, embarrassed even, and said the marriage break-up had been a mutual decision. It was time he pushed her for the truth. Being here in Strawberry Pond meant Heath was going around in circles, digging into the past even though he knew it was likely a bad idea, just as Tom had said.

As Heath listened to Josie's phone ring, he kept waving his arms and made more "shooing" sounds.

Once again, the animal turned its head and stared as if to say, "Are you talking to me?"

He gave it a dirty look as Josie's phone went

to voicemail and he left a message. Meanwhile, seemingly unconcerned, the cow moved on to munch on a low bush near the fence.

"No, Cookie, stay inside with me." He didn't know if she'd been around cattle but he wouldn't take any chances. What was he supposed to do now? He turned back to the phone to search online for cows and plants, all the while keeping one eye on the enormous bovine in his front yard.

"It looks like you got yourself a problem." A gray-haired man in denim overalls and a baseball cap with a tractor decal on the front appeared at the foot of the porch steps and spoke to Heath through the screen. "I saw her moseying along across the field so I hustled over. Mike Murphy."

"Hi, yes, you're Anne Sullivan's brother. I should have come over to introduce myself before now but I've been busy. Heath Tremblay."

"I know who you are." Mike came up the porch steps as Heath joined him outside. "I saw you with Josie Ryan and her girls at the band concert. The two of you have also been making the local news. Every time I read my paper there's another picture of you front and center." His bright blue eyes narrowed. "That's the Ryan cow, isn't it? Clarabelle?"

"How can you tell?" To Heath, all cattle looked the same, although, now that he took a closer look, this one did seem somewhat familiar.

Mike grunted. "Well, she's got an udder, for a start. Also looks like she'll soon be ready for milking."

"Yes, well, that makes sense." From behind Mike, Heath stole a glance at Clarabelle, who still ate vegetation as if too busy to give them the time of day.

"If you've been around cattle for a while, you get to know them by their markings and personality." Mike grinned. "I also raised Clarabelle from when she was a little one before I sold her to Tom. I know her and she knows me. Always more of a free spirit, this girl."

"I see." Heath bit his lower lip. There was no reason for him to be embarrassed. He didn't know cows or much else about agricultural life. He didn't have a reason to, either, since even before leaving Strawberry Pond as a kid he'd lived in a subdivision outside town.

"Not to worry." Mike chuckled. "I'll have Clarabelle out of there in no time. You might want to put netting over those blueberry bushes. Once they're fully ripe, the birds will be at them. Likely your dog will get in there, as well. Clarabelle got a head start is all."

"Good idea. I thought... Well, I didn't know what she was eating." Heath might as well be honest. "I worried it might be poisonous to her."

"That's smart but there's nothing around here

that'll hurt her or any other livestock. Bea made sure of it." Mike took off his hat. "She was a nice lady with a good heart. I had a lot of respect for Bea." He put his cap back on. "My wife and I miss her."

"I do, too." A missing greater than Heath expected. Bea had had a long life and her death wasn't a surprise. Yet, living here in her home among her possessions had helped him see her in a new light. Not only as his white-haired great-aunt whose gait was slow and face wrinkled, but as a person in her own right. Someone who had a full life in between her visits to them in Boston. Someone who listened to jazz music and read cozy mysteries, did needlepoint and made cucumber pickles, jars of them lined up on a shelf in the stone cellar. And someone who'd saved every card and letter he'd sent her from childhood on and, more recently, had printed out every one of his email messages and kept them in the top drawer of her night table.

"Well, time's a-wasting and you must be busy. That cow's not going to move on by herself. I'd best be getting her herded off."

"It was good to meet you and talk." Heath meant it. Despite Mike's gruff manner, there was something about the other man he liked.

Mike nodded. "Me and my son, Pat, will be over next weekend to help with that porch of yours." He gestured with his thumb to the lumber and tools Heath had covered with a tarp. "It's all well and good to be self-sufficient but there are times when you need to call in experts." He shook his head. "You got in over your head there, boy."

Although Heath was hardly a boy, he took Mike's point. "I..." He turned at a thudding noise coming from the field behind the house and drew in a quick breath as Josie appeared riding a horse. Beneath a helmet, her hair blew behind her in the wind, and she sat straight as she and the horse cleared a small ditch at the edge of the field with ease.

"Like Clarabelle here, Josie's always been more of a free spirit." Mike followed Heath's gaze. "I've known her from the day she was born and watched her grow up. Along with my nephews, Colm and Connor, you won't find a better farmer in these parts, or one smarter, either. But more than that, she's a good woman. She and Bea weren't blood kin but the two of them were cut from the same cloth."

As Josie drew the horse to a walk, Heath still couldn't take his eyes off her. He'd only ridden a pony once, as a young boy at a country fair, so horses had never been part of his life. But even he could tell Josie was as comfortable on horseback as she was anywhere else. And currently as annoyed as he'd ever seen her.

"There you are, Clarabelle." She dismounted and led the horse toward them. "I've a mind to sell her back to you, Mike, but you likely don't want her, either." Josie's face was red and her eyes sparked blue fire. "I can't spend my days chasing around the country after this cow." She pressed her lips together and tied the horse in the shade to one of Heath's newly repaired fence posts. "Heath, meet Trixie."

He glanced around. "Oh, you mean the horse." He took a tentative step forward.

"Not just 'the horse,' she's *my* horse." Josie took off her helmet, shook out her hair and gave the animal an affectionate smile. "I've had her almost half my life. We were out for a ride checking crops when Grams texted me Clarabelle had gotten out again. I hope she didn't cause too much mayhem."

"She's fine, I think." Heath dragged his gaze away from Josie's magnificent hair to glance at the cow. Clarabelle now stood in the middle of what had once been Bea's garden like the queen of all she surveyed.

"I came over to herd her back to your place but got talking," Mike said. "Even though she's a good milker, I wouldn't take that cow back if you paid me. She's your problem."

"Figures." Josie gave him a rueful smile. "I do love Clarabelle but she sure tries my patience."

Mike patted Josie's shoulder. "I'll take her home if you like. I planned to head over to talk to your gramps, anyway. The fellows and I missed him at bowling last week."

"That would be great, thanks." Josie shook her finger at Clarabelle. "You behave, hear me?" She turned back to Mike. "Gramps will be happy to see you. His back pain's a lot better but the doctor said he shouldn't overdo. The problem is Gramps isn't used to sitting around so he's bored."

"Getting involved in your work, I expect." Mike's expression was knowing.

"No surprise there." Josie rolled her shoulders and winced. "Grams threatened to shut him in the henhouse if he didn't stay out of her kitchen. She was joking, but I have to say the idea sometimes has a certain appeal." Her laugh was tired.

"You look like you could sit for a while." As Mike went to corral Clarabelle, Heath gestured to the porch chairs. "Do you want a drink or anything?"

"I'm okay but…" Josie took her phone from the pocket of her jeans and checked it. "I can stay for a few minutes, I guess." She perched on the edge of a chair and set her riding helmet by her side. "How's Cookie doing?"

"See for yourself if your horse, Trixie, is okay with dogs?"

"She loves them."

Heath opened the screen door, clipped Cookie's leash to her collar and the dog tugged him to Josie.

"Hey, girl." She bent to give Cookie a hug, and Heath's breath caught. What would it be like to have Josie's arms wrapped around him and have her hold him close? He never expected to be jealous of his dog but right now he was.

"Um… Since our last lesson I've been working with Cookie on those commands and exercises you showed us."

"Let's see." Josie gave him an expectant look.

"Okay." For a moment, Heath was back at school anticipating a teacher's feedback but Josie's approval was more meaningful. He dug in the pocket of his shorts for dog treats. "Sit, Cookie. Good girl."

As he took Cookie through the everyday commands they'd practiced, his confidence and pride in the dog grew.

"You guys are doing great." Josie clapped and gave them one of her beautiful smiles.

"We have a great teacher." He ruffled the hair at Cookie's neck and gave her a last treat. "Speaking of which, I want to ask you something." Heath hesitated and glanced around.

Mike had left with Clarabelle so they were alone. "Well, tell you something first." He took a deep breath. "I'm considering not selling this place but instead keeping it as a summer home. I'd rent it out when I wasn't here." He sat in the chair next to Josie, and Cookie sprawled on the porch floor between them. "I'd appreciate it if you'd keep it to yourself for now but I wanted to tell someone. Tell you." Josie was becoming important to him and he valued her opinion and needed her advice.

She fingered a strand of loose wicker on the chair arm. "What brought about that change of heart?"

"A lot of things." *You. Hearing about Bea. Getting to know this special place where I might belong.* He tried to make his shrug casual. "It's still only an idea but I've been learning about orchards, hayfields and all the rest." He raised his arm in a sweeping gesture. "I've also been thinking about what Bea might have wanted and what *I* want."

Whenever he'd let himself think about it, Strawberry Pond had always been a reminder of his fractured family, but in the past few weeks that'd changed. Or he'd changed, which meant his perspective was different. Now his feelings for the place were more nuanced. He didn't only have bad memories here. Some were good and now he was making new memories as well. *With Josie.*

"So what did you want to ask me?" She tilted her head to one side, and Heath was momentarily distracted by the soft curve of her neck and ear where a gold-colored stud earring glistened.

"If I keep Bea's place, and it's still a big *if*, I'd appreciate your advice. Not only a few web links, although those were fantastic, but practical tips. If Tabby Cat Hollow were yours, what would you do with it?"

"Honestly?" She wet her lower lip with her tongue.

"There's no other way." Heath's breathing stuttered. All of a sudden, their conversation was more nuanced and it seemed they were talking about more than a piece of land and run-down house.

"If this property *were* mine, I'd start thinking of it that way. Not as Bea's or anyone else's. The person you should be asking is you." She leaned toward him, her expression intent. "Like you said, I can give you advice about practical things like the orchard and hayfield and I'm handy with a paintbrush and basic repairs. But if this place is your home, act like it. Let yourself fall in love with it."

That was the problem. If Heath let himself fall in love with this place, he might get hurt. And he couldn't do that to the lost boy who was still part of the man he'd become. The man who'd already been hurt and had vowed to never fully open his heart again.

At nine on Sunday night, while listening to a farming podcast through her earbuds, Josie did a final check of the barn. She'd topped up water and hay for the horses, checked stalls were latched and fed the barn cats and Bella and Josie's bunnies. Another day was almost done and she'd made it through, although with way too many thoughts of Heath.

Since he'd crashed into her life the day of the Strawberry Festival, things hadn't been the same. Her usually predictable days had been upended, and even when she wasn't with him, he took up space in her mind and now, she had to admit, her heart. What if he did keep Tabby Cat Hollow as a summer home? Boston wasn't that far away. Hope flickered before she tamped it down. She was getting ahead of herself. He'd only asked her advice about what to do with the property as a friend and neighbor, nothing more.

Away from Laura and Alana, Josie's optimistic confidence that day at the diner to "take a chance" on Heath had faded. Her life was busy enough and, when rational thought returned, the memory of what had happened the one time she did take a chance was all too vivid. Yet, despite their superficial similarities, Heath wasn't Drew, and her ex-husband had no bearing on her present or future.

"How are you doing, Trixie?" Removing her

earbuds and the podcast she'd stopped listening to, she greeted the Morgan in the end stall nearest to the barn door.

Trixie nickered and nudged Josie's shoulder.

"I know you want my attention, sweetheart." She rubbed the horse between her ears. "It's our special time, isn't it?" This hour before bed was one of Josie's favorite parts of the day. As night drew in, the farm seemed to settle into itself and the landscape. With only night birds, the rustle of animals and wind to disturb the quiet, Josie also settled into herself. It was when she did her best thinking, and although she couldn't set the world to rights, this daily hour in the barn helped her resolve many of her own smaller problems.

In the distance, thunder rumbled, and Trixie cocked her head.

"It's okay." Josie kept her voice low and soothing. "I'll leave the lights and radio on when I leave." Both would be a distraction from the flash of lightning, rain hammering on the barn roof and the crash of thunder. Or maybe Josie would curl up on the tack room sofa until the storm passed. While Trixie wasn't usually troubled by storms, some of the horses they boarded weren't as calm.

"Josie? You still here?" The barn door creaked open and Grams came in carrying a feed bucket and Josie's rain jacket.

"I'm with Trixie." Josie stepped farther into the barn's central aisle to join her grandmother. "Why are you still up? I thought you'd gone to bed with Gramps."

"I did but I couldn't sleep. It's hot and with the storm coming, I guess I'm restless." Grams set the feed bucket on a shelf with the others and hung the jacket on a wall hook. "I checked on the girls and they're fine. They were sound asleep almost as soon as their heads hit their pillows. If only I could do the same." Her laugh turned into a sigh.

"Thanks for putting them to bed for me." Josie grabbed a broom and swept up loose hay. Although she always tried to be there for the girls' bedtime, tonight there'd been a problem with a hose on the milking machine and repairing it had put her behind.

"It's my pleasure, you know that. Lottie especially reminds me of your dad at that age." Grams found a dustpan for Josie to sweep hay into. "Always chattering and so curious. And Bella's such a serious soul and wise. The two of them keep me young."

"You think the girls are growing up okay, don't you?" Josie leaned on the broom.

"Of course they are. Why would you think they aren't?" Grams stared at her in astonishment.

"Because I'm their mom and their dad isn't

around. I'm working all the time to keep them fed and clothed and I doubt myself." While Josie might seem confident on the outside, inside she was a mass of insecurities, especially when it came to motherhood.

"That's nonsense." Grams took the broom from Josie and set it aside before clasping Josie's hands in hers. "Plenty of children raised by a single parent turn out fine. All moms doubt themselves at one time or another, but you're a wonderful mother. I've never heard Bella and Lottie talk about missing Drew, have you?"

"No, but that doesn't mean they don't." Heath's comments about missing his dad swam into her mind along with the loss she still felt for her own parents.

"You're doing the best you can and that's all the girls or anyone else can expect." Grams cupped Josie's chin in a gentle hand. "Including your gramps. We both know it's thanks to you and your work we've hung on to this farm."

"Is Gramps okay? He seems…not frail but not as strong as usual." Staring into Grams's face, Josie saw the worry in her blue eyes and new lines around her nose and mouth. "I know his back's still bothering him but you'd tell me if there was something else going on, wouldn't you?"

"Of course." Her grandmother's lips quivered.

"I suspect he's in more pain than he'll admit. Along with worrying about you and me and how we're coping with the extra work, well, he's not easy in his mind, either."

"How can we help him?" Josie wrapped her arms around her grandmother's sturdy shoulders and held her close. Growing up, Grams and Gramps had been her comforters, protectors and parents in all but name. Now their roles were beginning to shift and she wanted to give them the secure and comfortable old age they deserved and had more than earned.

Grams glanced around as more distant thunder rumbled. "I talked with Anne Sullivan. I thought she'd be able to help given what happened to her poor Howie. It's not the same, of course, but I had to talk to someone." She moved to a nearby stall to pat Snowball, one of the horses they boarded, who had a nervous temperament and tended to spook easily.

"And?" Howie Sullivan had passed last spring after a long illness. Like Josie's grandparents, Mr. and Mrs. Sullivan were devoted to each other.

"Anne said the most important thing for any of us, whether it's minor ill health like your gramps or something more serious, is to focus on and maximize what you can do rather than lamenting what you can't." Lightning flashed, and Grams found a stall toy to distract Snowball. "Anne's right, you know. I complain about that arthritis in my knees but I can still keep active so I should concentrate on that."

Josie nodded. "It makes sense." Not only when it came to medical issues. She had a loving family, two healthy, happy daughters, a comfortable home and way of life many people would envy.

"Anne also said to ask for help when you need it. Your gramps is independent, we all are, but maybe we've been too self-sufficient."

Josie's insides clenched. The bank needed more information to make a decision on that loan she'd applied for, and with each passing day she became more anxious about how to give them what was required. It had been a big step to apply for the loan in the first place, and although Gramps hadn't stood in her way, he hadn't supported her, either. But if they didn't get the loan, they wouldn't be able to implement technology and energy upgrades to make the farm more competitive and financially successful. It was a vicious circle and so far, she hadn't been able to find a way out.

"Gramps would be upset if we asked for help. We're all equal partners in this business." Josie worried her bottom lip. "We can't go behind his back."

"Yes, but he doesn't know I talked to Anne. She's my closest friend so we talk about lots of private things, but this is the first time I've spoken to her about worries in my marriage. For all these years, Tom and I have always been in sync. We've had disagreements like all couples but before now he never shut me out." Tears welled in Grams's eyes, and Josie hugged her close again. "If he won't listen to either of us, maybe it's time for an outside perspective."

Although Grams didn't say it, the future of their family's farm could depend on it. The reality she'd tried to ignore surged over Josie like fog rolling off the mountains. If she let things slide any longer, they'd be in even more trouble. Sometimes if you couldn't get through to a person you loved, you had to go around them. Not only for their own good but others, as well.

Bella and Lottie. Her heart gave a dull thud. The girls might not want to take over the farm, but they still needed a place to live. A home where they had roots, stability and animals like family. She glanced at Trixie, who paced restlessly in her stall. Even Clarabelle, despite the trouble that cow caused. Yet, Clarabelle was determined to get what she wanted and didn't let Josie, fences or anything else stop her. There was an important lesson there for Josie to heed.

"I'll figure something out, Grams. Don't worry." With a last reassuring pat, she released her grandmother.

"I know you will and despite my loyalty to your grandfather, I'm on your side." Grams studied Josie for a long moment. "We'd better get indoors before the storm hits." The thunder was closer now and shook the barn door and windows.

"I'll stay out here. I don't want to leave Snowball and the other horses on their own. It won't be the first time I've spent a night on that sofa in the tack room." She manufactured a smile.

"Then promise me you'll come in and sleep late afterward? Bella and I can manage the early milking." Her grams waggled a teasing finger in front of Josie's face. "Even though you may think so, neither you nor your gramps are indispensable. That's something else Anne said."

"Yes, Grams." Her grandmother wasn't comparing Josie to Gramps, was she? They were nothing alike.

"See you in the morning." After Grams left the barn, rain pattered on the roof and Josie went from stall to stall ensuring her equine charges were calm and comfortable.

While she could ask Laura and Alana for advice, they knew Strawberry Pond and her grandparents well so couldn't be objective. When it came to the loan application and everything else to do with the farm business, she needed someone else. Someone discreet who had strengths and knowledge she didn't. Someone like Heath.

CHAPTER TEN

"I REALLY WANT you to come visit, Mom." And not only because it would give Heath a chance to talk honestly with her about what had really happened with his dad. With his phone pressed to one ear, he opened the diner door with his free hand. "You, Jenna and the girls. It'd be fun."

His brother-in-law, a government lawyer, was working in Washington for the summer and from calls and texts with his sister, he got the sense she and her daughters needed a distraction. "My place is pretty basic, but you could stay in one of the inns or hotels in town. It's short notice but I could ask around. Maybe there'll have been a cancellation."

As Heath approached the Strawberry Spot's take-out counter, he stepped aside and gestured to the teenage girl behind the counter to serve the family behind him first.

"All right, I'll talk to Jenna again and see what we can do."

The hesitation in his mom's voice told him

she'd come here for him but not by choice. "I suppose Strawberry Pond's changed a lot in thirty-odd years?"

"I don't remember much about what it was like before but it's sure picturesque and people are friendly." He smiled at his neighbor, Mike Murphy, who helped a woman using a walker, presumably his wife, to a window table.

"I do miss you so I guess I can put up with Strawberry Pond for a few days." His mom's tone suggested it would be the equivalent of getting through a bout of gastroenteritis or dental surgery.

"Let me know what you'd like to do when you're here, and I'll make it happen. I miss you, too, Mom." He softened his voice. Although she'd dated occasionally, his mom had never shown any interest in remarrying. Now she'd retired and despite all her volunteer work and hobbies, she must sometimes be lonely in her apartment by herself. "I can't wait for you to meet Cookie." With Josie's guidance, he'd been working with the dog on crate training and today was the first time he'd left her on her own. Although logically he knew she'd be fine, was this anxiety how a parent felt the first time they left their baby with a sitter?

"How will you manage a dog when you're back in Boston?"

"I'll have to find dog day care, I guess." Heath didn't want to think about his city life right now. "I'll figure something out." Although she hadn't been part of his life for long, Cookie was family.

As he and his mom said their goodbyes, Heath glanced around the diner. Even on a Wednesday afternoon, most of the tables were full. In keeping with the fun retro vibe, the sound system blasted the Beach Boys' "Then I Kissed Her," and several white-haired couples swayed together on a small dance floor.

"Your usual?" When Heath reached the front of the line again, the teenage server, Liv, gave him a dimpled grin, her ice cream scoop already poised above the tub of maple walnut in the display freezer.

"Of course." He grinned back. He might be predictable but maple walnut ice cream was a classic for a reason. The Strawberry Spot's version, made with local maple syrup, was the best he'd ever had. "Why mess with perfection?" As he took out his wallet to pay, his gaze was caught by a flash of strawberry blond hair in a small booth for two near the take-out counter. "Thanks." He took the cone, paid and then moved farther into the diner for a closer look. "Josie?"

"Heath?" She spotted him the same time he saw her.

"I thought you'd be out in the fields or in the

barn. Doing farmer stuff." His face warmed. *Farmer stuff.* He wouldn't have said that if she'd been a doctor, hairdresser or did almost any other job.

"And I thought you'd be in your home office doing *financial analyst stuff.*" She raised her eyebrows and gestured to the seat across from her. "Want to join me?"

"Sure." He slid into the booth and licked a drippy blob of ice cream. "Sorry, I didn't mean anything by what I said about your job." He grabbed a napkin from the holder.

"Apology accepted." She eyed him from behind an old-style milkshake glass that held a jaunty red-and-white-striped paper straw. "Neither of us knows much about the other's work." She indicated the pen and spiral notebook by her side. "I needed to get away from the farm to do some planning so I came here. I could have brought my laptop, but something about writing by hand helps me think."

"Me, too." He tried to contain his ice cream cone and make sure it didn't end up on the front of his white polo shirt. "I spend more than enough time in front of a computer. I came into town to go to the hardware store for a break."

"I was wondering, not here but if you're free later this week… Could I maybe come over? I'd appreciate your advice on something." Her face went as red as the straw as she drank from her milkshake.

"Whatever day and time work for you. You've got milking and the girls and everything." Milking cows twice a day was the one part of her job he knew something about. He often saw the animals being herded across a field near his place toward the barn at Snow Moon.

"I've got a couple of dog grooming clients tonight so say seven thirty tomorrow evening? It's private, about the farm. You're smart and I thought maybe you could help. And in your job, well, you must have to be discreet." Her gaze darted everywhere but at Heath.

"I have a duty of confidentiality. It's both the law as well as the ethical standards of the professional organization I belong to." He leaned forward. "I know you're not a client but it applies anyway, even if I'm only giving advice. I won't charge you." Best to get the money issue out of the way first.

"No, I should pay." She twisted her fingers together.

"I wouldn't hear of it." He crunched his ice cream cone. "You're helping me figure out how to manage that hayfield and the orchard. We're friends, at least I hope we are." Except, part of him now wanted more. Josie made his life better simply by being herself. Despite her reserved and sometimes prickly nature, she was warm, kind and fiercely loyal to her family, friends and community.

"Yes, we're friends." She dropped her gaze to her milkshake and moved the straw around in the glass. "But thanks. That's really generous."

Heath shrugged. "Isn't that how things work in Strawberry Pond? Neighbors helping neighbors. Like your grams dropping off meals for Mike Murphy and his wife while Marcy was recovering from surgery. I've also heard how kind you and other folks were to Bea, maybe even when she didn't appreciate it."

Josie gave him a small smile. "Most of us want to help our neighbors, that's true, but it doesn't mean there aren't some cantankerous people here. The town's not perfect."

"No place is." But beyond its adorable outward charm, Strawberry Pond had a refreshing inner goodness that inspired Heath to look outside himself and give more to others. "However, most places don't have a social media account dedicated to sharing random acts of kindness, either."

"I guess not. That social media account's Alana's initiative through the library." Josie finished her milkshake and wiped her mouth with a napkin, which drew Heath's gaze to her lips.

They were full and pink, the same color as the wild roses that grew in the garden at Tabby Cat

Hollow. The hairs on the back of Heath's neck stood up, his mouth went dry and he cleared his throat. "Besides, I...what?" He caught her staring at his own mouth.

"You've got ice cream on your chin. Here." She took a clean napkin and leaned across the table. "Hold still." The sweetness in her voice mesmerized him and nothing short of a fire alarm would have persuaded him to move even a fraction of an inch. "There." She wiped his chin and, in the process, brushed his lower lip. The gesture was almost a caress. "All done." She moved away and crumpled the napkin.

"Thanks." He touched his chin and lip as if he could still feel the imprint and warmth of her touch.

"No problem." From the bench at her side, she grabbed a green tote advertising a farm equipment company and stuffed the notebook and pen into it. "I should get going. I have to pick up groceries. Bella and Lottie are having a growth spurt. They're always hungry." She rummaged in her bag for a pair of sunglasses and popped them on, hiding her eyes. "We grow most of our own food but some things we can't. Like nuts and Bella's favorite dried fruit. If only acorns tasted better. We'll sure have enough of them in a few months. Even though I could boil acorns to make them safe to eat, they're still not great."

Her smile was strained, and she spoke so fast and her words came out in such a steady torrent Heath couldn't get a word in edgewise.

Had she been as rattled as he was by that brief closeness? He stood as she left the booth and clasped his hands behind his back. "See you tomorrow night?"

"You bet." She caught her bag on the edge of the table and yanked it free. "See you then." She dashed out of the diner like Cookie did when she took off after a squirrel.

She was gone before Heath could say anything more.

Unlike that old Beach Boys song, which someone must be playing on repeat because "Then I Kissed Her" once again echoed through the Strawberry Spot, he hadn't kissed Josie but he wanted to—and soon. He only had to find the right time.

OUTSIDE HEATH'S FRONT DOOR, Josie dug a clip out of her purse to pull her hair into a high ponytail. After changing her clothes three times before she'd left her bedroom at the farm, she'd finally settled on her newest pair of jeans and a short-sleeved, blue-and-white-striped top she'd borrowed from Laura and hadn't yet returned. Since she had to walk across the fields, she'd worn sneakers but they were her best pair and not for farmwork.

She was as ready as she'd ever be and there was no need to be nervous. Unlike meeting with the bank's loan officer, this was Heath, her friend. Except, when she'd brushed that ice cream from his face, it had felt a lot more than friendly. Then she'd talked a mile a minute to cover her confusion. If his bemused expression was any indication, she'd only made things worse. Why, oh why, had she mentioned eating acorns? That was her nerves rather than her brain speaking.

Okay, here goes. She rapped on the door and it opened so fast that Heath must have been standing on the other side. "Hi." As Heath stepped aside to invite her in, he seemed taller and all around bigger than usual. She'd been in this house many times visiting Bea, but the elderly lady hadn't taken up as much space as her great-nephew. Bea hadn't made Josie jittery, either. "Hey, Cookie." She greeted the dog, who eyed her from behind Heath.

"I'd suggest sitting on the porch but we'd be eaten alive by mosquitoes." Heath glanced over his shoulder as he and Cookie led Josie through the hall and into the small living room. "They seem to be a lot worse around sunset."

"They are. Local hazard, I guess." She pressed her lips together so she wouldn't ramble on about

New Hampshire having more than forty different types of mosquito, most of them night feeders.

"I shouldn't complain. Massachusetts has lots of mosquitoes as well." Heath gestured to the sofa for Josie to take a seat and then perched on what had been Bea's favorite armchair. "Something to drink? Lie down, Cookie." As the dog sprawled by his chair, Heath gestured to the coffee table. It held a tray with several cans of soda, two glasses, napkins, plates and a white bakery box. "Or I could make coffee or tea."

"A soda would be great." She glanced around the room as Heath poured her drink. While it didn't look much different from when Bea had lived here, it felt different. From the lingering fragrance of Heath's citrusy-lemon aftershave to a laptop and charge cord on an end table, a large navy sweatshirt tossed over the back of the sofa and a red tartan-patterned dog bed under the window where floral curtains had been replaced with a wood venetian blind, this previously feminine room now had a decidedly masculine imprint.

"Blueberry bar?" She turned back to see him holding out the bakery box, a plate and napkin. "I can't take credit." Her stomach lurched at his slow smile. "I got them at the bakery in town."

"You can't go wrong with anything from Schuyler's. It's been family owned for almost a hundred years." She took a bar and then set the plate back on the coffee table, rolling the napkin between her fingers. The bakery was one of several successful and long-standing family businesses in Strawberry Pond. What set them apart from others that had come and gone? That's why she was here. To make sure Snow Moon Hill wouldn't be one of those business failures.

"Like your farm." Heath settled in his chair. "It's been in your family for a long time."

He'd given her the opening she needed so now she had to get the words out and in the right order. "Yes, for over a hundred years. It's what's called a 'century farm.' You may have seen that recognition on the sign at the end of our lane. It's been continuously owned by the Ryan family since the 1850s."

Unlike many nineteenth-century New Hampshire farmers who'd gone to the Midwest or taken jobs in New England's textile mills, Josie's family had hung on to this rocky patch of wooded land through drought, economic depression and other calamities large and small. She wouldn't be the one to lose that legacy.

She straightened on the lumpy sofa. "That's why I wanted to speak to you. The farm needs to evolve and I thought maybe you could give me some advice."

"I see." Heath tented his hands behind his

head. "Why me? I'm far from an agricultural expert."

"But you know about business and finance." She wouldn't be disloyal to Gramps but she also had to be honest. "We're facing increased agricultural production costs, and I'm trying to get a bank loan but they've asked for more information before they make a decision. It's not the bank's fault. I get it. The farm's a risk." She sipped soda and the silence lengthened between them. Heath was listening to her, not interrupting or jumping in to solve what *he* thought was the problem.

Unlike her ex. Drew didn't know anything about farming, either, but that hadn't stopped him from butting in and telling Josie what he thought she and her grandparents should do.

She set her soda glass back on the coffee table, using one of the quilted coasters Grams had given Bea for Christmas several years ago. "The farm business needs to change but Gramps doesn't understand why we have to adopt more climate-resistant and commercial approaches. We also need to diversify, try new products, specialty products like organic milk and cheese. We need to keep learning and adapting. There's lots of resources we can access from colleges and universities but Gramps… Well, he's not keen."

"I see." Heath's nod and attentive gaze encouraged Josie to go on.

"We also need a farm succession plan, but whenever I try to talk to him about it, Gramps changes the subject." Josie rubbed at the familiar tightness in the back of her neck. "He wants me to take over the farm, but he won't give up even a bit of control." Most of the time she felt as if she was walking a tightrope, wobbling and about to fall. "I need to do what's best for the farm business, but I also don't want to upset Gramps. I love him."

"What about your grandmother?"

"She supports Gramps, of course, but she also understands the farm has to change. She knows where I'm coming from but she hasn't had any luck talking to Gramps and getting him to see things how we do. So, we're stuck. Maybe it would be different if my parents were still alive, but it's only me and I don't know what to do to support the loan application or anything else."

Josie hugged herself and looked out the living room window. Night was drawing in and in the shadowy dusk a whippoorwill called, its song echoing in the warm humid air coming through the window screen. Leaves rustled, and in the soft light of a table lamp, Heath's thick, dark hair gleamed with red and orange tints like New England maple trees in fall. And when his blue eyes met hers, they held understanding, compassion and something else.

Something that looked a whole lot like attraction.

"You're in a tough spot for sure, but it's not unusual. Lots of operations, even successful ones, sometimes have problems mixing business and family. Here." He reached for his laptop and turned it on. "Let's look at some numbers. First, to address the information the bank needs for your loan application and then to tackle your gramps. If we take things step by step, hopefully they won't seem so overwhelming. Does that sound like a good plan?"

"Yes." Josie swallowed. "You'll really help me?"

"You bet." He moved to sit beside her on the sofa, pulled the coffee table closer and put his laptop on it between them. "But you'll be doing most of the work. It's your farm and your family. I'm only here to give you an outside perspective and, I hope, share some expertise and give you options. You're in control, Josie. Always. Do you trust me?"

She nodded and her heartbeat sped up. She trusted him when it came to business, but now she also wanted more.

CHAPTER ELEVEN

"WHAT DO YOU THINK?" Several hours later, Heath pointed to the notes and charts on his laptop screen.

"You're amazing." Josie stared at him wide-eyed. Her face was flushed, her rosy lips parted, her blue eyes sparkled and her hair, half out of its ponytail, gleamed against the dark green sofa. She was beautiful and, even more appealing, she seemed entirely unaware of it.

"No, you are." His voice caught, and he almost reached out to touch her hair before pulling his hand back.

"Well, I guess *we're* amazing. What a team." She smiled. "You really think this new financial plan will help convince the bank to give me that loan?"

"You won't know unless you try, but it'll certainly strengthen your case." Was it his imagination, or had she lingered as he had when their gazes connected. Heath stretched and leaned back.

"And Gramps?" She followed his lead and settled back into the sofa, moving closer.

"That's why with him you need to downplay the numbers and focus on the family legacy." He gestured to the piece of paper with the basic tree diagram Josie had sketched when Heath had asked about the Ryan family history on the farm. "Ask him what he knows about John Ryan and his wife, Bridget. They were his great-grandparents so even though they passed before he was born, maybe he remembers his folks talking about them. There might even be family pictures somewhere."

"Gramps is all about family." Josie ran a hand through her hair and more of her ponytail tumbled around her heart-shaped face.

Heath's mouth went dry, and he made himself look away to Cookie curled up in her bed and snoring. "There you go, then. Appeal to his emotions and family pride."

"Of course, I knew family was important to Gramps, but I got so caught up in the farm business and numbers, I forgot what matters." Her smile was rueful.

"No, you'd never forget your family." Josie's devotion to her grandparents and daughters was one of the things Heath liked most about her. "You want to save your farm so it's natural to focus on costs and profit."

"I've been so frustrated with Gramps, but he's likely been as scared and worried about the farm's future as me." Her warm breath skimmed Heath's cheek. "As for succession planning, I didn't understand how hard that must be for him. I still can't understand it, not really, because I'm not him, but he's bound to be looking back on his life and thinking about his legacy. It's natural, I suppose, at his age. Like all of us, he wants to be remembered by those who come after him."

"Yeah." There was a bitter taste in Heath's mouth. What would *his* legacy be? Tom Ryan had a legacy beyond the farm. He had Josie and the girls. He loved and was loved and supported by a good woman. He had friends, community ties and deep roots in this rock-strewn landscape. He was also honest and upstanding, as solid and stalwart as the surrounding mountains. Heath wasn't anything like Tom, who'd spent his whole life on a small New Hampshire farm. Yet, in some ways, Tom's life was richer than Heath's. Had Heath also forgotten what mattered?

"I should get going." Josie's voice broke into his thoughts. "Gramps is doing the morning milking but that doesn't mean I don't have to be up early."

"I'll drive you." Heath grabbed his key fob from a bowl on the coffee table.

"No need. It's only across the fields. I probably won't even see a rabbit, let alone a coyote." As Josie reached for her purse, she bumped his leg. "Sorry." She drew back.

"It's late, almost eleven. I want to see you get home safely." Heath drew in a shaky breath. "Indulge me." Josie's face held the same surprise and vulnerability as when they'd gone to the baseball game and she'd hopped out of the car before he could open her door.

"Okay, thanks." She gave him a dimpled smile.

"I'm used to looking out for others." Heath held her gaze. "That's what my mom taught me, anyway."

"Your mom sounds great. And thank you. Everything you've done for me tonight, it's fantastic. I feel like I have a fresh start with both the farm and Gramps." Her face turned a pretty shade of pink.

"I'm happy to help. Anytime." Heath's throat constricted.

"Well, I don't know what to say, so…" Josie flung her arms around him in a hug.

For a second, Heath stilled and then his arms went around her, too. As he held her close, time seemed to slow. "Josie, I…"

"Yes?" She tilted her head back.

"Your hair's so lovely." He touched one of the red-gold curls by her cheek. It was as soft and silky as he'd imagined and had a faint scent of fruit and vanilla.

She smiled. "That feels nice."

"For me, too." Holding her felt good, even better than he'd dreamed.

She traced the outline of his chin with her forefinger, and he trembled. Her face hovered close to his and he bent his head. "Josie, may I kiss you?"

She nodded and then their lips connected, as if they'd moved closer together at the same time, almost as one. He tasted the blueberry squares they'd shared along with the sweetness that was Josie.

It wasn't his first kiss. After all, he was forty, not fourteen, but this first kiss with Josie was one he'd remember forever. And part of him wanted to keep kissing her, maybe even for the rest of his life.

THE NEXT MORNING, Josie hummed along to the easy-listening music on the radio and opened the gate to let the last cows back into the pasture. In single file, the cows moseyed from the red barn that housed their small milking parlor. "There you go, Clarabelle." She rubbed the animal's back. "You, too, Daffodil." She nudged the smaller cow into line with the rest of the herd.

At six in the morning, the world was fresh and washed cleaned with dew. A patchwork of green fields stretched into the distance, bordered by woods and a sailor-blue sky. *Home.* She closed the gate with a flourish and drew in a lungful of crisp air.

"You're in a good mood." Grams gave Josie a sideways smile as she passed Josie carrying one of the metal scrapers they used to clean the parlor after milking. "I hated to wake you but your gramps needed help." A worried frown puckered between her eyebrows. "His back's still not right but he won't call the doctor. Or even admit he's in pain although I know he is."

"I'll talk to him." In overalls, gloves and barn boots, Josie began washing the outside of the milking units by hand. Nothing, not even her concern for Gramps, could dim her happiness. While she hadn't intended to kiss Heath, it had been surprising, wonderful and exactly right and she wanted to do it again as soon as possible. "As for waking me up, it's not a problem."

Josie brimmed with energy and while she'd hardly slept, she'd sprung out of bed eager for the new day. In her imagination, she could still feel the warmth of Heath's embrace and tenderness of his lips against hers. The strength in his back and arms beneath her hands. And his gentleness and awe as he'd touched her hair.

She smiled to herself as she scrubbed a bucket and air hose, swaying in time to the music. Relaxing tunes had always made for happy cows and higher milk production at Snow Moon. A text message chimed, and she set aside her cleaning equipment and took off her gloves to fish her phone out of a deep pocket.

Morning. Hope you slept well and I didn't keep you up too late. Heath's message included a smile emoji and picture of a sleepy-looking Cookie.

Josie's smile broadened as she typed a quick reply. He'd kissed her again after walking her to the front door of the farmhouse. Like a teenager, she'd almost floated up the stairs to her bedroom and then watched from her window as with one last wave he drove away.

See u later? This time, he attached a selfie.

Her breath caught as she studied his tousled hair and hopeful expression, a coffee mug cradled between his hands.

Around ten thirty? Your orchard?

After the milking parlor was clean, she had to do a few other farm chores and shower before having breakfast with the girls. She planned to head out to check the cornfield around midmorning, though, and it would be easy to take a side trip to Tabby Cat Hollow.

Sounds good. I'll bring coffee.

"Josie?"

At a tap on her shoulder, Josie covered her phone screen and whirled around to face Grams. "Yes?" Her face heated. She wasn't doing anything wrong and she was a grown woman. Despite living with her grandparents, she was entitled to a private life and didn't have to explain herself to them or anyone else.

Grams gave her a small smile. "I didn't mean to interrupt, but your gramps is in the main part of the barn. If you want to catch him, I'll finish cleaning up here." She glanced from Josie's phone to what must be her pink cheeks. "You said you'd talk to him so—"

"Right, of course." Josie stuck her phone back in her pocket. "No problem." She made her expression neutral. "I'll go and—"

"I'm not interfering in your life." Grams stopped Josie with a gentle touch on her wrist. "I wasn't waiting up for you last night, either, but I still heard you come in and vehicle noise. Old habits die hard, I guess."

"I understand." Josie was a mom, too, attuned to her girls no matter whether they were awake or asleep. "I was over at Heath's and he drove me home since it was late. He had some good ideas to help us with the farm and... Gramps." She shifted from one foot to the other. "I said I'd figure things out and I will. Heath's smart and he won't go talking about our business around town. In his job he has to keep things confidential."

"I'm sure he does." Grams studied her for several seconds. "You had a good idea talking to him but be careful."

"Of course." Josie gave a light laugh. "We were only talking business." But then that business had become personal. "I better catch Gramps before he's off somewhere else. You know what he's like going here, there and everywhere."

"He sure is." Grams turned back to her cleaning.

Yet, after Josie left the milking parlor and before she found Gramps, she took a few seconds to reply to Heath's text.

See u soon. I'll bring snacks.

Her face heated again when he replied, almost immediately, with a single red heart.

CHAPTER TWELVE

"You want to see Josie, Cookie? Come on." Heath held out a treat to encourage the dog to move along. "More walking and less sniffing." Whom was he kidding? They had plenty of time to reach the orchard before Josie got there but Heath was impatient.

He smiled and glanced around to savor the gorgeous morning. Sunlight filtered through what he now knew were old maple trees lining the lane from the house to the orchard. Overhead, the sky was a cloudless vivid blue and tall yellow blooms poked their heads out of the bushes by the path. Taking out his phone, he snapped a picture. When he got back to the house, he'd use the New England wildflower app he'd downloaded to identify them.

First, though, he'd see Josie, the woman he'd hardly been able to stop thinking of since he'd dropped her off last night. He'd drifted through two conference calls in a daze, taking notes when anything related to his work projects had come up, but otherwise letting the presenter's words swirl around him like tendrils of morning mist above the hayfield.

It was only a kiss, at least that's what he kept telling himself, but it meant much more than he'd expected. The warmth and tenderness of Josie's touch, and the sweetness of her lips against his had shifted something profound not only in his heart but in the depths of his soul.

His phone rang and he answered on the first ring without checking call display in case it was her. "Oh, hi, Mom." He continued along the lane with Cookie now walking sedately by his side.

"Sorry I wasn't who you were expecting." His mom's voice held a hint of laughter.

"It's not that." *Liar.* "I'm in the middle of something." True but not related to work, which is what he wanted his mother to assume.

"I'll be quick. One of the inns on that list you sent us had a cancellation so your sister and I booked to come visit. We've got a family suite for seven nights arriving a week from Sunday."

"That's great." This time he meant it. "You'll be more comfortable there than at my place, especially with the kids. I'll book some vacation." He had more than enough time and had already told his boss he'd likely need to take some days off at short notice.

"Greg might even be able to join us. I'll have

my whole family together." The elation in his mom's voice was unmistakable.

"It'll be good to see all of you." Heath liked Greg, his brother-in-law, and his sister and nieces missed him when he had to work away from home.

"I'll email you the details. I know I said I didn't want to come to Strawberry Pond but it will be different now. I'm different. We all are."

As Heath ended the call, he spotted a flash of light-colored hair near the orchard. "There's Josie, Cookie." The dog tugged on her leash and, their training forgotten, Heath broke into a jog.

He wanted his family, his mom especially, to have fun here and she was right, they were all different now from what they'd been back then. But some of the biggest changes in Heath had only happened in the last month and were because of Josie.

"Hey, you." He went into the orchard and took her hands in his with Cookie bouncing between them. Josie's smile warmed Heath all the way through. "You're early."

"I didn't have to spend as long checking the corn crop as I expected."

"I'm glad." He gave her a quick kiss.

She returned his kiss and then glanced around as if afraid someone might have spotted them.

With reluctance, Heath took his hands away.

"Here." He slid his backpack from his shoulders and opened it. "Your coffee." He produced a blue thermos, followed by a picnic blanket and two stainless steel travel mugs.

She opened her own pack and took out a tin with a picture of horses on top. "Hermit cookies. Grams made them." She sat on the blanket under the shade of an apple tree and handed him the tin. "I didn't have time."

"How would you?" She wasn't apologizing, was she? Now that he had some understanding of what her working day was like, he wondered how she'd found time to make that strawberry-rhubarb pie she and the girls had brought over his second day here. "You work harder than anyone I've ever met."

"That's life on a farm, especially in summer. I don't usually stop for a coffee break but this is fun." Sitting cross-legged, and in denim shorts, a pink T-shirt and with her hair loose, she looked younger and, for a brief moment, more relaxed, almost as if a weight had been lifted off her shoulders.

Had he helped lift that weight? New and unexpected tenderness rushed through him. He wanted to make her life easier, protect her and keep her safe. Because he cared about her. His hand shook as he poured coffee into a mug for her. "There you go."

"Thanks." She took a sip and closed her eyes. Her eyelashes, darker than her hair, fluttered against her cheeks as delicate as a butterfly's wings. "I needed a hit of caffeine and that's good coffee. Not like the slop we make in the barn." She opened her eyes and grinned. "Small batch, specialty blend, right?"

He nodded, caught up in the vision of Josie with her eyes closed and at rest. How peaceful and happy she'd looked. What would it be like to be the man who helped her feel that way all the time?

Heath cleared his throat and rummaged in his pack for a treat for Cookie. "Is small-batch, specialty-blend coffee bad?" Just when he thought they'd reached a new understanding, there'd been an edge to her voice that reminded him of her initial prickliness.

"No, not at all." She eyed him over the mug. "We come from different worlds, that's all."

"So? It doesn't matter." He'd make sure of it. Josie was different from other women and that was part of her appeal. Besides, their differences complemented each other. Next time he went into town, he'd go to that coffee shop and buy a pound of this blend for her. Josie shouldn't have to drink "slop" anywhere, even in a barn.

"It does matter. Despite that kissing."

She didn't enjoy kissing him? "I'm sorry, I

won't kiss you again." His body chilled and his heart stuttered.

"That's not what I meant." She shook her head and took a cookie. "I like kissing you."

"I like kissing you, too." He let out a relieved breath and his heart resumed its normal functioning. In fact, he liked kissing Josie more than he'd ever liked kissing any woman. Now, in the light of day, he could face the truth and it wasn't as scary as he'd expected.

"Good." Her smile disappeared and a troubled expression took its place. "But you're a city guy who drinks coffee made from whole beans you likely grind and weigh yourself. Whereas I'm a grab-whatever-instant-brand-is-on-sale-at-the-grocery-store-and-scoop-it-into-a-coffeemaker kind of girl."

"I drink instant coffee sometimes." When there wasn't any other option but he wasn't snobbish about it. How had she guessed he had a coffee grinder and scale?

"Forget I said anything. I'm worried about Gramps and it's making me weird." Josie's initial jubilation and lightness had deflated like a punctured balloon. "I talked to him after morning milking. Even when he agrees with me, it's like I'm primed for him to argue. And now I'm even more worried about him because he was actually meek, nothing like his usual cantankerous self."

"Aw, Josie. You should've said something before." Heath exhaled. "What can I do to help?"

"Nothing." She brushed cookie crumbs from her hands and then reached out to link her fingers with his. "When I said making sure the family legacy continued was the reason why I wanted to change some of how we do things on the farm, he seemed to understand. He still has concerns, but he said he trusts me. He's never said that before." Her eyes glistened and she blinked. "Then he talked a bit about his parents and he's never done that, either."

"Don't cry." He brushed tears from her cheeks. "It's good, isn't it? That your grandfather listened to what you want to do?"

"Yes, but he even agreed to go into debt to hire a few hands to help us implement new farming practices, and he also encouraged me to take an online agricultural management course through a community college this fall. Between the cost and being needed to help on the farm, I never had a chance to go to college. All the learning I've done has been ad hoc. This course will give me something more formal, and the professor's an expert. I'll learn from the other students as well because there are discussion forums and a group project."

Heath studied her bent head. "Lots of smart people don't go to college."

"Yeah, but I wanted to." Her voice was husky. "Anyway, a college degree doesn't matter now and this course will help some."

Given Josie's dejected posture, college clearly mattered a lot but wouldn't be an option with two kids and a farm to run. Another way Heath was privileged. Thanks to his mom and Bea, and although he'd still worked multiple student jobs, he'd gone to the college of his choice and earned an MBA, as well.

While he couldn't solve Josie's problems, Heath could listen and maybe that would help. He squeezed her hand, and she squeezed back. "That course sounds great and who knows, maybe when you complete it there'll be other options."

"Yeah, I'd have taken it earlier if Gramps had okayed some of my changes around the farm before now. He's so stubborn, I mean, independent."

Heath suppressed a smile. Tom Ryan wasn't the only stubborn, independent one but that didn't mean he liked Josie any less.

"I want to learn as much as I can." She held Heath's hand tight. "But I can't shake the feeling something's really wrong with my grandfather." She sniffed and brushed her free hand across her face. "He even let me call the doctor's office to make an appointment for him about his back."

"I still don't understand. You got what you wanted." Heath set his coffee mug aside and drew her into a hug.

"Yes, but I didn't realize talking about the family legacy would mean...maybe make him think I expected him to pass soon." Sobs shook Josie's body and she buried her face in Heath's shirt. "I'm scared of losing him and Grams. They're not getting any younger."

"They still seem active and healthy." Heath didn't know any other people their age who did as much hard, physical work as Josie's grandparents. "Hopefully they'll both be around for a long time yet."

It was natural she worried about her grandparents. Apart from her daughters, they were her only close family. He wanted to help more, but how? He lived in Boston. Even if he spent a few weeks each summer in Strawberry Pond, as much as he wanted to think it didn't matter, he and Josie did live in different worlds. Coffee was a small thing but it represented something bigger. A gaping chasm neither of them might be able to bridge.

"What's wrong, Tom?" On Friday afternoon, Martha glanced from her husband to Buster and Honey, who'd followed him in from the barnyard. Even without the scent of roast chicken wafting through the farmhouse, both dogs had an internal clock that told them it would soon be dinnertime.

"Nothing." Tom winced as he pulled off his boots. "Why do you always think something's wrong?"

"Likely because it is. After being married to you for so long, I know the signs." After checking on the chicken, Martha wiped her hands on her apron and met Tom in the kitchen doorway. "Why don't we sit on the front porch? The meal won't be ready for a while yet. Not until Josie gets back from town with the girls. She'll text me when they're on their way." The three of them had gone to a family afternoon movie being shown at the library. "It's nice for them to get away from this farm now and then. Like a—what do they call it now? Staycation."

"We should be able to afford a real vacation." In his sock feet, Tom padded from the kitchen through the hall and out to the porch.

"We can't so there's no use thinking about it. It's not so bad. Lots of people come to this area on vacation and we're lucky to live here all year around." She followed Tom onto the porch, plucking a dead leaf from a pink geranium as she passed.

"You've always tried to make the best of things. Lots of women would've complained, but not you." He turned and gave her a grateful nod.

"It's no use complaining and it'd only make me unhappy." Although it wasn't always easy to practice, Martha did her best to hold to a positive mindset.

"You've made it real pretty out here with the flowers and such." Tom sat in one of the two wooden rocking chairs that had belonged to his parents. He gestured to her container garden, the small seating area with blue-and-white cushions and a blue rag rug on the white-painted floor. "It's peaceful."

"Thank you." Tom didn't often notice small details so when he did, the praise was even more meaningful.

Martha sat in the other rocker and took her knitting bag from a shelf. The wind chimes Bella and Lottie had given them for Christmas tinkled in the breeze. And since the screened porch overlooked the front lawn with its tall trees and a small pond with a wooden wishing well, it *was* peaceful. Although she loved Josie and the girls, she also cherished these quiet times with her and Tom together.

His chair creaked and he let out a heavy sigh. "Josie and those plans of hers worry me. Talking about what she calls the 'family legacy' got me all stirred up."

Martha checked the pattern for the pink variegated winter scarf she was making for Lottie and then picked up her knitting needles to start a new row. It wouldn't do any good to ask Tom why he was "all stirred up." One of the many things she'd learned about her husband over the years was he'd tell her in his own time.

"Talking to Heath like she did was a real good idea. I'm proud of her for asking his advice but it can't have been easy." Martha rocked back and forth as she knit, the motion of both her hands and the chair calming. "Despite his family coming from here, that man's a square peg in a round hole. I heard he spent almost five hundred dollars on a dog bed at the pet store in town. The owner ordered it in specially for him."

"At least he shopped local, and if he has the money, why not?" Tom patted Honey's head. "It's not our business, anyway."

It wasn't but that didn't mean Martha hadn't thought about all the things $500 could buy if it had been theirs to spend. A new computer if she got it on sale. Back-to-school clothes and supplies for the girls with enough left over to take them to that waterslide Bella kept talking about. Spa pamper treatments for her and Josie. A new recliner for Tom. The list was endless and she hadn't even considered what the farm needed.

"Josie's changing and that's a good thing." Although Martha didn't want to think about how Heath might have influenced those changes and what that could mean when he returned to Boston. "She's always been smart and independent but now she's… I don't know…more confident but also not afraid to let her softer side show. I often worry she keeps her emotions bottled up." In that way, she was like Tom.

"I look at her and see a lot of her dad." His voice roughened. "How our Nate might have been if he'd lived long enough."

"Me, too." Martha dropped a stitch. Even so many years later, the loss of their son was still a raw wound that would never fully heal.

"What if Josie's plans don't work out? When she started talking about my folks and how the farm had evolved since their day because it had to, it was like seeing a ghost. A couple of ghosts. You and me, when we first started out, we had all those big ideas, remember?" He raised his hands and dropped them back onto his lap.

"How could I forget? We were younger than Josie is now and I remember your parents… Well, it's no good talking about the past." Although Tom likely didn't recognize it, his dad had been as resistant to change, too. "You did the right thing with Josie. She still needs us, but when it comes to this farm, it's more than time to let her show what she's made of." Martha looked over the top of her glasses and gave him a teasing smile. "She learned from the best in having you to guide her."

"In you, as well." Tom reached for her hand, and Martha set her knitting aside. "Life didn't work out like we planned, did it?"

"In a lot of ways, no." The dull ache of loss slid through her. Although they'd planned on having a big family, they'd only had Nate. And when he'd been killed, if it hadn't been for Josie being so young, Martha didn't know how she'd have gone on. "You have to take the rough with the smooth and we've had some good times." She clasped his hand. "And we're both still here and have each other so we're better off than many."

"We sure are." Tom's face with its familiar lines softened. "I'm not planning on going anywhere soon, either. My back's bothered me ever since I fell off that shed roof and I was only forty then. It's a weak spot is all. I'm going to see the doctor next week to please you and Josie, but he's not going to tell me anything I don't already know."

"I'm sure you're right but I'm still glad you're going." Except, as she returned to her knitting, Martha wasn't sure of anything. Everything was changing, not only Josie, but neither they nor the farm could stay put.

After a life filled with twists and turns, she'd learned to expect the unexpected. She glanced again at Tom, who stared out at the lawn as if seeing those ghosts of family members who'd gone before. However, no matter what happened, it wasn't the end of their story. It was only the next chapter.

CHAPTER THIRTEEN

"Hurry up, Bella." Holding Lottie's hand, Josie stood at the bottom of the library steps and waved to her older daughter. "Aren't you hungry for roast chicken?" She rubbed her stomach. Despite popcorn and other snacks at the movie, after a busy day and only a small field lunch, Josie was ravenous.

"I wish we lived in town." After saying goodbye to her friends, Bella joined Josie and Lottie.

"Why so?" Josie kept her voice light as they made their way to the parking lot where she'd left the truck.

"It's more fun and there's more things to do."

Bella's mouth was set in a stubborn line reminiscent of Drew. Why her ex, who'd been born and grown up in New York City, thought rural life could be for him was something Josie still couldn't understand. He must have temporarily deluded himself—and her.

"There's lots of things to do on the farm." Lottie's warm hand, sticky from the s'mores bars

Alana had made for the kids, was comforting in Josie's. "We couldn't have our cows if we lived in town."

"We wouldn't have to milk them, either." Bella scuffed her sneakers along the asphalt. "When I grow up, I'm going to move to New York City like the girl in the movie. Like Dad. I won't have to muck out stalls, weed gardens or hunt for eggs ever again."

"Whatever you choose to do when you grow up, I'll support you, but you have lots of time to decide." The girls didn't often mention their father but it made sense that after seeing a movie set where he lived that Bella would think of him. Josie unlocked the truck and the girls climbed into the rear seat.

Except for that dream of going to college and during her marriage, she'd never wanted to live away from the farm, but things were different now. It wasn't surprising if Bella looked at Josie's life and decided it wasn't for her. Sometimes it was a life Josie wanted to escape but she couldn't picture herself living in a city, either. Her roots were here and that was more important.

"I'm also gonna take taxis or the subway everywhere. Not ride in an old muddy pickup truck." Bella made a face as she buckled the straps on her booster seat. "Why do I still have to use this thing?"

"Because you're short." Lottie elbowed her sister.

"So are you." Bella elbowed back.

"Girls, please." Josie pressed her lips together as she rummaged in her bag for a moist wipe so Lottie could clean her hands. "Both of you will likely have a growth spurt soon. I did when I was around your age."

"How tall is Dad?" Bella held out her hands for a wipe.

"About the same height as me." Her daughters should know how tall their father was. But to know things like that about him, they'd have to see him more often than once every few years. "Ready to roll?"

Drew wasn't Josie's problem, and it was up to him to make the effort to be part of Bella's and Lottie's lives. Still, she should email him the picture she'd taken of the girls on their last day of school. Since he made child support payments, she felt she owed it to him to send brief monthly updates in return.

"Yes, but why doesn't Dad—"

"Look! There's Heath and Cookie." Lottie interrupted her sister and, as she pointed, in her exuberance she almost whacked Josie in the nose. "Heath, over here!" Lottie waved again.

"Watch your arm." Josie took a step back from the open truck door. Lottie had given her a reprieve from answering questions about Drew, but Bella likely wouldn't let the subject rest. She was getting older and it was natural she'd ask about him and Lottie would as well so Josie had to be prepared to answer. "Heath." Her breath caught as he reached them.

"Ladies." He smiled at Bella and Lottie before his gaze lingered on Josie.

"Hi." Josie greeted him as Cookie barked, and the girls spoke over each over, both trying to tell him about the movie. "What brings you to town?" He'd texted her earlier and said he was working at home all day. Unease prickled in the pit of her stomach.

"Nothing exciting. Not like you guys." He held Cookie back from climbing into the truck with the girls. "Cody Bailey, the lawyer, called about some paperwork I needed to sign. It wasn't urgent but I decided to combine a trip with stopping by the tourist information place. My mom asked me to pick up some brochures for when my family visits." He indicated the paper bag with handles tucked over one arm. "I parked here because it's nearby."

"Makes sense." Josie let out a breath. Heath wasn't Drew. There was no reason to think he'd lied to her in that text. His plans had changed, nothing more. And he'd already mentioned his mom, sister and her family would be here soon so it wasn't like he'd hidden anything from her there, either.

"Does your family have any girls our age?" Lottie leaned around Josie to talk to Heath.

"As it happens, we do." He looked between Bella and Lottie to include them both. "My sister has three daughters. My oldest niece, Ava, is thirteen, but the younger two, Taylor and Sadie, are eleven and nine. I've told them about you so if your mom says it's okay, maybe you can make friends with each other."

"Are they from Boston like you?" Bella sat forward with an interested expression.

"As good as. They live in a suburb but come into the city a lot." Heath chuckled as Cookie once again tried to get into the truck. "No, you don't, puppy dog. Our car is over there." He gestured several rows over.

"It'd be great for the girls to meet your nieces. They're welcome to visit our farm or—"

"Boring." Bella shook her head.

"Not for Taylor and Sadie and maybe even Ava." Heath glanced at Josie. "Seeing your place would be fun. I don't think any of them have ever visited a working farm."

"I can show them everything." Lottie beamed. "Except they'll hafta be careful they don't step in cow poop."

"Lottie." Josie made a silencing face at her daughter.

"What? You always say poop's natural." Lottie's face was innocent.

Heath laughed. "It's fine. I'm sure we can find boots for them."

"Whatever." Bella tossed her hair over her shoulders and frowned.

"We should get going." Josie looked between her daughters and Heath. This conversation was getting more uncomfortable by the moment. "Let me know when you'd like to bring your nieces over."

"Of course." Heath stepped away from the vehicle and tugged Cookie with him. "But I'd also..." He lowered his voice. "I'd like you to meet my mom and sister, not only my nieces. My brother-in-law as well, if Greg's able to be here. I've met your family and we're neighbors, after all." He glanced back at Bella and Lottie.

"You want to bring your whole family to our farm?" Josie's blood pounded in her ears.

"Sure, why not?"

"Well, it won't be what they're used to." Even though she hadn't met them, they were from the city and, from the sounds of it, his brother-in-law was a high-powered lawyer. Her thoughts whirled. The farmhouse was home and she loved it but it wasn't new or modern.

"Don't worry." Heath's expression reassured her. "They're good people, and you already know my mom grew up in the White Mountains. They won't judge you or the farm." He leaned nearer and his words were for her alone. "Meet me for a coffee break tomorrow morning? I miss kissing you."

"It's only been a day but yes. I'll text you later." She missed kissing him, too.

His blue eyes gleamed before he stepped away and waved at the girls. "See you."

She couldn't let her daughters guess there was anything between her and Heath but neighborly friendship. Besides, apart from a few coffee dates and earth-shattering kisses, what else was there? As she got into the truck and double-checked the girls had their seat belts buckled, her stomach churned.

Heath couldn't be certain his family wouldn't judge her or the farm. Even if they didn't say anything to her face, she'd sense their disapproval. Like the chill that had emanated from Drew's family the few times they'd met. She suppressed a shudder and started the truck. Although she'd only recognized it in retrospect, Drew had criticized her, too, so Josie had begun to judge herself. But she wasn't that person anymore. She'd moved on and, thanks to her grandparents and

Laura and Alana, she'd rebuilt her life. If people judged, that was their problem, not hers.

She pulled out of the parking space and pointed the truck toward home. Whatever she and Heath had was casual. His family shouldn't matter to her because after this quick visit, she'd likely never see them again.

Despite a brief pang of disappointment, that was for the best. It had to be.

"You're here. Finally." On the wide front porch of May House, a cozy boutique inn nestled in the center of Strawberry Pond near the town green, Heath hugged his sister, Jenna. "Where's Mom?"

"She'll be down in a minute. She wanted to freshen up after the trip." After returning his hug, Jenna sighed and tugged her sandy-brown, blunt-cut bangs away from her forehead. "My guess is she wanted a few minutes to herself. If I hadn't been driving, I had the feeling she'd have turned around and headed home before we even reached the New Hampshire state line. Let's sit." She moved to several chairs grouped invitingly around a table covered with a lace cloth. "We can keep an eye on the girls from here and we won't miss Mom, either, unless she finds a back exit."

"Surely not." Heath glanced at the inn's front lawn where he'd greeted his nieces moments earlier. Sadie, the youngest, turned cartwheels across the grass while Ava and Taylor sat on a white-painted lawn swing absorbed in something on Ava's phone. "I wouldn't have pushed Mom to come here if I'd appreciated how hard it would be. I know Strawberry Pond isn't her favorite place, but she and dad split up more than thirty years ago."

He'd either been naive, or so caught up in his own life he hadn't stopped to consider his mom's feelings. Or listen to her in the way he should have. Guilt punched his chest. He needed to make it up to her, but how? She was here now. "Do you think she needs to stay somewhere else? Over in Conway, maybe? It's not too far and I'd pay the cancellation fee here."

"As if we'd find somewhere there or anywhere else nearby for all of us to stay at this point. It's peak tourist season. We got lucky with this cancellation. Otherwise we'd be with you at Bea's house. Mom came here for you." Jenna reached for two glasses and poured them both lemonade from a jug on the table. "She's worried about you. We both are." His sister studied him from behind blue-framed glasses that were new since the last time he'd seen her. "You look different. Better."

Heath turned away to pick up a glass plate with a domed lid that held a selection of miniature strawberry, chocolate and lemon tarts. Jenna was three years older than him but despite what had at times seemed like a large age gap, they'd always been close. She'd looked out for him when they were kids and those sisterly instincts hadn't diminished once they'd reached adulthood. If only he'd listened when she'd expressed doubts about Danielle when he'd first introduced them. He'd have saved himself a lot of heartache.

"I've been working outside. I don't have my usual office pallor." He tried to joke because his sister was too perceptive. "Here, have a tart." He took off the lid and held the plate out to her.

"No, you looking good is something else." Jenna chose a strawberry tart and cocked her head to one side. "You look happier. Before, it was like you had the weight of the world on your shoulders."

"Gee, I wonder why?" He set the tarts aside. In the past few years, his wife had cheated on him, he'd gotten divorced and now Danielle had a baby with someone else. "Sorry." He softened his voice. "It's a sensitive subject." And likely always would be.

"I know. I'm on your side, remember?" Jenna patted his clenched hand. "All I'm saying is it's good to see you looking more like yourself again. So, tell me everything you've been up to. I can't wait to see Bea's place. Your place now, I guess."

It was, although Heath still had trouble claiming that "ownership" Josie had talked about. He shifted on his chair. He didn't want to tell Jenna everything. Those kisses with Josie were private.

"You've met someone, haven't you? She must be special because you're trying to avoid looking at me." Jenna finished the tart in two bites and sat back in her chair with a satisfied smile.

"That's a big assumption and I'm not avoiding looking at you. I was putting the top back on that cake plate thing. You don't want it to get broken, do you?" He made himself strike a casual pose. He was babbling but if he kept talking perhaps Jenna would be diverted.

"Heath." His mom's voice rang across the porch as she came toward them.

"Mom." He stood to embrace her, breathing in the sweet freesia scent she'd worn as long as he could remember. "How are you doing?"

"Better than I expected, actually." She took him in from head to toe. "You look great."

"So do you." In white denim capris, a turquoise top and modern silver jewelry, Diane Tremblay looked stylish as ever. However, her blue eyes, the same color as Heath's, were dark-shadowed and the lines between her nose and mouth were more pronounced than usual.

"I need to apologize." He took his mom's arm and led her to a chair between him and Jenna.

"What for?" His mom took the glass of lemonade Jenna poured for her.

"I should have paid more attention to your doubts when you talked about coming here. I know Strawberry Pond holds lots of bad memories for you and I shouldn't have pushed." He covered one of her hands with his. "How can I make things better?"

"You already have." She glanced at Jenna and then back to Heath. "No, I didn't want to come back to Strawberry Pond, but I've also spent years avoiding this town and entire area. I should have faced it a long time ago because in the meantime my fear only got bigger." She fiddled with a paper napkin. "So, I'm here and although it isn't easy, today I've taken the first step in overcoming that fear and taking control. I guess it's never too late."

"I'm proud of you, Mom." Heath's throat was thick.

"We both are." Jenna took their mom's other hand.

"The two of us will be right here with you on this trip. If there's something you find extra hard, say so." Heath glanced at the charming three-story white clapboard inn. "We can bring you back here to take a break."

"Thank you, both of you." His mom's eyes filled with tears. "The three of us have always been close and I'm grateful. After your father left, I don't know what I'd have done without you kids, my folks and Bea."

"I don't know what we'd have done without you." Tears welled in Jenna's eyes, too. "This summer when I've been mostly on my own with the girls, I've realized how strong you were for Heath and me. It's not the same because Greg's only away for work, but being a single parent is tough."

"It is." Their mom nodded. "But when you don't have a choice you do the best you can because your kids come first. I sure learned how to juggle work and home."

Like Josie did with Bella, Lottie and the farm. Maybe for the first time, Heath understood the strength it must take each and every day for her to parent those girls and take care of Snow Moon Hill. While her grandparents helped, Josie cared for them in many ways as well, and that would only increase as Tom and Martha grew older.

Their mom's tender smile was like the warm hug Heath needed. The kind that comforted and reassured him and reminded him to be grateful. A family looked different for everyone, but his mom had made a new and loving family for him and Jenna and he should never have taken it for granted. Still, maybe he could get answers to some of the questions that troubled him.

"Coming back here, it's made me think about

our family. Dad's family as well. You always said you and Dad splitting up was a mutual decision and Dad needed to 'find himself.'" Heath chose his words with care. "But why didn't Dad keep in touch with Jenna and me more often? And why didn't we ever have any contact with Dad's family?" He darted a glance at his sister. Should he have talked to her first?

"I tried to shield you kids. No, Jenna, it's okay." Their mom shook her head when his sister would've interrupted. "I should have told you both the truth long ago, but I was either a coward or I wanted to pretend things were different than they were. Probably both. But looking back it was the only way I could protect myself from being even more embarrassed."

"Why would you be embarrassed?" Heath asked. "Marriages break up all the time. People lose jobs. Families get estranged as well."

His mom stared at the tablecloth. "I told you your dad needed to 'find himself' which is true. He was also a 'rolling stone' like I said. However, that 'finding himself' and wanting to move on meant he didn't want a relationship, at least not with me and you kids. He'd lost touch with his own family soon after Jenna was born, although he never told me why, and then they moved away. Foolishly, I thought our family would be enough. It wasn't." Her voice hitched. "He abandoned all of us. For a long time, I thought it was something I'd done."

"Oh, Mom." Heath exchanged an agonized glance with his sister.

"It took years for me to realize that it was your dad's problem, not ours," his mom said.

"But you loved him at first?" Jenna's voice was choked.

"I did, and we both loved you kids. One of the last things your dad said to me was he couldn't be the father you two deserved." His mom paused. "Maybe it was because of his own family. I was also too young and inexperienced to see the problems right in front of me."

"Is that why you never remarried or even dated much?" Something else Heath had wondered about.

"In part." His mom's smile was wistful. "But I guess I was scared to let myself get serious about anyone else."

"It's not too late." Heath spoke around a lump in his throat.

"Don't either of you start matchmaking." She looked between him and Jenna. "I'm happy with my life, and the past is the past. However, if you want to try to find some Tremblay relatives—"

"Of course not," Jenna said.

"No." Heath nodded agreement. His family—the one that he had now—was the one that mattered. "Okay then. Like life, raising you two was a journey, but despite the hard times, here we are." His mom squeezed each of their hands and then released them to help herself to a lemon tart. "Now, tell me about Bea's house and everything else."

"Well, with help from a neighbor and his son, I've been fixing Bea's porch." Heath made himself return to the present. "Maybe you remember the family? Mike and Marcy Murphy?"

"I haven't thought of Mike Murphy in years." His mom wrinkled her forehead beneath her silver-blond hair. "He's older than me but played football for the high school team before taking over the family farm. Marcy was a cheerleader and worked part-time at the diner." She chuckled. "I expect there's still lots around here I'll remember."

"Everybody's been friendly and welcoming to me so I expect they'd be happy to see you. If you're comfortable reconnecting, of course." Now that his mom was here, he'd take things as slowly as she needed. "You already know I've adopted a dog and have gotten to know the people who live on the farm next door."

As he told them more about Cookie, and Tom and Martha and Josie and her girls, his mom and Jenna asked questions. Like always, and before he'd retreated into himself before and during his divorce, they were interested in him and his life because they loved and missed him.

"Since Josie's daughters are close in age to Taylor and Sadie, we thought it would be fun for them to meet. Maybe at their farm? See the animals?" Under Jenna's intense scrutiny, Heath was having second thoughts.

"That sounds good. Tomorrow maybe?" Jenna paused, raised her eyebrows and grinned. "Or whatever works for Josie…and you?"

It was too much to hope his sister had missed that reference to "we." Neither had his mom, judging by the sideways look the two of them exchanged. The women in his life were smart but he loved them for that and so much more.

"I'll text Josie now and ask her about the timing." He pulled out his phone and then took the last strawberry tart. His face must be as red as the tart's jam filling but all of a sudden he didn't care. He liked Josie and wanted her to meet his family, the most important people in his world.

Although he hadn't recognized it at first, with Danielle he'd been isolated from his family and many of his friends because she wasn't comfortable spending much time with them. He wouldn't make that mistake again, but there was no reason why his mom, Jenna and Josie wouldn't like each other. He was making too big a deal out of this meeting before it even happened. Yet, as he scrolled to Josie's number and listened to her phone ringing, he also knew this first get-together was important.

Like his mom coming to Strawberry Pond, by introducing a woman who was important to him to his family, he'd have to face his own fears. And that would make him vulnerable.

CHAPTER FOURTEEN

"I ASKED YOU once already. Now I'm telling you. Go and change, Bella. You can't wear that dress to play in." Josie checked her hair and makeup in the mudroom mirror and pulled on her boots. "Scoot, get upstairs as quick as you can. Heath and his family will be here any minute."

"But his nieces won't be wearing—"

"I told Heath to tell his sister that her daughters should wear old clothes so it's not a problem if they get dirty." All Josie's mom friends would know what she meant but maybe Jenna was different. Who knew what city moms were like? She sure didn't.

Bella's feet stomping up the farmhouse stairs echoed in time with the pounding in Josie's head. Although she kept telling herself it didn't matter if Heath's family liked her, it did. At least she didn't have to face the scary-sounding lawyer brother-in-law. To Josie's relief, he wouldn't be here until later in the week. What would she talk about with a guy like Greg who'd gone to

Harvard and worked alongside a member of the United States Congress? She'd have to think of something to say before his visit.

"Mommy?" Lottie tugged her hand. "Don't worry. You look really pretty."

"Thanks, honey, but I'm not worried." Her anxiety must be bad if an eight-year-old noticed it. "Shall we go out to the barn? Heath texted me they're on their way."

"Okay, but I bet Heath thinks you're pretty, too." As they went out the back door of the farmhouse, Lottie's voice once again broke through Josie's spiraling thoughts.

Out of the mouths of babes. What had Lottie seen? The few times they'd all been together, Josie had been so careful to treat Heath as any ordinary neighbor. "Heath's too busy with his job, Cookie and working on his house to pay any attention to me." Given their regular morning coffee break dates, that wasn't strictly true, but having been put on the spot it was the best Josie could manage.

"When we saw Heath after the movie at the library last week, when he looked at you his face went all soft and gooey. Like how Gramps looks at Grams before he says she's his best girl." Lottie wrinkled her nose. "That's good, isn't it? You said when Bella and me grow up we should look for someone who looks at us like Gramps looks at Grams and treats us nice. Like in our princess movies."

"I did and I mean it but that doesn't mean Heath looked at me that way." Josie fumbled with the latch on a farm gate. "Maybe you and your sister have watched too many princess movies. It's good to have an imagination but there's a difference between movies and real life, remember?" Real life didn't always bring Prince Charming and a happy-ever-after or even a happy-for-now. She opened the gate and ruffled Lottie's hair. "Do you hear a car? Listen." She cupped both ears, and Lottie did the same.

It was ridiculous to think Heath looked at her the way her grandparents looked at each other. Grams and Gramps had been married for years while Josie had only met Heath last month. It was also ridiculous to think a girl Lottie's age would be so attuned to adult emotions.

"They're here." Lottie waved as Heath's car pulled into the farm lane followed by an unfamiliar SUV.

Josie switched to a welcoming smile as vehicle doors opened, and Heath and Cookie joined an older woman who must be his mother. That left the brunette and three young girls as Jenna and her daughters.

"Hi, welcome to Snow Moon Hill Farm." Out of the corner of one eye, she spotted Gramps coming out of the barn with Grams. "I'm Josie Ryan and this is my younger daughter, Charlotte. We call her Lottie."

"It's so nice to meet you." The older woman, who introduced herself as Diane Tremblay, took both of Josie's hands in hers. "Heath has told us all about you."

He had? Josie darted a glance in his direction but he was bringing his sister and her girls forward to meet them.

"My grandparents and my older daughter, Isabella, Bella." In the hubbub of greetings, Josie hadn't said a word to Heath but then he was at her side.

"Breathe." In the guise of bending to pat Cookie, he spoke into Josie's ear. "My family won't bite, you know?" His low laugh feathered the hair at her nape.

"I know." She had to laugh because it was both wonderful and silly at the same time. "Look at Gramps."

In the midst of exchanging introductions, her grandfather was already leading Jenna and her oldest daughter, Ava, toward the barn. And since Gramps's default speech volume, particularly when he was nervous, tended to be on the louder side, Josie cringed as he launched into a monologue about dairy cow welfare.

"He is who he is. Jenna's a middle school

teacher and an artist so she's used to talking with all kinds of people." Heath nudged Josie's elbow so she turned in the direction of the garden. "And see the girls? They're already paired up. How long did that take?"

"Less than five minutes." While Lottie showed Sadie the tomato plants, Bella, now dressed in almost identical denim shorts and a T-shirt to those worn by their young guests, had taken Taylor to gather eggs.

"Diane and I are heading over to the porch." Grams nudged Josie's elbow. "She's a crafter like me."

"Now I'm retired, I have more time for handiwork." Diane glanced between Heath and Josie. "Martha's offered to help with a knitting pattern I'm having trouble with." She patted her large shoulder bag. "Isn't it lucky I brought my wool and needles with me? You two are welcome to join us."

"Josie?" Heath's eyes twinkled.

"We will later. I don't want to leave Gramps on his own." Rather, she didn't want to leave him alone with Jenna and Ava because who knew what he might talk about. Tom Ryan was a farmer from the tips of his work boots to the brim of his peaked cap and from his favorite rural colloquialisms to the intimate details of a cow with mastitis, once he got going there was no stopping him.

"Go on, then." Grams gave Josie a one-shouldered hug. "We'll keep an eye on the girls, but don't be too long. I'll be bringing out cold drinks and cake soon."

"We won't." Even if Josie had to forcibly drag Gramps from the barn.

"I hope you'll like my strawberry cake. The recipe was my great-grandmother's and is a family secret passed down from mother to daughter." Grams's voice faded as she and Diane moved from the farmyard toward the house.

"See? You were worrying about nothing." Once his mom and Grams were out of sight, Heath gave Josie's shoulder a comforting squeeze.

"That obvious, was I?" She let out a breath as they walked along the fence and into the cool, shadowy barn. Her grandparents had always been hospitable but they usually entertained family and friends. Not strangers to whom their way of life would be alien.

"Likely only to me." Heath stopped by an empty stall. "You can tell me it's none of my business but I want to get to know you, the real you." He paused for a beat and then took Josie's hands in his. "Did your ex-husband have a problem with your family?"

"Drew, my ex, was polite but our families are

from different worlds and I don't only mean New York City and Strawberry Pond." Josie leaned on the stall door and stared at the dust motes that hovered in the sunshine above fresh straw. Who was the real Josie? It wasn't who she'd been with Drew, that's for sure. Now she was comfortable in herself but maybe she was still evolving and always would be with Heath or anyone else. "At first, I thought our differences didn't matter, but I was naive." She took her hands away from his and picked up a lead rope that had fallen off a hook outside the stall. "All that doesn't matter now. Your family's great, and my girls are going to have fun with your nieces."

"Yes, but—"

"Let's find Gramps and your sister and Ava," Josie rushed on. She hadn't answered Heath's question but she couldn't. Not only did Drew's attitude still hurt, it was also a reminder that Heath and his family came from a different world, as well.

And once again she'd begun to let herself care for a man who might break her heart.

"Josie's fantastic." Stretched out on a beach towel next to his, Jenna looked at Heath from under the brim of her straw sunhat. "It's great she and her daughters could join us today. Bella and Lottie are wonderful girls." She gestured to the trio who played in shallow water bordering the sandy beach at a state park half an hour from Strawberry Pond.

Heath dug his bare feet into the sun-warmed sand, seeking the coolness below. Although happy his sister liked Josie and her daughters, he wasn't ready for a heart-to-heart with her about his own feelings for them. "Josie's really busy on the farm so today... I guess it's because of Bella and Lottie. She wants them to have fun."

A smile played around Jenna's mouth. "Josie's devoted to her daughters, but I suspect today's about more than wanting to give Bella and Lottie a good time." She huffed like she'd done when they were kids and considered Heath an annoying little brother. "You're always the last to see the obvious. Josie likes spending time with *you*. With the sparks flying between the two of you at lunch, I swear I could have lit a campfire and toasted marshmallows."

"Okay, I like her." Heath stared at the green-sloped mountain across the lake. "But neither of us is rushing into anything."

"That's smart but Josie's nothing like Danielle. Thank goodness." Jenna scooped a handful of sand and let the grains slip through her fingers.

"She's not but..." Heath studied Josie and her daughters again and his heartbeat sped up. He'd taken vacation this week to spend time with his family and while it'd been fun, it was even better when Josie had been able to join them.

"But what?" Jenna sat up, found Sadie's pink sand shovel and dug a trench.

"You married your college sweetheart and are living happily ever after." Heath sat up as well and found another shovel. "It's not so simple for me."

"I get that but no relationship is simple. Not even me and Greg." Jenna's gaze drifted to her husband swimming with their daughters.

"Everything's okay with you two, right?" Jenna and Greg were the most solid couple Heath knew. If they couldn't make their relationship work, what hope was there for him?

"Of course, but this summer is tough with Greg having to be away so much. Besides..." Jenna's usually bright expression dimmed. "With what happened between Mom and Dad, it's like I have to work even harder to have a good relationship."

"I know what you mean." Without a positive model of marriage from his parents, Heath had felt adrift when things had started to go wrong for him and Danielle.

"But Danielle wasn't right for you and Josie could be. Even from the little I've seen, she's the reason you're different. Josie makes you happy and there's nothing complicated about that."

Jenna clapped as Ava executed a graceful forward dive off a floating dock. "The right partner makes all the difference. Greg 'gets' me, all of me, and we're a team. No matter what happens, I know he'll always be in my corner."

"You're lucky."

"I am but it's not as if there isn't enough luck and happiness to go around." Jenna finished making a small moat and began heaping the sand she'd dug into a pile. "You deserve the love of a good woman, but you'll never get it unless you open your heart."

"Uncle Heath!" Sadie called and skipped across the sand to him followed by Lottie. "You like hiking, don't you?"

"Sure I do." The girls had saved him from replying to Jenna, but her words needled him. Could he take that next step with Josie?

"Lottie's mom loves hiking. She said so." Beneath her pink sunhat, Sadie exchanged a knowing look with Lottie. "Dad said there's lots of trails in this park. You and Josie should go hiking together."

"Why not?" Jenna beamed at the girls and then turned back to Heath. "It'd be fun, and I'd be happy to watch Lottie and Bella."

"Don't you guys want to hike, as well? It's a family vacation." Ever since his family had arrived, Heath felt like he'd been caught up in a whirlwind. His younger nieces and Josie's girls had become fast friends so Bella and Lottie had shared lots of outings with them this week. His mom had bonded with Josie's grandmother, choosing to visit Martha today instead of coming to the beach. And despite Josie's initial wariness, in the past few days she and Jenna had talked and laughed together like they'd known each other for years.

"Greg's knee still bothers him from that skiing accident last winter so hiking's out for him. As for me?" Jenna's face suffused with love. "All I want is to be near Greg and our girls. The five of us together as a family."

Heath's stomach knotted. *Family.* His sister had the nuclear family the two of them had longed for as kids and he was happy for her, but that family also highlighted his own solitary state.

"I'll go talk to Josie now." Before he could stop her, Jenna jumped to her feet and jogged across the beach with Sadie and Lottie close behind.

It looked like Heath and Josie were going hiking, and as much as he loved his relatives, it would be great to have some time alone with her.

But whether they were alone, with the girls or Heath's family, it felt right. Maybe even like he was part of Josie's family and she was part of his, and they were building something important together.

CHAPTER FIFTEEN

"Doesn't the view make that steep part of the climb worth it?" Josie put her hands on Heath's shoulders and turned him in a slow circle. Her hands quivered at the warmth of his skin beneath his T-shirt as they took in the panorama of sky cradled by forested mountains.

"It sure does." The awe on his face must be reflected on hers. "I appreciate you showing me this part of your world. We're only about twenty minutes from the beach, but wow. Hang on." He dug in the pocket of his shorts for his phone. "Let's take a selfie."

Josie smiled as he put one arm around her, positioned his phone and snapped a picture.

"I'm so used to being on the farm, I sometimes forget what magnificent scenery I have almost on my doorstep." Even after he'd taken the photo, Heath kept his arm around Josie's shoulders, almost like they were a couple. "If we were dressed right and had the gear and more time, I'd take you on a longer hike over near Mount Washington.

It's amazing. From here, though, we're still in the park and can see the lake and beach. Look." She gestured. From this vantage point, both were mere dots in the middle distance.

Heath nodded as he followed where she pointed. "Except, they can't see us or see me do this." He dipped his head and gave her a quick kiss.

"No." Josie rested her head on his shoulder. "Although if they could, I expect Lottie and Sadie would think their plan had succeeded." Over the past few days, the two girls had made a concerted effort to get Josie and Heath together at every turn, from being seated next to each other at the impromptu barbecue Heath had hosted to this short hiking expedition. Heath might be oblivious, but Josie sure wasn't. Lottie especially wasn't exactly subtle.

"You mean we were set up?" His low chuckle vibrated against Josie's ear. "I wondered but then I thought maybe I was being too suspicious."

"Nope." Josie inhaled warm mountain air, pine needles, sunshine and a faint whiff of Heath's aftershave. "Those two aren't as cunning as they might think, but I'm also wise to Lottie."

"No matter how they did it, I'm glad to have this time with you." Heath sat on a flat rock wide enough for Josie to nestle at his side.

"Me, too." She rarely took time off so today

was special anyway, but spending it with Heath made it extra special. "Gramps assured me he could handle the late milking, but I asked Colm Sullivan to check in on him. Colm will be driving past the farm on his way home from town so it's not out of his way. That wasn't too sneaky, was it?"

"No, it's caring." Heath's voice was husky as he hugged Josie. "Family's important to you like it is to me."

"I like your family." Enveloped in Heath's strong arms was fast becoming Josie's favorite place.

"They like you, too." As the wind blew Josie's hair across her face, Heath caught the loose strands and rested his head against her cheek. "You sounded surprised. Didn't you expect to like them?"

"It's not that." She couldn't tell him about her ex's family. "I wasn't sure I'd have anything to talk to them about. Greg especially and even Jenna. Instead, it's easy. Which is a good thing," she added. "I thought I'd be uncomfortable with Greg because of his job but he's so friendly." Heath's family had been kind and interested in Josie's grandparents, as well. Seeing how they'd accepted Grams and Gramps had warmed her heart and melted her worries away.

"Greg's a good guy. I got lucky in the brother-in-law department."

His sister got lucky in the husband department. As Josie watched the couple together, it was obvious they made a good partnership. Their girls had a solid family unit to guide and nurture them as they grew and, unlike Josie's daughters, a dad involved in every aspect of their lives. "Do you know what Jenna asked me last night when you were busy barbecuing?"

"How would I?" Heath shifted to shelter Josie from the breeze and gave her a teasing smile. "She wasn't talking to me, was she? My family kept you so busy I was old news."

"Never. Your nieces adore you." Heath more than returned that adoration and was a big part of their lives. "Anyway, Jenna asked if I'd ever thought of offering cow cuddling at the farm with our herd. It's a trend in mental health therapy and helps relieve stress. She and Greg have friends who pay what's to me lots of money to go to a farm and hug cows."

"Who knew? If you're asking my advice, I'd say go for it." He gave her shoulders an encouraging squeeze. "What do you have to lose?"

"Nothing except for time to set the scheme up." Ever since Jenna had mentioned the idea, Josie had been formulating a plan. "Gentle cows like Clarabelle, Daffodil and a few others would be perfect. When you and I talked about diversifying the farm's income, all I could think of were tangible products like organic cheese and milk. I'm already putting those plans in place, and Gramps has agreed to convert an old shed into a small farm store, but cow cuddling is a service we could offer more quickly. I'd want to start small and see how things go, but why not? I've already done some research online and had ideas for designing a flyer to advertise at local tourist information centers. I also plan to talk with the marketing and business studies teacher at the high school. She takes my fitness class, and I bet I could trade a free class in exchange for advice on how best to reach the kind of people who'd want to cuddle cows."

"I'm proud of you, Josie." Heath rested his chin on top of her head. "You're smart, savvy, proactive and a force to be reckoned with. If anybody can turn Snow Moon around, it's you."

Warmth suffused her body. Josie was used to pep talks from Laura, Alana and Grams but they were family. Heath was different. He didn't have to believe in her but he did and that meant more. "I'm not doing it on my own. You're helping me with financial planning, and Jenna suggested cow cuddling."

"Don't sell yourself short. You're the one in the driver's seat and you've got good people skills.

Although he still has reservations, you even got your gramps on your side." Heath's voice held a smile.

"Begrudgingly but yes." Jenna laughed. "But that's before any cow cuddlers turn up. Can you imagine what he'll have to say about that idea?"

"It doesn't matter. Look at me, Josie." Heath drew her around to face him. "Whether it's your gramps or voices in your head like maybe your ex who said you weren't good enough, if you trust your instincts you won't go far wrong."

How had he guessed Drew had belittled her? Still, Heath was right and Josie straightened her shoulders. "Okay, let's add cow cuddling to the plan. Although we've started moving toward organic practices with planning for soil testing and learning about what's needed for certification, that transition will take a year or more. It's the same with my other new initiatives, crops and so on, which will take time to implement. As for a farm store, Gramps and I have just started working on the shed. We won't be up and running with anything until Thanksgiving at the earliest. However, I've already worked out costings versus anticipated revenue and we could launch cow cuddling for leaf season in the fall."

"You bet. Let me know what you need but you've got this."

"Yeah, I do." And for maybe the first time, she

believed it. "We should head back." Even without checking her phone, she could read the sun and, as it dipped down in the sky, this perfect day was drawing to a close.

"It'll be quicker going downhill." Heath shrugged into the hoodie he'd wrapped around his waist. "We should be back at the beach in what, fifteen minutes or so?"

"If you don't dawdle looking at plants like you did on the way up." She gave him a joking smile and pulled on her sweater. "Who'd have guessed a city guy like you would be interested in horticulture?"

"Not me, for sure." Heath returned her smile and added a too-brief hug. "Next year, I'm going to grow tomatoes in pots on my condo balcony. I'll email you pictures."

"Sounds good." Josie kept her voice light. Whatever they had was temporary, and she wouldn't let herself hope for more. They were working together because she needed his help to save the farm. And even though that farm and her other jobs didn't offer their usual distraction, she wouldn't lose her heart to him.

She wouldn't let Bella and Lottie get too attached to Heath, either. They were already a tight-knit family with Grams and Gramps. It had to be enough. None of them could risk the hurt of being abandoned again.

"We'll text when we get home." Heath's mom spoke out the half-open front passenger window of Jenna's SUV. "Don't forget to take that gift bag over to Martha and Josie and thank them again for their hospitality."

"I won't." His mom had left the sparkly purple gift bag tied with an enormous pink bow on Heath's dining room table beside his laptop. "Safe trip."

Cookie barked as Heath's family called out their goodbyes. Then the SUV rumbled up the lane to the road before disappearing around the curve by Mike Murphy's cornfield, leaving Heath and the dog alone.

"What are we going to do now, girl?" It was Sunday afternoon so he didn't have to work, but after Greg had left earlier and now with Heath's mom, Jenna and his nieces gone, he felt oddly flat. Or was that "flatness" because he no longer had plans with Josie and her girls to look forward to?

He'd seen Josie daily this past week. Even if she hadn't joined Heath and his family doing what he thought of as "all the tourist things," Bella and Lottie and Heath's nieces had run back and forth across the fields to play with each other. He'd seen Josie when she picked up or dropped off her daughters and they'd had lots of time to talk.

Together with that hike at the state park and

almost without Heath noticing, their relationship had evolved and deepened. Josie was more than his neighbor next door. She was important to him in ways that went beyond being a sounding board for the farm's business plan and offering advice when she needed it.

He returned to the house and grabbed the gift bag and his keys and, after locking up, unhooked Cookie's leash from the fence post where he'd kept her tied so she wouldn't chase after Jenna's car. "Want to go on an adventure? You like visiting Josie, don't you? And Buster and Honey?"

Cookie wagged her tail and gave him the wide smile that clutched at Heath's heart. Back in June there were a lot of things he'd never have guessed he'd have fallen for. Gardening, Cookie, Strawberry Pond. And after this past week he could admit it. He was well on his way to falling for Josie, too.

As he stuck his keys in the pocket of his shorts and set off on the well-trodden path alongside what he now knew was a fallow field, Cookie whined and tugged on the leash.

"What is it, girl?" Heath glanced around. Now in early August, the heat hung heavy in the air and life seemed slower. Or maybe it was because he'd slowed down, taken a vacation and stopped to pay attention to the rhythm of the seasons. "Tom?" He raised a hand to wave at Josie's gramps, who approached from the opposite direction. "Are Josie and Martha around?"

As Tom reached Heath, he gestured over his shoulder toward the house. "They're on the porch with the girls. Beyond regular chores, we try to keep Sunday as our day of rest and for family time."

Although he walked at a steady pace, Tom appeared more stooped than he had before his back had begun bothering him. "Why aren't you with them?" From everything Heath had seen and heard, family was central to Tom's life.

"They sent me fishing." Tom patted a long tube he carried over his shoulder, likely a fishing rod case and held up what must be a tackle box. "Said I hadn't gone once this summer and they're right. Mike Murphy's joining me. Come along if you want. We'll be at the pond beyond your hayfield."

"I've never fished, but sure." Heath had never had a grandfather in his life. Those intergenerational relationships were important and getting to know Tom and Mike was a reminder of what he'd missed. "I'll catch up with you after I drop off this bag from my mom." He eyed Tom over the beribboned confection.

"Women stuff. I get it." Tom gave Heath's shoulder a fatherly pat. "If you want, Mike and me can set you up with a rod and reel and show you the ropes. My dad taught me when I was young. There's nothing better than fishing and time in nature to settle your mind."

As Tom continued to the pond and whistled an aimless tune, Heath resumed his own walk. Did his mind need settling? Before this summer, he'd have scoffed at the idea but perhaps Tom had a point. In Boston, Heath rushed from home to work and back again barely pausing to breathe. While working out in the gym was good for fitness, like in the office he was goal driven. It could be fun to give fishing a try.

The field path ended behind the Ryans' barn and although they were behind a fence, he gave several cows in the pasture a wide berth. As he came out by the house where tall pink-and-white hollyhocks bordered Martha's vegetable garden, voices sounded from the front porch.

"That's right, Bella." Josie encouraged her daughter. "Great job finding that missing piece of sky."

"I finished the bird. See?" Lottie's high treble spoke over Josie and Bella.

"One at a time, remember?" Josie spoke again.

"Hi, everyone." Heath came around the porch and rapped on the wood-framed screen door. Josie and her daughters sat around a card table that held a puzzle while Martha was in a rocking chair with knitting.

"Heath." Lottie, who was nearest, opened the

screen door for him while both girls knelt at Cookie's level and Buster and Honey came to greet her, tails wagging.

"Hi." Josie's smile as she lifted her head from the puzzle made everything right in Heath's world. "Did your family get away okay?"

"They did." He made his feet move around the table to join her and Martha. "Here." He held out the bag. "My mom and Jenna asked me to give you this gift from all of them. It's a small 'thanks again' for making them feel welcome."

"It was our pleasure." Martha took the bag and set it on her lap as she and Josie pulled out pink, purple and white tissue paper.

"Presents for us?" Lottie inserted herself between her mom and grandma.

"No, you already had presents from Ava, Taylor and Sadie, remember?" Josie gave Lottie a reproving look. "Your mom and Jenna are so kind," Josie exclaimed as she took out a box of local artisan chocolates.

"And generous." Martha showed a set of handcrafted pottery coasters and beeswax candles. "Diane must have caught me admiring these the day we went shopping in town. They'll be perfect here on the porch. And my favorite, maple caramel corn." She patted the package and turned to Heath. "We'll write thank-you notes, of course, but it's very thoughtful of your mom and sister."

"They appreciate how thoughtful you were to them. I do, as well." Josie's family had opened their hearts and home to the people he loved most in the world because that was their way. Now, having seen his family through Josie's eyes, he understood it was his mom's way, as well.

"Moose! Those two chocolate figures have to be for me and Lottie." Bella squealed as Josie took the last presents out of the bag.

"Here you go." Josie handed the popular New Hampshire souvenirs to the girls. "No chocolate around the dogs, remember? Put them on your treat shelf in the pantry."

"I'll go with them." Now holding the box of chocolates, Martha glanced between Heath and Josie before following her excited granddaughters.

"I won't interrupt your time with your grams and the girls." Although these few minutes alone with Josie were an unexpected gift for him. "I met your gramps on my way over and he invited me fishing."

"You should be honored." Josie's eyes twinkled. "Gramps doesn't invite just anyone to fish with him and Mike."

"I doubt I'll catch anything." Even if he did, Heath wouldn't know what to do with a fish except for throwing it back.

"That's not the point." Josie studied him.

"While I'll never say no to fresh-caught pond trout fried up for supper, fishing's more than that, at least for Gramps. You'll see."

"I guess I will." He hesitated but Martha and the girls were still in the kitchen. If he wanted to take the next step with Josie, now was his chance. "I wondered… Anne Sullivan mentioned it to me when I bumped into her in the grocery store yesterday. I hear there's a pie social coming up. It sounds like fun. Would you like to go? With me?"

"To the pie social?" Josie stared at him and then, belatedly, closed her half-open mouth.

"Yes, next weekend, isn't it?" He held his breath. There was no reason to be nervous. She'd say yes or no and it would be fine either way. She likely had other plans and—

"Sure, I'd love to." She hugged the purple gift bag and an edge of the ribbon bow grazed her cheek. "I'm already making a pie."

"I look forward to sampling it." He stepped closer.

"Mom? Come quick," Bella hollered from the kitchen. "Lottie knocked her glass of milk over and it's going everywhere, even on Grams."

"Coming." Josie made an exasperated face. "Sorry, I have a really busy week ahead but—"

"Go on, I understand. Text me when you can."

Her girls and the farm came first, but the pie

social would be another chance to connect with her and see where things might go between them.

And unlike the other times they'd spent together, it would definitely be a date.

CHAPTER SIXTEEN

Josie set her blueberry pie with its intricate lattice-top crust under a mesh net at the end of one of the long tables scattered around the town green. Grams had taught her to make that crust, and against the blue-checked tablecloth and small, vintage milk glass bowl Josie had filled with extra blueberries, it made a simple but effective display.

"Looking at this spread, my mouth's already watering." Alana set her pie, a classic strawberry rhubarb, under another net to the right of Josie's. "I haven't seen you in ages and you canceled our regular breakfast. What's up?"

"Oh, I've been busy with work." Josie turned to Laura, who'd finished setting up a stylish glass pedestal plate surrounded by lemons and greenery, ready for her lemon meringue pie which needed to be kept in a cooler until immediately before serving. "You can tell she's used to staging homes, can't you?"

"Don't try to distract me." Alana tugged Josie

and Laura away from the table. "We saw you arrive with Heath."

Laura nodded agreement. "We told you so." She and Alana gave Josie matching teasing smiles.

"We did," Alana added. "And so we want details."

"Heath invited me to the pie social. Big deal." Josie looked away, noticing the busy green filled with townspeople and visitors for a key event in Strawberry Pond's summer calendar. Luckily, the weather had cooperated with blue skies, sunshine and comfortable warm weather.

"It's a big deal and you know it." Laura leaned toward Josie and spoke softly so nobody would overhear. "It's a date and how long has it been since you had one?"

"You're also in public as a couple." A wistful expression flitted across Alana's face. "Heath's happy for people to see the two of you together. That's important."

"Okay, it's a date. At least, I think it is. I mean I dressed for one." She looked at the sleeveless blue linen summer dress she rarely wore but had pulled from the back of her closet because Heath mentioned blue was his favorite color.

Josie also hadn't missed the covert looks she and Heath had attracted as they'd arrived here together without her grandparents and the girls.

It was different from when they'd gone to the baseball game. Then, she'd been welcoming a new neighbor to town and Heath had sat with her family. Today, although they were here, her family was nowhere to be seen.

"You look beautiful, and Heath looks smitten," Laura said.

Although she hadn't gone on a date in years, Josie still recognized an admiring look, and that's what Heath had given her when he'd picked her up earlier. "Okay." She drew Alana and Laura into a huddle. "I'm enjoying spending time with him."

"And?" Laura's eyes were wide. "The suspense is killing us. Don't you know we're living vicariously through you?"

"And nothing." Josie shrugged. "He's here for the summer, and I'm not worrying about what the future might bring."

"Josie?" At Heath's voice, she turned and he touched her arm. "Hi, everyone." He greeted her friends while she tried to recover her composure.

He hadn't heard what she'd said, had he? No, he couldn't have. She'd as good as whispered it against lots of background noise.

"Sorry to keep you waiting on your own. I met Alana and Laura while I was setting out my pie." She jerked a hand toward the table.

"I can't wait to taste all your pies but I wasn't

alone." Heath's mouth quirked into an easy smile. "I've never been to a pie social before so Mike Murphy, Anne Sullivan and a few others told me all about it. They said it was good I'd brought my appetite." He rubbed his flat stomach beneath his white golf shirt.

"We'll leave you both to enjoy the social." Laura tugged Alana away.

"Don't mind my friends." Heath still held Josie's arm and didn't seem to have any intention of letting go.

"I don't, I like them." He led her over to the pie table and took a picture of her pie with his phone. "I'll send this photo to my mom and Jenna. Too bad they aren't here to taste your pie. I'm sure it's even better than it looks."

"I hope so." Josie let him lead her to a quiet spot beneath a shade tree away from the crowd.

"It was hard for my mom to come back here but you and your family helped make it good for her. She's now got some happier memories of Strawberry Pond and the White Mountains. Rather than the ones of my dad leaving." He drew her closer and kissed her cheek. "You've given me happy memories of this town, too."

"I'm glad." Josie stared at him, the noise from the rest of the green fading until it was as if it was only the two of them.

He swallowed. "I care about you, Josie, and I'd

like us to keep in touch over the winter. I know it's not winter yet, but the summer seems to be flying by."

"I'd like that." She swallowed hard. "And I care for you." She stopped as if by giving him even a hint of her feelings the sky might fall in. It was too soon to use the word *love* but the feeling surging through her felt a lot like it. "Maybe I could come to Boston and see you this winter. Jenna already invited the girls and me to spend a weekend with them."

"That'd be great." Heath cleared his throat. "I could show you around. We, you and me, could go out for dinner. There's this great place in Little Italy. I'd like to share it with you."

"That sounds fun." He'd remembered her mentioning she liked Italian food. While she loved Strawberry Pond, its restaurant options were limited. "Sorry. What did you say?" She pulled her thoughts away from a happy daydream of her and Heath at a cozy table for two with candlelight flickering between them. Unlike today, nobody would notice or care that they were on a date.

"I said it looks like the mayor's going to say a few words and then they're going to cut the pies." He indicated a wooden platform where the mayor stood and held a microphone.

"That's usually how things work around here. Fred's already got his camera out." She pointed to the newspaperman, who'd hopefully have enough picture options today without snapping her and Heath.

As the mayor started her speech, excitement fizzed inside Josie that had nothing to do with the prospect of sampling delicious pies. There were many ways to have a relationship, and Heath's return to Boston didn't mean she'd never see him again.

Maybe she could have what she'd hardly let herself think about. A real and loving relationship with a man who'd put her first—and come to love her daughters like his own.

"Enjoy yourself?" Tom came up beside him and clapped a hand on Heath's shoulder.

While Josie and her friends collected their pie plates and other items, Heath had waited for her here at the far side of the green. "It's been great."

Though the pies Heath had eaten had all been tasty, he could've eaten cardboard and still had fun because he'd been with Josie. They'd talked and laughed as they'd shared childhood memories and life experiences large and small, everything from first jobs to favorite sports and funniest Halloween costumes. Heath felt like he belonged in a place and with a person who wasn't family.

"Good." Tom took Heath's arm. "While the

women are busy, I'd like a word. If you don't mind?"

"Sure." Tom hadn't asked a question but rather issued an order.

"It's about my granddaughter." Tom drew closer to Heath and glanced around as if to make sure nobody would overhear what he was about to say.

"What about Josie?"

"I want to ask what your intentions are toward her." Tom stuck his thumbs in the front pockets of his navy chinos and gave Heath a searching look.

"My intentions?" Had Heath suddenly slipped into some alternate reality, more nineteenth than twenty-first century? "I like Josie. I care about her."

He loved her. And he wanted Josie and her girls to be a more permanent part of his life. Heath pressed a hand to his chest as the warmth and rightness of that realization slid through him. But what would loving her mean and could he let himself trust in love again?

"I reckon Josie cares about you, too." Tom continued to study Heath. "Back when Martha and I were young, if a man invited a woman to this pie social, it meant he was serious about her. Everyone knew they were stepping out. Times have changed, but folks, older ones especially, will still have noticed you and Josie coming here together."

"I see." Heath swallowed. Josie would've understood the significance of today as well, although she'd likely have cut him some slack. After all, there was no way Heath could have known he'd as good as made a public declaration they were a couple.

"Martha and I want Josie to be happy." Tom moved closer, and Heath made himself stand his ground. "So far, we like you well enough. At least, you haven't given us any reason to dislike you."

Coming from a blunt-and-crusty man like Tom, Heath supposed that was a compliment. "Like you, I want Josie to be happy."

But was he the one to make her happy? At heart, they were still different people, and while variety was supposedly the spice of life, were they *too* different? Despite wanting to revitalize Bea's orchard and grow heritage apples, Heath liked good restaurants and going to concerts, plays and professional sports events. That was only one example of their different worlds.

"I'm sure you want to make Josie happy now, but when you go back to Boston, what happens then? Martha worries you could break our girl's heart." Tom wagged a bony finger in front of Heath's face. "You might not think so because she doesn't often show it but underneath all her bluster Josie's got a real softness inside. She hurts deep."

"I don't… I wouldn't…" Heath stopped.

"You can't say how Josie will feel nor her daughters, either. All three of them were hurt bad by that ex of hers, but Josie's made a fresh start and gotten back on her feet. Martha and me don't want to see her knocked back again. You understand what I'm saying?"

"Yes, sir." Heath understood more than maybe Tom intended.

Although he loved Josie, could he be a good stepdad to an instant family and help raise children who weren't his by blood? He liked kids but Bella and Lottie already had a dad. And if Tom meant what Heath assumed, keeping in touch with Josie over the winter from Boston wouldn't be good enough. That was casual and Tom was all about commitment. The guy had been married for more than half a century to prove it.

As a kid, Heath's mom had taken him and Jenna skating on a frozen pond and sledding. It'd been fun.

But the isolation. You can't imagine how lonely it was in the winter especially. How cold. Apart from a small carnival, there was nothing to do.

His mom's words echoed in Heath's head, one of the rare times she'd talked to him about life here.

For a city guy, you almost look like a real farmer. Now Josie's words. Joking but still truth in them.

"Gramps, I hope you aren't boring Heath with stories about your pumpkin patch." Josie appeared at Tom's side and rolled her eyes. "Gramps is growing some big ones this year, but he can go on about those pumpkins to anyone who'll listen."

"Pumpkins?" Heath's voice cracked. He'd gotten so caught up in his thoughts whatever else Tom said hadn't registered.

"Yes, as Gramps has likely told you, the pumpkin is New Hampshire's official state fruit. That's the main reason he grows them." Josie huffed out a breath. "I'm ready to leave if you are. Laura, Alana and a few others are having a barbecue at Laura's farm. We've been invited to stop by. Grams already said she can look after the girls and put them to bed."

"Sure, sounds fun. We can make a real day of it."

For now, Heath would push away his doubts. It was early days and if he and Josie loved each other, maybe long distance could work.

Still, as they said goodbye to Gramps and walked back to Heath's car, he was conscious of the older man's gaze following them.

CHAPTER SEVENTEEN

THE AFTERNOON AFTER the pie social, Josie, alone in the barn, gripped her phone and read Drew's email again.

Her ex couldn't mean... Words jumped out at her at random until the walls spun and her vision blurred. She collapsed onto a bench outside the tack room and tried to catch her breath.

Bella had turned ten in April and Lottie would be nine in November. For almost nine years, Drew hadn't wanted anything to do with Josie and their girls. Nothing meaningful, anyway. Apart from the child support payments that appeared in her bank account, they hadn't heard anything from him in over a year.

Now, in less than twelve hours, he was coming to visit.

Cautiously, she raised her head, and the barn's familiar scent of horses, hay and old wood came back to her but didn't bring their usual calm. *Think. Be rational.* She pressed a hand to her forehead.

"Josie? Are you finished with—" Grams came around the barn door and stopped. "What's wrong?"

There was no point in trying to hide the truth. Grams would know soon enough anyway and, like Josie, she'd need time to prepare. "It's Drew. He's coming here. Tomorrow morning."

"Tomorrow morning?" Grams sank onto the bench beside Josie and raised her hands in a helpless gesture.

"Don't worry, he doesn't expect to stay with us. He booked a room at that boutique hotel in town. But all of a sudden he wants to see the girls and be what he calls 'a real part of their lives.' He says he's changed." She glanced back at the email. "And become 'a new and better man.'"

"Where's he been since Lottie was six months old?" Grams gentle expression hardened. "Bella and Lottie hardly know him. They've only seen him for what, a handful of visits?"

Josie nodded and tried not to cry. "Brief visits at that. I send him email updates when I get a child support payment, but he hasn't replied to any of those messages in over a year. He said he didn't want to be a parent, remember? I took him at his word." She choked back a sob.

"How could I forget?" Grams's arms went around Josie in a fierce hug. "You won't let Drew see the girls on his own, will you?"

"Of course not." Thank goodness her gramps had agreed to hire extra help. With two more people now working alongside them to lay the groundwork for what Josie called their farm's transition and futureproofing plan, her taking some time off wouldn't have as big an impact as it could have. However, she'd still do regular chores and fit as many tasks as possible into early mornings and late evenings. "It's typical Drew. He comes up with an idea last-minute and expects everyone to fall in with what he wants."

Once she'd found that impulsiveness exciting. Now it was one more thing that made them too different to make a relationship work.

"It'll be hard but Gramps and I are here for you and whatever you and the girls need." After another hug, Grams let go but still held on to Josie's hand.

"I know." They'd also be there to pick up the pieces after Drew left again. "On the bright side, while there's never a good time for Drew to make an impromptu visit, I can think of lots worse. Like when we're in the middle of harvest or back to school and the girls are getting used to new teachers."

"That's my girl. It'll all work out somehow." Grams's voice was as soothing as when Josie was a child and skinned her knee or argued with a friend. "I've always admired you for keeping things civil with Drew and never saying a bad word about him around Bella and Lottie."

"It's easier when he's not around, but the girls are my priority. They should have a relationship with their dad and since Drew's coming here—"

"Dad's coming here? When?" Bella bounced through the open barn door to where Grams and Josie sat. "Gramps asked me to get another lead rope so I heard." Her face was flushed with excitement and her eyes sparkled.

"Your dad will be here tomorrow." Josie wouldn't give a time as Drew was often late. "He just sent me an email." She waved her phone to forestall Bella's next question, which would be why Josie hadn't told her about her dad's visit before now. "I was going to come out to the paddock to tell you and Lottie in a minute." The girls were watching Gramps give a lesson to a new rider who'd begun boarding her horse with them.

"Did Dad say anything else?" Bella's eyes narrowed.

"Not much. It's a last-minute trip so I imagine he'll want to make plans with you when he gets here." Although Drew had mentioned going to the water park Bella kept talking about, Josie wouldn't tell her daughters anything that would get their hopes up only for their dad to disappointment them.

"How long's he staying?" Bella glanced between Grams and Josie as if she suspected them of hiding something from her.

"Three or four days, I think, but he's not staying here." Josie kept her voice neutral.

"Did you tell Dad he couldn't stay here?" Bella put her hands on her hips.

"No, of course not. He already booked a place in town." It was understandable Bella would want to spend as much time as she could with her father. Lately, however, she'd seemed to resent Josie, idealizing her absent father versus her mom, the parent who set boundaries and rules.

"Oh." Bella paused. "Well, can me and Lottie stay there with him?"

"No." Josie sat straight even as soul-deep weariness weighed down her body.

"Why not?"

Josie took a deep breath. Bella was curious, strong-willed and determined. All of which were good qualities in theory but sometimes not reality. "You and Lottie live here at the farm with me. That's what the judge said, remember?" Drew hadn't contested the custody ruling, either. In fact, he'd seemed almost relieved by it.

The girls also hadn't seen their dad in a long time and needed a chance and supervision to get to know him again. "Supervision" wasn't one of Drew's strong points. She suppressed a shudder at a memory from his last unexpected visit.

He'd taken the girls to a park, gotten talking to a group of hikers and hadn't noticed Bella and Lottie wander off. Luckily, Anne Sullivan had been picnicking nearby and spotted the girls before they reached the bank of a fast-flowing river, but Josie still had nightmares about what could have happened.

"But Dad wants to see us, and I want to see him." Bella's voice rose in a whine.

"Which you will, I promise."

"You know your mom keeps her promises," Grams said. "Now, why don't we leave your mother to finish here and you and I take that lead rope to your gramps and get Lottie. How'd you like to make and decorate cupcakes for your dad?"

All this time, Grams had stayed quiet, but now, when Josie was at the end of her own metaphorical rope, Grams had her back. She sent her grandmother a grateful look and found the lead rope Gramps wanted.

"You've moved on, don't forget." Grams spoke in Josie's ear as Bella darted away to tell her sister about their dad. "And you love your girls way more than you're angry and upset with their father."

"Yeah, I do." Which meant Josie would bite her lip when she needed to, think before she spoke and wouldn't do anything to upset the girls. "Thanks, Grams."

"No problem." Grams patted Josie's shoulder before calling for Bella to wait.

Maybe Drew *had* changed and become the new and better man he wanted Josie to believe he was. She walked along the barn aisle and leaned over the door of Trixie's stall. "What do you think, girl?" Josie laid her head against the horse's warm neck.

Trixie whickered in greeting and nuzzled Josie's hair.

She wanted the girls to get to know their father. As they grew older, Bella and Lottie would figure out for themselves what Drew was like, the good and bad.

Josie had also made a fresh start in every other part of her life, including with Heath. Warmth flooded through her at the memory of the fun they'd had at the pie social and barbecue afterward, and those kisses that made her feel as giddy as a teenager.

Drew was only visiting for a few days. She wouldn't let him open up old wounds or think about the bad choices she'd made. She'd put the past firmly behind her. Nothing and nobody, not even Drew, would change who Josie was now or the new life she'd built out of the ashes of the old.

HOLDING COOKIE'S LEASH, Heath came out of the pet store on Strawberry Pond's main street and turned left to head toward the diner. He'd pick up a milkshake before going home and one of the diner's "pup cones" made with dog-safe ingredients for Cookie.

"What do you say, girl?" Thanks to Josie's training sessions, and Heath's hours of practice with Cookie, she was now a model dog, at least most of the time. He smiled as she yelped at Fred Sinclair and his beagle as they came around the corner, and the beagle returned her greeting with a characteristic howl.

"Haven't seen an entry from you and Cookie for the fall 'Pond Pets' photo contest." Fred stopped at Heath's side as their dogs sniffed each other. "Did you miss the announcement in last week's paper?"

"No, I saw it but isn't that pet photo contest for children?" Heath had scanned the headline and moved on like he usually did with the weekly local newspaper. While he checked it to make sure he wasn't featured, there was something appealing about living in a place where regular front-page news was a new stop sign or report on a fundraising dinner for a local war veterans' organization.

"There are categories for adults *and* children." Fred studied Cookie. "Meeting you was that hound's lucky day. I wouldn't have said so at the time, mind, but now she's gained a bit of weight and had proper care, she's a fine-looking dog. Glossy coat, bright eyes." He bent to pat the top of Cookie's head. "You should enter a picture of her, but even if she doesn't win I'll do a story on you both. Readers like a happy-ever-after."

As Fred and his beagle continued on their way, Heath gaped at their retreating backs. Meeting Cookie had been his lucky day, too, but that didn't mean he wanted them to feature in a newspaper story. The bond he shared with Cookie was private. Still, he supposed he could think about entering the contest. Apart from when his family visited, almost all the recent photos on his phone were of the dog. Maybe the one of her on the porch looking around a red hollyhock bloom. Or that funny shot where she—

"Heath."

He raised his head at Lottie's voice. Absorbed in his thoughts, he'd reached the diner where Josie, her girls and a man he didn't recognize stood in a line by the outside order window. "Hi, girls. Josie." He glanced at the man and then back at Bella. With their dark hair and eyes, the two resembled each other. However, when Josie had texted to cancel their morning coffee date, she'd only said something had come up. Not that her ex was visiting.

"Hi." Josie seemed distracted and as she turned to greet him, her tote bag whacked Heath's arm. "Sorry."

"No problem." When she was nervous or upset, Josie became clumsy. Not that she'd told Heath but it was one of those endearing quirks he'd noted as he'd gotten to know her. Now it put his inner radar on alert. "What's up?"

"Oh... This is Bella and Lottie's dad. My ex-husband, Drew Miller. He arrived unexpectedly last night." As she made the introductions, telling her ex that Heath was their next-door neighbor from Boston, Josie avoided his gaze.

"Great to meet you." Drew shook Heath's hand with a firm grip.

"Daddy's from New York City," Lottie said. "He doesn't like dogs." She tugged Cookie away from sniffing Drew's trendy gray-blue sneakers. Like his navy tailored shorts and white polo shirt, they were similar to the pair Heath wore so Heath should've felt some affinity for the guy. Yet, between Josie's unsettled manner and Drew's overly enthusiastic greeting, he didn't.

"I never said I didn't like dogs." Was Drew's booming laugh too hearty? "I'm not used to them, that's all. I thought those two you've got out at the farm were going to take a piece out of me last night. I've never heard such barking and growling."

"That's because it was late and Honey and Buster were protecting their territory." Josie's voice had a tight edge. "They see our family as their pack so they were protecting us."

"I couldn't wait to see my sweet girls so I caught an earlier flight. You didn't mind me waking you, did you?" He ruffled Lottie's hair and put an arm around Bella.

Although both girls giggled, they also darted glances at Josie, who rummaged in her tote with a stony-faced expression. "Have you decided what you want, girls? We're getting close to the front of the line."

As the girls chattered about ice cream choices with their dad, Josie took a step back. "I'm sorry. I meant to tell you but Drew was supposed to arrive this morning, not last night. He didn't give much notice for his trip and it's all been a bit last-minute. He'll be here until the middle of the week. Anyway, the girls are thrilled to see him so I guess that's all that matters." Her voice trailed off and she bent to pat Cookie.

Heath stole a covert glance at Drew. "It's fine, don't worry about it. Whatever's good for the girls." Josie clearly wasn't thrilled her ex had turned up but she was making the best of the situation for Bella and Lottie. It also wasn't like he and Josie shared every aspect of their lives with each other. Today was Saturday so Josie wouldn't be around for a few days. Heath would miss her, but he could handle it. Drew was part of their lives so Heath should make an effort to get to know him.

"What do you want, Jo? A strawberry milkshake as usual?" Drew grinned. "You've always been a woman of habit."

"No, I'd like a chocolate surprise sundae. With extra nuts." Josie's smile was strained. "It's new this summer and I've wanted to try it."

"Sure." Drew turned back to the teenager serving behind the order counter.

"Can Heath join us?" Lottie tugged on her dad's arm. "Please?"

"It's our family time, Lottie. Us four only." Bella took her dad's hand.

"I need to head home anyway." Heath gave them a bland smile so as not to embarrass Josie any further. "I'm installing a new storm door so the house is ready for winter." While he no longer wanted a milkshake, Cookie recognized the diner was where she often got a treat and he didn't want to disappoint her.

"I spent a few winters here but never again. The skiing's great but that's for a vacation. Along with the cold, it's the isolation, man." Drew gave Heath's shoulder a friendly slap like they were buddies. "Boston and New York are cold, sure, but there's lots to do. I'm in advertising. Creative director. I head up my own agency. What kind of work are you in?"

The cold. The isolation. Nothing to do here in winter. Almost verbatim, Drew had repeated what Heath's mom said.

"I'm in finance." Heath made himself focus on Drew. When he named the company and briefly explained his role, the other man's eyebrows lifted.

"We should talk more." Drew paid for his order and continued talking over one shoulder to Heath. "My team might be able to help you guys with a campaign. Does Jo have your number?"

"She does." Heath would leave it up to her whether she gave that number to Drew or not. While Heath had heard Laura and Alana call her Jojo, he'd never heard anyone call her Jo. Did she like it? Or was Drew the only one who called her by it? There was a burning sensation in his chest and he clenched his teeth.

"See you around." With a friendly wave, Drew followed Bella and Lottie to a patio table shaded by a green-and-white-striped umbrella.

"Yeah, sure." As Heath took his place at the counter and gave his order for Cookie's pup cone, Josie nudged his arm.

"I'll text you later," she said almost under her breath as she grabbed extra napkins before rejoining the others.

Then Heath was alone with an excited dog and pup cone to go while Josie and her girls were at a table with Drew. A family, just as Bella said. One where he'd always, like now, be on the outside looking in.

CHAPTER EIGHTEEN

"You're sure there's nothing else I can do?" On Monday morning, sitting across a desk from the bank's loan officer, Josie clenched her hands together to keep them from shaking.

"Not unless you win the lottery. Sorry, bad joke." Carly, who'd been a few years ahead of Josie in school, slid the bulging file of paperwork back across the desk. "I tried, I really did, but I couldn't get your loan approved." Her dark brown eyes softened in sympathy. "A lot of farmers are struggling. I know it doesn't help but you're not alone."

"Yeah." Josie stuffed the file folder into her tote bag. She might not be alone when it came to her financial situation, but even though she was surrounded by other people, she'd never felt more isolated. The big milk contract she'd counted on was delayed. If it fell through, she'd be well and truly sunk. The only woman to run Snow Moon Hill in almost two hundred years and she might be the one to lose it. "Thanks for all your help."

Carly nodded. "I'll let you know if anything changes. The bank's risk averse and, well, it's a tough time."

Not for Carly, who could count on a regular monthly salary and whose husband had a steady job as a police officer. Josie mentally shook herself. She wasn't being fair. Carly had done her best and it wasn't her fault Josie hadn't gotten the loan. All that work on the business plan Heath had helped with was for nothing because the farm's financials weren't good enough. Adding cow cuddling, organic milk production, a different crop rotation sequence, trying new irrigation techniques and everything else wouldn't make a meaningful difference right now or maybe ever. Without the loan, they couldn't afford the equipment upgrades she'd planned on, either.

Leaving Carly's office, Josie kept her head down as she walked through the main area of the bank and out onto Strawberry Pond's main street. What was she going to do? One problem at a time. She'd think about the farm's situation after Drew was gone.

Heading to the library, where she'd left her daughters with Drew for a magic workshop, other worries circled like flies at a picnic. Drew wasn't the featured entertainment Alana booked, but Josie's ex was a magician all right. In less than seventy-two hours, he'd charmed her girls like he'd once charmed her.

"Jo?" Drew stood by the library steps and held out a hand to her.

"Why aren't you inside with the girls?" She clutched her bag and didn't take his hand. In the space of five minutes, her life had gone from bad to worse.

"Alana and some other woman said they'd keep an eye on them and—"

"Some other woman?" She bit back the rest of an angry retort. "Drew, you can't leave—"

"It's someone who knows your grandmother. Anne Sullivan? She was with her family and Alana said it was fine so... I wanted to talk to you."

Josie exhaled. She'd sensed this chat was coming but had avoided it as long as possible. "Okay." She gestured to a bench in a shaded garden area beyond the steps. While private, it wasn't secluded and they'd be able to see caregivers and kids leaving the library when the workshop ended.

"I'm sorry, okay?" Drew sat on one end of the bench and Josie sat beside him with her bag in between.

"For leaving the girls in the library? You already apologized. It's fine." Maybe she'd overreacted, but Drew had arrived so much earlier than expected. And from then on, despite her best intentions, he'd once again turned her world upside down.

"No, I'm apologizing for everything else." He scrubbed a hand through his hair, giving it a tousled look that made him even more attractive. "Not being there for Bella and Lottie. Leaving you to raise our daughters on your own. Sure, I make child support payments, but the amount hasn't changed in years even though I'm earning a lot more. I'm not proud of myself but I've changed. I swear I have."

"If that's true, you need to prove it to all of us." Her voice hitched and she fiddled with the handle on her tote.

From the moment Drew had arrived at the farm, waking them out of a sound sleep, all Josie had seen were his similarities to Heath. Not so much physically, although both men were tall and good-looking, but in what they wore and their general manner. They were both city guys, and while Josie had long wondered what she'd ever seen in Drew, were they the same qualities that now also attracted her to Heath?

"I know it'll take time and words are easy but I want to show you I've changed." Drew's voice was low. "What I'm trying to say is I want to take responsibility for my mistakes and do better. Back then, after the initial fun and excitement of babies, I wasn't ready for the reality of kids so I panicked and ran."

"You did." Josie's thoughts whirled. The girls were thrilled to spend time with their dad, Bella especially. But if he let them down again, it was Josie who'd have to deal with the repercussions. The tears, anger and disappointment.

"Life was a big adventure back then. It still is in lots of ways but now I see some things differently, more like a grown-up." He gave her a sheepish smile. "It took me long enough, I know, but I'll turn forty in a few years and that has a way of changing a guy. Also, my older sister got sick. Colleen's doing better now but life's short. In the end, family's all you have."

"True." Josie hesitated. "I'm sorry about Colleen. She was kind to me but we lost touch."

"That's my fault. With my parents, as well. I should have taken a stand with all of them sooner. You were my wife and Bella and Lottie are our children, their grandchildren. My parents shouldn't have... Well, they're sorry for judging you harshly." He exhaled. "One day, if it's okay with you, they'd like to see the girls again."

Better late than never, and Josie was all for healing a fractured family if it meant the girls would be loved, respected and welcomed. "While I'd like the girls to have a relationship with your family, let's take things slowly, okay?"

"I get it. That's more than fair." He put a hand to his face, vulnerable in a way Josie had never imagined he could or would be. "I've messed up and I'll do whatever it takes to make amends. I've never been good with keeping track of details. I'm a big-picture guy. It didn't cross my mind we needed to review what I'm paying for child support. Lottie told me you said there wasn't enough money for her to take figure skating lessons this fall. I feel really bad, but it's not something I'd ever think about. Next time, call me okay?"

"Okay." Maybe Josie's stubborn pride had also been part of the problem. The months when Drew's money for the girls wasn't enough, or there was something extra, like Lottie wanting to figure skate, instead of standing up for herself, she'd seethed with silent anger. That hadn't done her any good or the girls, either.

"You're doing a great job with Bella and Lottie and your grandparents are fine people." Drew's gaze never left hers. He meant well and he was telling her the truth but would his good intentions and promises last?

Josie's throat tightened. "In your text you said you wanted to be a real part of Bella's and Lottie's lives. What does that mean?"

Josie stared at the weathered gray trunk of a nearby maple tree. It had been there long before she was born and without a storm or other disaster, it would remain long after she was gone. Trees and other elements of the natural environment helped put her own life into perspective. For peace of mind, she'd tried to let go of her anger toward Drew and his family, but as soon as he'd arrived, it had all come rushing back.

"It means I want to make plans to see the girls on a regular basis and stick to them. Get to know them and be there for stuff at school as often as I can. I left you to do all the heavy lifting so I can't expect to be an instant dad."

"No, but you're sure the fun parent." Josie tried to keep the bitterness out of her voice. "It would also mean you consider me and my grandparents. Our lives are here, on the farm and in Strawberry Pond." That routine made her feel safe. Now, with Drew's unexpected reappearance and superficial similarities to Heath, she didn't know what to do. All she wanted was for her life to go back to how it was before but that wasn't going to happen. "You can't turn up when you feel like it and expect us to welcome you with open arms."

"I know but I didn't expect you to all be in bed and sound asleep by nine on a Friday night. Maybe the girls but—"

"You never really understood farm life, did you?" It was a rhetorical question but one Josie had to ask. "I'd been up most of the night before with a sick cow and had set the alarm on my phone for two the following morning to check on her again."

When she and Drew had been together, they'd rented an apartment in town. He'd worked as advertising manager for an outdoors company but also had time to ski in the winter and lead hikes in the summer. Josie, meanwhile, had worked a nine-to-five job in an insurance office. In those days, the farm hadn't been as big a part of her life and, at least for Drew, life had been like one big extended vacation. Josie's pregnancy with Bella had been a surprise, and at first Drew was excited to be a dad and wanted to have two kids close together, but after Lottie was born everything changed.

"I'm sorry for not waiting until Saturday morning to turn up at the farm. I didn't think and that was inconsiderate." Drew's voice was laced with regret. "I can't promise I won't make more missteps but I'll try harder, including increasing what I pay you in child support. Spending time with the girls and you has been great. It's good for us to be a family, don't you think?"

"For the girls, yes." Josie and the girls were already a family. She didn't need to play mom and dad with Drew.

"Mommy, Daddy. See what we made?" Lottie ran toward them followed by Bella as Alana watched from the library steps. "Do you like my sparkly magic wand?" She waved a wooden stick topped with a cardboard cutout star decorated with pink and gold glitter.

"It's gorgeous. Yours, too, Bella." She admired Bella's green-and-silver wand.

"The magician had a rabbit, a real one, and he made it disappear. He also did some great card tricks. Why did you have to talk to Mom?" Bella wrapped her arms around Drew.

"Because I want to see you two more often. What do you say?" Drew hugged both girls.

"Yes, please." Bella and Lottie squealed and talked over each other.

"Before we go to the water park, I have presents for you." Drew dug in a backpack he'd stored beneath the bench for two parcels wrapped in the same sparkly pink paper Heath had chosen that day at the jewelry store for his niece's birthday necklace.

As Josie moved along the bench so the girls could sit between them and unwrap their gifts, her heart sank. Their excitement was natural. Drew was like a shiny, new toy they hadn't tired of yet. And he hadn't disappointed them, which despite his promises and apologies, she still couldn't trust him not to do.

"What did your dad give you?" She forced a stiff smile as the girls opened matching blue-velvet jewelry boxes.

Bella raised her head from her box with an awed expression. "Is it a real diamond?"

"It sure is. Nothing but the best for my girls." Drew lifted Lottie's hair to clasp the thin yellow-gold necklace with the petite diamond around her neck. "I got the same one for each of you. Remember that song and the movie, Jo? 'Diamonds Are a Girl's Best Friend'?" He laughed.

"It sparkles even more than our wands. See, Mommy?" Lottie held the necklace out for Josie to admire.

"It's beautiful. They're beautiful." She admired Bella's necklace, too. And expensive. As for that song, Drew was in advertising, that's for sure. He had the perfect quip for every occasion and likely didn't remember he'd once said the same thing to Josie when he'd given her those diamond earrings for their wedding, which now, after she'd worn them once, sat in her jewelry box. She'd kept them in case the girls wanted to wear them at a graduation or wedding but maybe she should sell them instead.

As the girls talked about their necklaces and the four of them made their way back to Drew's sporty rental car, fear seeped through Josie's body and she bowed her head, her mind numb. Her ex-husband was a big success and could afford to give the girls whatever he wanted. Meanwhile, she couldn't even get approved for a small loan to help the farm through fall and winter. Her shoulders slumped and she held the tote in a death grip.

She couldn't tell her grandparents, Laura and Alana or even Heath about the loan being turned down, the delayed milk contract or now a new and even more terrifying worry. If Bella and Lottie continued to be dazzled by the dad they hardly knew, where did that leave her relationship with them? The three of them had always been close, but she couldn't deny them a relationship with their dad and his family, either.

"Jo? You need help putting that stuff in the trunk?"

"I can manage." She pulled out her wallet and stuck her tote and the girls' backpacks in the trunk Drew had opened remotely. She hadn't been a "Jo" since he'd left, reverting to "Josie" or "Jojo" like her friends and grandparents had always called her. Now the name "Jo" was foreign, as ill-fitting as the skirts, blouses and high heels she'd worn for those brief years in that office job.

After making sure the girls were settled in their booster seats in the back, she got into the front passenger seat for the trip to the water park Drew had promised.

Bella leaned between the two seats to show Josie her necklace again.

"Isn't it fun being all together? We're like a real family."

There were all kinds of families, each one valid, but Josie understood what Bella meant. Her daughter hankered for a family with a mom and dad living in the same house as their kids.

Maybe from the outside the four of them looked like that happy family but it was a lie. Josie had never been more solitary or afraid or felt more like a failure.

COOKIE DIDN'T NEED GROOMING, but Heath had to find a reason to talk to Josie. She still hadn't called, even though Drew should have left by now. On Wednesday evening, he parked his car outside the yard at the farm and got the dog out of the back seat. "Here we go, girl."

Cookie wagged her tail and gave him an expectant, bright-eyed look as he gathered up her leash and they made their way to a shed behind the house Josie used for her dog grooming business. He'd made the appointment online and since he'd gotten an automatic confirmation, she must be expecting them. If she'd heard the car, why hadn't she come out to say hello?

"Hey, stranger." He poked his head around the half-open shed door.

"Hey." Josie turned from a pet-size sink and patted Cookie, who strained at the leash to greet her. "Nail clipping, ear cleaning, brushing and a bath and blow dry tonight?" She lowered a metal table and helped Cookie onto it.

"Yeah, I guess." He'd bathed Cookie a few days ago when she'd rolled in something smelly but if it would give him time to talk with Josie, another one wouldn't hurt.

Josie picked up a brush and ran it through Cookie's fur. "She seems nice and clean and an unnecessary bath would strip healthy oils from her coat." Josie studied him. "What's really going on here?"

"Okay, you've been kind of distant. I know with Drew visiting you're busy but..." Heath rubbed Cookie's ears as Josie took a pair of clippers from a drawer. "Is everything all right?"

"It's fine." She focused on Cookie's nails. "Relax, baby." She continued soothing the dog while wielding the clippers. "Bella and Lottie want us all to spend time together. Drew was only supposed to be here until today but now... He's staying over the weekend. Are you busy at work?"

Heath shrugged. "Same as always. I miss our morning coffee breaks."

"Easy, Cookie." Josie focused on the dog's rear feet as far away from Heath as possible.

"I'm worried about you, that's all." He studied her bent head. "You haven't texted me in a few days and if things are hard or uncomfortable with your ex, I'm here for you."

That's what a friend did. Having had more than a week to get used to the idea of loving Josie, he'd gotten more comfortable with the notion. However, even if any relationship between them was currently on hold, they were friends first.

"Thanks, but like I said, everything is fine. Good girl, all done." Josie straightened and gave Heath a bright smile. "Let's look at your ears, Cookie." She lifted the floppy, velvety folds. "Not bad but they could use a bit of cleaning." She took a bottle from the shelf and several cotton pads from a lidded jar. "The weather's been great this week, hasn't it? So sunny and warm."

Heath's stomach knotted. Josie was pretending everything was fine and talking about meaningless things. Exactly what his ex-wife had done in the last year of their marriage when she'd already been involved with someone else. "Now the porch is fixed and Mike Murphy's son screened it in for me, I've been working out there. It's nice and shady and no mosquitoes."

"Great." She finished cleaning one of Cookie's ears and moved to the other. "The girls have spent so much time outside with me and Drew, they're tired. They even went to bed early tonight without complaining."

"Is Drew still here? At the farm?" Was her ex the reason she was so edgy?

"No, we had supper in town with him and then came home. Since he extended his vacation, he needed to answer work emails tonight." Josie patted Cookie's back. "All finished, sweetheart. We'll leave the bath for today, then?"

"Sure." Heath could wait around for another half an hour and pretend to make conversation, but it would be even more of a waste than giving a clean dog another bath. "What do I owe you?"

"Forget it." Josie lowered the table so Cookie could hop off. "It's always a pleasure to see this sweet girl."

"No, I insist." Heath pulled some bills out of his pocket and gave her what nail clipping, ear cleaning, brushing *and* a bath and blow dry had cost before. "I hope you don't run your farm business that way. If you give too many freebies, you won't make a profit." He smiled so she'd know he was teasing.

"No." She didn't return his smile. "I'll see you around, I guess?" Her voice hitched and after stuffing the money in the pocket of her shorts without counting it, she twisted her hands together. It was the first real emotion Heath had seen from her except for when she'd been focused on Cookie. "I have to check on a cow."

"Give me a call or text when you're free."

Heath followed Josie out of the shed. "But if you need to talk about anything, I meant what I said when I—"

"Yeah, I know. I can't..." Pain mixed with what might have even been love flashed across her face. "Anyway, that cow." She turned and almost sprinted to the barn while Heath stood by the shed staring after her.

"That went well, didn't it?" If only dogs understood sarcasm. He let Cookie walk on a loose leash to sniff as she pleased while they headed back to the car. Josie was avoiding him and there wasn't anything Heath could do about it. Unless... He veered toward the farmhouse, where a light shone from the kitchen window, and rapped softly on the side door.

"What are you doing knocking... Oh, Heath, it's you." With her hair wrapped in a towel and wearing a dressing gown, Martha opened the door and gestured him into the bright and cozy kitchen. "Hurry up, you'll let the bugs in. Bring Cookie with you. Our two are in the barn with Tom."

"I'm sorry to bother you but I saw the light on." He sat in the chair she offered and savored the warm scent of chocolate, cinnamon and fresh bread. A cheerful yellow cloth covered the table, and bright copper pans hung from hooks on the ceiling.

"Cup of tea and a cookie? No, it's no bother. The kettle's already on the boil." Martha waved away his protest. "You're here about Josie, aren't you?"

"How did you guess?" Heath rested his elbows on the table.

"She hasn't been herself since Drew turned up. Tom and I are worried about her." Martha spoke over the boiling kettle before she warmed a teapot and added tea bags and more hot water. "She keeps saying everything is 'fine' but I didn't bring her up from a little one not to know what's what." She shook her head.

Heath got up to help her bring the tea things to the table and then gestured to the seat beside him. "Chocolate chip cookies are my favorite." He eyed the plate Martha had filled. Something about this evening would go right.

"They're Josie's favorite, as well. I made them to try to cheer her up."

Heath took a cookie and bit into its buttery chocolate goodness.

"I don't think it's Drew that's the problem, at least not entirely." When he nodded, Martha poured tea into Heath's mug. "Of course, he's bound to unsettle her and the girls, but even so there's something else going on."

"Is it the farm?" Heath finished his cookie.

"Josie hasn't said anything more to me so I let her get on with the plan we put together."

"I don't think so. There's no problem with the bank loan I know of and we've been promised a big new commercial milk contract. Things are still tight but manageable." Martha's blue eyes narrowed. "Unless there's something she's not telling us."

"Why wouldn't she tell you? This farm's a family operation." Maybe Josie wouldn't talk to him but her grandparents were different.

"No reason." Martha's shoulders slumped. "It's a mystery. When Josie said you'd booked a dog grooming appointment, I wondered if she'd talk to you but I guess she didn't."

"No, I tried but didn't get anywhere with her. Then she went to the barn so fast it was like she was being chased by a bear. Said she had to check on a cow."

"Well, that's true enough. Little Ming, Clarabelle's calf, is doing better but she's not out of the woods yet." Martha drank some tea. "Still, Tom already went out there to check on Little Ming and Josie knew it. I tell you, I can't wait until Sunday when Drew leaves. Maybe then things will get back to normal."

Voices echoed in the barnyard, and Heath stood quickly. "Josie can't know I talked to you."

"Fair enough, but I'll say I wanted to see you

and Cookie and invited you in. Which is also the truth." Martha drank more tea. "I'm not about to hustle you out the front way like there's something suspicious going on. Besides, your car's still out there, isn't it?"

"It is." Heath laughed for the first time that evening. "You'd make a good detective."

"I've raised teenagers and in a few years there'll be two more of them in the house." Martha's face creased as she smiled. "Not much gets by me."

"I should go. You have an early start in the morning."

"That we do. Here, take another cookie." Martha handed him the plate. "Josie will come around. She's not usually secretive."

But as he said a stilted good-night, brushing past Josie and Tom at the back door, Heath could only hope Martha was right.

CHAPTER NINETEEN

"I wish Dad could stay even longer, don't you?" Bella tucked her arm through Josie's as they waited for Drew and Lottie under a striped awning outside Strawberry Pond's lone toy store. Bella had said she was too old for toys but Josie sensed her daughter also had another agenda.

"Well, since he already changed his plans once, he can't." *Thank goodness.* "You need to make the most of the rest of the time he's here." Josie had forced a smile so often this endless week her face ached. She also couldn't answer Bella's question truthfully because, unlike her daughters, she was counting the hours until Drew left.

"You and Dad like each other." Bella's face wore the same hopeful expression it had for several days now. "You've been spending lots of time together."

Only because the girls wanted them to do family things. "Your dad and I are having fun with you and Lottie, sure." To give him credit, Drew was making an effort and together they'd put on a united front for their daughters.

"Dad doesn't have a girlfriend. I asked him." Bella leaned into Josie's side. "And you don't have a boyfriend. Heath's only a friend, right?"

Maybe she should have told the girls there was something between Heath and her but now it was too late. Besides, she'd been rude and messed things up with Heath so badly when he'd brought Cookie for dog grooming he probably never wanted to speak to or see her again. "Bella, you—"

"Look what Daddy bought me." Lottie came out of the store carrying a shopping bag almost as big as she was, followed by Drew with another bag.

"Drew, it's too much." Josie shook her head at him. "Everything you bought them for back to school and Bella's new bike and Lottie's figure skates and—"

"I have some catching up to do." Drew's smile cajoled her.

Once she'd have fallen for that smile but not now. "No more shopping, all right?" She glanced at the mini karaoke machine for kids and art kits and games Lottie showed her. "We need to go home for lunch."

"Then we're going to the beach and swimming again." Lottie bounced between Drew and

Josie. "Dad wants to go to the state park where we went with Heath."

"And Heath's family when they visited," Josie said in response to Drew's raised eyebrows. Her heart twisted. They'd gone to that park less than a month ago, but in some ways it felt like a lifetime. Despite their superficial similarities, Heath was nothing like Drew and she'd been foolish to think he was. For a start, he'd never bought Bella and Lottie things as a shortcut to try to secure their affection. "Come on, girls. Grams texted. She made us egg salad sandwiches for lunch."

"I hate egg salad sandwiches." Lottie's voice came out in a whine. "Dad said we could go to the diner."

"You did?" Josie glanced at Drew. "I thought we agreed you'd check with me first before making plans."

"We did but Lottie said she wanted to go to the diner so I said we'd ask you." A strand of Drew's hair flopped onto his forehead, making him look more like the man she'd fallen in love with. "It's only lunch." He wrapped his arms around both girls. "I guess we have to go back to the farm. What do you say we get milkshakes to take back?"

"No, Drew. If the girls have milkshakes they won't eat lunch." Lottie was a picky eater and Josie struggled to get her to eat a balanced meal at the best of times. "They've also had lots of treats this week. They need their routine, especially with back to school soon."

"But, Mom—" Bella and Lottie spoke in unison.

"Your mom's right." He hesitated. "I'm sorry. I was wrong." He spun Lottie and Bella around in a circle as if the three of them were on a dance floor.

Josie pressed a hand to her chest. Despite what he might say and even think, Drew had never grown up. Although she hadn't seen it before, she did now and instead of her usual anger and frustration, all she felt was pity. Maybe his folks had never set boundaries, or maybe they had but with his charm and good looks, in the end they'd let him have his own way. And unlike today, he hadn't often said he was sorry or admitted fault.

"Why don't I text Grams and ask her if she could pack the sandwiches in a picnic for us? We could take our lunch to the park instead."

"And get ice cream after the park and swimming?" Lottie looked between them.

"If it's okay with your dad, sure." Josie wanted this discussion and the day to be over. She texted Grams about their lunch. As the four of them made their way back to the lot where Drew had parked his rental car, her thoughts churned like clothes in a washing machine.

Drew had made a start in trying to do better and although she was grateful, she had another motive for having lunch at the park. So far, Josie had managed to divert him whenever the subject of Snow Moon's profitability had come up and she needed to keep it that way. While he'd never said or implied he wanted the girls to live even part of the time with him, what if he or his family got the idea she wasn't managing financially?

As they passed the bank, she ducked her head in case Carly, the loan officer, happened to be near the door or windows. Without that loan, Josie had to find another source of revenue, but how? She didn't want to ask Heath for more advice. He'd believed in her and been optimistic about her loan application being approved. She hadn't only let herself down but him, as well. Then there was Gramps. She'd convinced him to hire extra help they couldn't really afford and now they were in worse financial shape than ever.

"Yes, Bella? What is it?" In the library parking lot, Josie stopped with one hand on Drew's open car door. "Why didn't you go with your dad and Lottie to pick up her library book?" Josie glanced over her shoulder at the library entrance. She'd counted on a few minutes alone in the car to settle herself.

"I wanted to talk to you." Bella slid into her seat. "Alone." She gestured Josie closer and as

Josie crouched outside the car, Bella lowered her voice. "I want to know. Are you and Dad getting back together?"

"Whatever gave you that idea?" Josie tried hard to stifle her shock.

"Well." Bella rolled her dark-lashed eyes, so much like Drew's. "Like I said before, you don't have a boyfriend, and Dad doesn't have a girlfriend. I want you to get back together. We could all live in New York City with Dad."

Josie swallowed. A child's logic was simple. "Your dad and I are divorced, sweetheart. But even if we weren't, we couldn't leave Grams and Gramps here on the farm on their own."

"Dad's rich. I bet he could buy a house near us for Grams and Gramps to live in. Then they wouldn't have to be on the farm at all. I heard Grams say Gramps needs a rest." Bella wrapped her arms around Josie's neck. "Please, Mommy. Some divorced people get married again. I know a girl at school whose parents did."

"Bella, I can't—"

"You can't what?" Drew appeared behind Josie.

"Oh, it's nothing. We'll talk later."

"I want a cheese sandwich." Lottie continued to complain.

Bella grinned at her dad and then made an impudent face at Lottie. "You have to eat egg salad like the rest of us."

"Bella." Josie shook her head. "That's enough. Lottie, get in the car and don't argue. You ate an egg salad sandwich fine last week."

"Listen to your mom, girls." Drew went around the car to make sure Lottie had buckled herself in.

While Drew had backed her up, she now had an even bigger problem. This family together time, and Josie's pretend happiness, had given Bella and maybe Lottie the wrong idea. Although she'd always said she'd do anything to make her daughters happy, that'd never included getting back with their dad. But now she also understood why she'd pushed Heath away. She was afraid.

When Josie got into the front passenger seat and Drew started the car and pulled out of the parking space, Josie sat rigid as if frozen. If she let herself love Heath and gave him her whole heart, she risked becoming the woman she'd been with Drew. One who relied on and trusted someone else to only be let down. She and Heath had shared a few kisses, and along with affection and friendship, she'd started to believe in a love that likely wasn't real.

Josie glanced over her shoulder where the girls chattered with excitement about an inflatable water toy Drew had given them. She wouldn't reunite with their dad but taking things further with Heath wouldn't help, either. In fact, it would likely make things worse.

"Cookie, come." Heath gave the dog a treat when she trotted over to join him on the path through the trees. "It'll be cooler once we get to the water. Want to go for a swim?"

Thanks to a company-wide half day of vacation, Heath had this Friday afternoon in late August off so he'd decided to head back to the park he'd visited with his family and Josie and her girls. He hadn't heard anything from Josie since that awkward dog grooming appointment. Not that he'd expected to but the silence still stung.

He dug in the pocket of the shorts he'd worn over his swim trunks for his phone. "Hang on, girl. Sit." Cookie sat as he checked directions. "If we take this left fork, it's a shortcut to a beach where you're allowed." While dogs couldn't use the main beach in summer, the ranger had directed Heath to a pet-friendly one alongside the park boundary.

As they set off along the path, Cookie wagged her tail as if she understood.

Heath laughed to himself. He'd gotten used to talking to his dog and if anyone heard and thought it odd, their opinion didn't matter. He'd heard Josie talk to Honey and Buster often enough. His heart skipped a beat. Even when he didn't intend to think about Josie, she was never far from his mind.

"Oh, wow." He said the words almost under his breath as he took in the stunning vista. The trees opened up into a grassy picnic area partlysurrounded by mountains with the sparkling azure lake below.

"Great view, isn't it?" A man who looked to be in his late fifties stopped cleaning a public barbecue grill and gestured to the panorama. "A hidden gem. I come here because it's quieter. Usually with my wife but she had to work today. You local?"

"Sort of. I'm here for the summer." Heath introduced himself.

"Kevin Murphy." He grinned beneath a baseball cap advertising the Strawberry Spot Diner. "I knew your great-aunt Bea. You've got a nice piece of land in Tabby Cat Hollow. My cousin, Pat, helped fix your porch. He said it was a tricky job."

Although Heath should be used to it by now, he was still taken aback when complete strangers already knew a lot about him and what he considered to be his private life.

"If you need any other work done around the place, I'm a painter and decorator. Here." He went over to a nearby picnic table and rummaged in a backpack. "Take my card." He held it out to Heath.

"Thanks." Heath took the card and tucked it in his pocket. He wasn't used to paper business cards, either, but in an area with patchy cell service, he supposed it made sense.

"Well, I won't keep you." Kevin returned to cleaning the grill. "If you're looking for the pond, it's a minute or so that way." He jerked one thumb. "There's another beach below here so mind the signs. Dogs only allowed on that one out of season."

"Great." Heath shepherded Cookie away from an open cooler and in the direction Kevin pointed. As they neared the edge of the picnic area shaded by more trees, children's voices and the splash of water grew louder and a sandy path led down a gentle hill to the lake. "No, we're not going there. You're not allowed."

Cookie's ears pricked and she wagged her tail.

Heath stopped and stared. From their vantage point near the trees, he and Cookie were mostly hidden from view but he could still see the beach.

"Hurry up, Lottie." Bella splashed through shallow water at the edge of the sand followed by Lottie, both girls wearing bright pink swimsuits. "It's us against Mom and Dad." She tossed a red-and-white beach ball toward Josie and Drew, who stood farther out in the lake.

Josie caught the ball and swam toward Drew. "That's right, Lottie." Her voice carried over the water. "Swim to Dad and me," she encouraged.

Heath's stomach contracted. They'd gone for a family swim and were playing a game to entertain the kids. It didn't mean anything important. Although he should keep going, some inner force compelled him to stay and watch.

Drew wrapped one arm around Josie's shoulders, almost hugging her, as they both jumped up and down in the water and cheered on their daughters. Then all four of them made a circle, laughing, talking and splashing each other.

Cookie whined. His dog's anxious brown eyes stared at him and he bent to pat her as if on autopilot.

"Sorry, no swimming today." If they continued on their current route, Heath risked being seen. He couldn't face any of them right now, Josie most of all.

"Hey, I thought you were going to the pond," Kevin called from a picnic table as Heath retraced his steps to the woods.

"Change of plans but..." Heath took a deep breath. "I may want some painting done. I'll call you."

Kevin gave him a thumbs-up, and then Heath hustled Cookie onto the path that led the short distance back to the Forest Service road where he'd left the car.

With the vehicle in sight, he fumbled for his key fob. This time next week, he'd be home in Boston where he belonged. If nothing else, he thought he and Josie were friends. He'd trusted her, but she'd brushed him off. Abandoned him, betrayed him, even? Those were strong words but given the possessive way Drew held her... Images of his wife and, in a different way, his father rose from his memory.

Yet, despite appearances, Heath was a different man from what he used to be, one who didn't want to doubt Josie or be too quick to judge and jump to conclusions. This summer had changed him, and people and situations were more complicated than he'd once thought. He needed to give Josie one last chance to explain herself—or say goodbye for good.

He got into the car and when Cookie hopped onto his lap, he held her tight and buried his face in her warm fur. "It's okay. Everything'll be fine."

He didn't know if he was trying to reassure the dog or himself.

CHAPTER TWENTY

THE LATE-AFTERNOON SUN cast wavy ribbons of light across the green pasture where black-and-white-patterned cattle grazed, cocooned by darker green hills and a soft blue sky. As always, the familiarity of the scene brought Josie comfort, reassurance and a bone-deep sense of belonging. It was home and she'd work to her last breath to keep it.

She clambered down from the tractor and opened the gate that led from the field to a shaded lane. Since Drew had left the day before, both she and the farm had settled back into a familiar rhythm, one that undulated with daily chores and the seasons.

Too bad she couldn't say the same for her daughters. Their dad's visit had turned Bella's and Lottie's lives upside down, and Bella especially was acting out, disagreeing with everything Josie said and asked her to do. Meanwhile, Lottie seemed much quieter, which was so unlike her normal self.

"Hey, Clarabelle. How're you doing, girl?" Josie greeted the cows crowded around the gate. Bringing them in for milking was one of the best parts of the day, a constant that grounded her and gave simple joy.

Clarabelle nudged Josie's arm while pushing the smaller Daffodil out of the way.

"Now, now. Mind your manners." Josie laughed at how cows were a lot like people. Clarabelle was determined to be first while some of the others were content to stay in the middle of the group or bring up the back of the line. "There you go, Daffodil. Don't worry, I'll look out for you."

As several cows continued to jostle for position, Josie left the tractor where it was for one of the new hands they'd hired to pick up later and called to Buster, the border collie who'd followed her from the barn. Together, they herded the cows into line and then, leaving Buster to guide the group at the front, Josie gathered up the last stragglers. "Come on, coboss, that's right."

Bella and Lottie would also settle in time. She'd talk to them after milking and then text Heath. No matter how difficult or uncomfortable, she owed him an explanation. Or at least a goodbye. Her stomach lurched so she put in her earbuds and pulled out her phone to scroll to one of the oldies playlists she'd made for Gramps.

As distractions went, jogging along a rutted country lane to Bobby McFerrin's classic song, "Don't Worry, Be Happy," was as good a start as any. Even if she didn't feel it, maybe she could *think* herself happy.

Turning a corner where the lane narrowed toward the farmyard, and the trees on either side made a leafy green canopy, Josie hummed in time to the music. "Almost there, Buster. Good job." The collie loved his work and, like Josie, looked forward to this time of day.

She waved to Gramps, who stood by the farmyard gate, and then almost tripped over her feet as she stumbled to a stop.

"Heath." She yanked the earbuds out of her ears and jammed them in a pocket of her jeans. "What are you doing here?"

"Waiting for you." He placed a hand atop one of the wooden split rail fences that marked a field long ago taken over by forest.

"But the cows. It's milking time." Although Josie wanted to talk to Heath, she didn't want it to be here or now.

"I already spoke to your gramps. He said he and that new part-time farm hand could cover for you." As Gramps and the remaining cows disappeared, Heath came around a piece of broken fence to join Josie in the lane. "Long time, no see."

Was that hurt and disappointment in his eyes and expression? Josie's mouth went dry. "With Drew here, life got busy. The girls wanted us to do family things. I couldn't disappoint them." All of which was true but not the whole truth.

"It looked like you and Drew were close. Really friendly." Heath's voice had a sharp edge.

Sweat trickled down the back of Josie's neck. Drew had always been tactile, but no matter how many times he put an arm around her or gave her a hug, it meant nothing. "It's better for the girls if their mom and dad can get along. Drew and I are divorced, but he's an exuberant, larger-than-life guy who sweeps everyone along with him. A big kid in lots of ways."

Which Josie realized had been the biggest problem in their marriage and one Josie couldn't ever have fixed. Drew would likely be the same impetuous man he was now when he was eighty. Fun to be around for the good times but nowhere to be found when life was hard.

"I see." Some of the stiffness in Heath's demeanor eased.

"Yeah, he's a hugger and playful so if you saw or thought… It was nothing, only that Bella and Lottie have to come first. They need a mom and dad who can co-parent effectively. Drew and I talked and since he wants to be more involved in their lives, I have to help make that happen."

"I understand the girls need Drew and it's good if he can be the dad they deserve. I would never stand in the way of their happiness, but I care for you, Josie. My feelings haven't changed, and I'd still like to see where things go between us, even long-distance. You visiting Boston this winter like we talked about." He scrubbed a hand across his face.

It was a handsome face and, along with Heath's gentle, yearning expression, Josie's heart cracked a bit more.

"I'm sorry. I can't." She cared for Heath but she couldn't drag him into this mess with the girls, Drew and the farm. "We had a wonderful summer and I'll always cherish our time together, but now we have to return to our real lives." With each word that came from between her numb lips, she hated herself even more, but it was for the best. Heath had to go home to Boston and forget her.

"So this it, then? Goodbye?" His voice cracked.

"Yes." She didn't trust herself to say anything more, even though the devastation on Heath's face almost stopped her.

But while his tortured look would be imprinted into her brain—and on her soul—forever, she forced herself to harden her heart, turn away and keep going. Alone.

Heath stowed his overnight bag in the trunk of his car and returned to the house for Cookie, who waited inside the screen door. Although he'd planned to leave Strawberry Pond the next day, given what Josie had said he no longer had any reason to extend his stay.

Or see that horse tomorrow morning at Laura's. After the town's pie social, he'd asked her to keep her eyes open for a Morgan suitable for a new rider like him and she'd come through quicker than he'd expected.

His cell phone rang and for a second his heart leaped. Had Josie changed her mind? No, it was Kevin Murphy, the painter Heath had hired to redecorate.

"I'm heading out soon. Start tomorrow as early as you want." He listened as Kevin confirmed final details of the work. "Sure, get me quotes from that kitchen and bathroom contractor you mentioned. The heating and air-conditioning company, as well." If Heath was going to rent out Tabby Cat Hollow to vacationers, the house needed to appeal to city people who expected top-of-the-line appliances, underfloor heating and a power shower.

People like he'd once been. His heart pinched as he gathered up Cookie's leash, portable water bottle, blanket and favorite squeaky toy. While Heath still liked modern comforts, home was more than having the latest conveniences. It was roots, family and the people you shared your life with that mattered.

"Want to go for a car ride, Cookie?" He clipped the leash to her collar, and as they went out to the porch, Heath turned off the hall light and locked the front door.

He'd been foolish to let himself think about him and Josie making a family and future together. She already had a family, one that didn't include him. As she'd said, the girls came first and how could Heath, who'd grown up without a good dad for a role model, be the stepdad those precious girls needed?

He opened the car's rear door and got Cookie buckled in. "There you go, sweetheart. You can nap until we get to Boston. You're going to be a city dog. What do you say to that idea, hey? Bright lights, a park a few blocks from my condo and fun at dog day care." Or, as the center he'd picked out advertised itself, a place for quality canine enrichment, learning and creative play.

Cookie turned away to look out the other window where lights from Snow Moon Hill Farm twinkled through the trees.

A wonderful summer. Josie's words ricocheted in Heath's head. It'd been a lot more for him but somehow he had to move on. She sure had. She'd run the rest of the way from the lane to the farmyard, and although Heath had stood hoping and waiting, she hadn't looked back once. That told him how much he meant to her.

He swallowed the rawness at the back of his throat and stared at the twinkling lights. Even though he didn't want to, he loved Josie and always would.

Before getting into the car, he pulled out his phone again to cancel his appointment to see that horse.

Laura replied to his text in seconds.

Sorry tomorrow won't work. See u when u r next in town? ☺

His stomach knotted at her cheery message and smiley face.

I've decided not to look for a horse after all.

He'd wanted to ride with Josie not by himself.

2 bad. R U ok?

Fine.

Along with Alana, Laura was Josie's best friend. Heath wasn't going to pour his heart out to her or anyone else.

U sure? Do u know what's up with Josie's loan? Haven't heard from her in days.

No. Gotta go.

Heath switched off his phone. He had to stop this exchange before Laura got the truth out of him. Not about the loan, because Josie hadn't mentioned it to him, either, but the rest of it.

But now that he thought of it, Josie should've had a decision on her loan application. He'd helped her put together that financial plan. Without the bank's help, Josie would struggle to keep the farm going through the winter and maintain the upgrades she'd already initiated. And because he loved her, there was one last thing he could do to make her life easier.

He got into the driver's seat and took a checkbook, piece of paper and envelope and pen from his computer bag. Although checks were old-school, he wanted to have left town before Josie received this gift. He didn't need the small financial legacy Bea had left him so why not give it to someone who did? Someone who'd also done more for Bea in practical day-to-day terms than he ever had.

After writing a brief note, he made out a check to Josie, signed it and stuck the check and note in the envelope and sealed it. Then he wrote Josie's name on the front and started the car.

When he reached the mailbox at the end of the Ryans' farm lane, Cookie whined from the back.

"Sorry, girl." He glanced over his shoulder. "You can't play with Honey and Buster or Bella and Lottie." His dog would miss Josie, her family and their dogs almost as much as Heath. "You'll make new friends soon." But they wouldn't replace the old ones for Cookie or him.

Heath got out of the car and, leaving the driver's door open, dropped the envelope into the mailbox that glinted silver in the moonlight.

Then, with one last look up the lane, he slid back into his vehicle and pointed it toward the highway. The fastest route to Boston. Whatever he thought he and Josie had shared was over. Now he had to make a new life without her.

CHAPTER TWENTY-ONE

Josie finished checking the milking machine and rubbed a hand across her hot face. Having hardly slept, she'd gotten up half an hour before her alarm and worked so fast she'd completed morning chores in record time.

So far, though, all that work hadn't stopped her from thinking about Heath or numbed the hurt in her heart. She didn't only care for him. She loved him with her entire being. Somewhere around two this morning, she'd finally admitted the truth, which made her feel even worse.

He must have left early because when she'd herded the cows around the long way back to the field, Kevin Murphy's painting and decorating van was parked by the porch, and Kevin had waved at her from a ladder outside the back door.

Josie had waved back, then huddled in Fifi's cab as the tractor rattled along the lane.

"Why don't you take a break?" Across from her, at a stainless steel sink, Grams washed and dried her hands before joining Josie. "You've been working nonstop since before sunup. I expected you'd come in for breakfast with the girls and when you didn't... What's wrong?"

If she stopped working, Josie would start crying and never stop. She'd thought she'd done the right thing by sending Heath away but she'd never been so unhappy in her life, not even when Drew had walked out.

"Nothing's wrong but I need to change the spark plugs on the lawn tractor."

"Surely your gramps can handle—"

"I already said I could." Gramps stood at the barn door holding a sheaf of mail. "Changing a few spark plugs is nothing. Thanks to that help you hired, these days I hardly do anything around here. You ladies even stopped me from finishing repainting the girls' playhouse yesterday. It would've taken less than an hour." Still, he gave Grams and Josie a fond smile and kissed Grams on the cheek as he handed her a seed catalog and several other envelopes.

Although Josie didn't know how she'd keep paying for that hired help, it was a blessing to see Gramps doing and sounding so much better. "We only want you to follow the doctor's orders. He told you to slow down, remember?" She shook a finger at him in mock admonition.

"Yeah, yeah. This here one must've been hand-delivered." He passed Josie an envelope with her name scrawled on it in unfamiliar writing. It was rare enough to receive personal mail these days, let alone someone stopping by to put it in their mailbox. "Who's it from?" He studied her expectantly.

"I don't know. Give me a chance to open it." Josie cleaned her hands and dried them on a towel before sliding a finger under the envelope's seal. "It's..." She was so stunned that she focused on the words a second and then a third time. "From Heath. Here, you read it. He says..." Tears threatened again. "We can't accept the money, of course."

"Come sit outside on the bench." Grams took Josie's arm and led her into the fresh morning air. Josie blinked as the blue sky, green grass and barn, house and outbuildings swam together.

"That's mighty fine and generous but we can't take a penny from Heath nor Bea neither." Gramps put the note and check back into the envelope and sat on one side of Josie while Grams sat on the other. "We don't need it anyway, not with that loan you got."

Josie's heart seemed to drop to her feet. "Well, you see...about that loan. I—"

"Turned you down, did they?" Gramps patted Josie's hand as Grams suppressed a gasp.

"Yes." There was nothing else to say.

"We can try again, can't we? Make a new application?" Grams sounded close to tears.

"Not anytime soon. We don't have the right profit margins. Carly, the loan officer, tried her best, but even with what Heath suggested I call a 'return to profitability plan,' the higher-ups still said no." Josie slumped on the bench.

"Banks these days." Gramps shook his head and slapped one hand against the barn wall. "Looking out for themselves, most of 'em. If Eugene Dobay was still in charge you'd have gotten your loan. He'd have known we'd be good for the money. Not like today when decisions are made by folks in some city who wouldn't know a cow from a heifer or even a bull."

"Now, Gramps." Josie forced a pained smile. Eugene Dobay had been dead for at least ten years and hadn't managed the bank branch in Strawberry Pond since Josie was in grade school. "The decision's been made. Nothing we say or do will change that."

"Oh, honey." Even Grams's soothing embrace didn't feel as comforting as usual. "Why didn't you tell us before now? We're a family. We face the good and bad together, remember?"

Josie choked back a sob. "I was ashamed. I keep thinking what if I could've cut costs sooner or we hadn't bought the new milking machine last year?"

"We had to buy that machine. We couldn't have kept up with our milk orders otherwise." Gramps's bushy eyebrows drew together. "The new contract with that corporate supplier should help."

"I didn't want to tell you but it's delayed. That business is having problems, as well." It was like a chain reaction. Farmers depended on others and if one of their customers was in financial trouble, it impacted everyone connected to them. While Josie understood the reality of farm life, it didn't make this situation any easier. "None of us want to take Heath's money, but I also don't know what else to do."

"Where are the girls?" Grams glanced beyond Josie to Gramps.

"On the back deck, playing with the dogs and that karaoke machine thing Drew gave them. Why?" Gramps raised his hands and dropped them back on his lap.

"It's time for a family meeting." Grams stood and gestured to them to follow her to the house. "There's no need for Josie to shoulder these burdens on her own."

"Grams, I—"

"Don't say another word unless it's to agree with me." Grams gave Josie a half smile. "You're miserable and you're well on the way to making the rest of us miserable, too. Bella and Lottie won't be happy without a happy mom so it's more than time we put our heads together to a find a way through."

"Listen to your grams, Jojo." Gramps gave her an awkward hug. Not usually a demonstrative man, when he showed physical affection Josie knew it came from his heart.

"I thought you'd be disappointed. In all this time, nobody's come close to losing this farm but me." Walking between her grandparents like she'd done as a child, for the first time in weeks the tension in Josie's shoulders eased.

Gramps snorted. "Sure they did but they didn't talk much about it if at all. My grandparents almost lost the place in the Great Depression of the 1930s, and we had some lean years during the farm crisis in the 1980s."

"I never knew." Josie glanced between her grandparents as they reached the front porch steps.

"That's because we kept going like we will now." Gramps opened the screen door and ushered Josie and Grams onto the porch ahead of him. "And we'll involve the girls. They're young and while they don't need to know the details or get scared that they'll lose their home, it's never too early to learn that in tough times we pull together and they're part of a team."

Her grandfather was right. While the girls

might have been dazzled by Drew and all the money he'd spent on them, that was a vacation. Real life was different. Josie sat on one of the porch chairs as Grams went to find Bella and Lottie.

"There's one other thing." Gramps sat in the rocker across from Josie. "I'm an independent old cuss. Oh, yes." He nodded. "You're right in thinking I am. You're also right I don't like change. If it ain't broke, don't fix it has always been my motto."

"But…" Josie stammered. "This farm has to change to survive."

"I reckon it does and that's why in the past month or so I haven't stood in your way. But I also know with me and you, the apple don't fall far from the tree."

"You mean, we're alike?" She put a hand to her face. Gramps was right again. "I guess I can be independent. And perhaps a bit stubborn."

"Like a mule." The rocker creaked. "I'm not saying it's always a bad thing. Far from it, but if you're so set on doing things your way on your own, it can make life harder. Asking Heath for help, now, you didn't get the loan but you'd have had no chance at all without his input. If we can somehow find the money, that plan the two of you came up with *will* keep us going."

Heath. Josie's heart pinched. Less than twenty-four hours later, she already knew she'd made a terrible mistake in sending him away. It had been her fear speaking, not her heart, but now he was gone and it was too late.

"Something wrong between you two?" Gramps continued rocking.

"You could say that." Josie shook her head. "It's all my fault."

"If it is, then you need to fix it. Simple."

If only. As the girls and Grams joined them on the porch, Josie pasted a smile on her face.

"Grams said we need ideas to get money to help the farm." Those were the most words Lottie had spoken at one time since Drew had left. She rushed over to Josie's chair. "Me and Bella could sell the necklaces Daddy gave us. They have real diamonds."

"Oh, sweetheart. Thank you, but things aren't that bad." She squeezed Lottie's hand.

"Dad said he'd call us before breakfast but he didn't. We waited and waited." After hanging back, Bella now sat cross-legged at Josie's feet with Buster and Honey sprawled across a rag rug.

Typical Drew but Josie was done apologizing and making excuses for him. "Then you should call your dad and ask what happened."

"Maybe later." Bella fiddled with Buster's collar. "I miss Heath. *He* called us today like he promised."

"He did?" Over Bella's head, Josie raised her eyebrows at Grams.

"Sure thing." Grams nodded. "Heath said goodbye to the girls yesterday while he waited for you with the cows. It was then he said he'd call today when he got back to Boston to tell them how Cookie was settling into city life."

Nobody had thought to tell her? Josie's breathing constricted. "Did Heath say anything else?"

"No, should he have?" Bella studied her.

"I guess not." After what she'd said, Josie shouldn't have expected him to leave a message for her.

"If we need money, why don't you rent land to Connor and Colm Sullivan?" Bella rolled onto her back and played with Honey.

"What?" Josie stilled.

"When they helped us with the hay, I heard them talking. They need more land, but Connor said you and Gramps would never go for the idea so it wasn't worth asking." Bella rolled her eyes. "People always think kids don't know anything but we do."

"You sure do." And why hadn't renting out a couple of fields ever occurred to Josie? Likely because in all her planning, she'd neglected to consider the obvious. Maybe she was more like Gramps than she thought. "While I wouldn't want to rent land to just anyone, Connor and

Colm would be perfect. They're committed to sustainable agriculture and smart and up on all the latest techniques."

Gramps slapped his hand against his jeans. "Bella, you may have saved the day. The Sullivan twins are fine fellows. There's no reason we can't cut back on our operation for a few years and maybe expand in other ways. Like that cow cuddling Heath's sister talked about. I'll admit I was skeptical but if we can give people something they want and make money from it, why not?"

As excited voices rose around her, Josie sat back and watched her family. With her worry over the loan application and delayed milk contract, she'd put the cow cuddling idea to the back of her mind and only mentioned it to Gramps in passing, sure he'd dismiss it.

Yet, although she should've been honest with him and the rest of the family from the start, once she'd told them the truth, they'd been there for her. It hadn't been too late for the farm so maybe it wouldn't be too late with Heath, either. But first, she had to make sure the girls understood something important.

"Everyone." She raised a hand to rejoin the conversation. They quieted and the girls and her grandparents turned toward her. "It's about Drew." She beckoned Bella closer. "I know you wanted your dad and me to get back together but you need to understand that's not happening. Not now or ever. We can visit your dad if you want but we're not moving to New York City."

For a moment, Bella's face clouded but then she took Josie's hand. "That's what Dad told me before he left. He also said Heath's nice and he hoped you guys would be happy together."

"What?" Josie put a hand to her mouth.

"Everybody knows you like him, Mom." Lottie cuddled on Josie's lap. "And he likes you. He wouldn't have kissed you behind a tree at the pie social if he didn't. Mrs. Sullivan saw you and told Grams."

"Lottie." A small smile played around the corners of Grams's mouth. "What have I told you about listening in on adult conversations and certain things not being any of your business?"

"Well, if Heath's gonna be our stepdad, it *is* our business, isn't it?" Bella defended her sister. "He's okay and I could get used to him being around more. Boston would be almost as fun as New York. It's also way closer."

"You're getting ahead of yourselves and we're not moving to Boston, either." Josie's cheeks burned. "Okay" was high praise from Bella. "Heath left and he—"

"Won't come back unless you ask him to," Gramps interrupted. "The man has his pride."

Josie was proud, too, but one of the things this summer had taught her was that there were times when she needed to swallow that pride and admit she'd been wrong.

"Here." Lottie took the phone from a pocket of Josie's barn dungarees. "You should text Heath. I wanted you and him to get together from the beginning but you kept saying he was just a friend."

"Out of the mouths of babes," Grams murmured.

"Okay." Her heart still raced, and with four pairs of eyes making sure she did what she said, Josie tapped out a brief text telling Heath that while they couldn't accept his money, she needed to talk to him. "There." She hit Send.

Now it was up to him.

HEATH HAD BEEN back in Boston less than twenty-four hours and already he missed Josie and her daughters, Tom and Martha and even the Ryans' cows, each with their own personalities. No restaurant, big-league sports game, museum, play or other urban attraction could compensate for love, family and a community like Strawberry Pond.

In his small condo kitchen, he half listened to his sister as Jenna helped him put away the groceries he'd ordered online and that had just been delivered.

"Mom bought symphony tickets and… You're

not paying attention to anything I'm saying, are you?" Jenna turned away from the pantry and, hands on her hips, stared Heath down.

"Of course I am. Mom, symphony tickets. Not a surprise. She likes live orchestral music." He bent to pat Cookie, who didn't want to let him out of her sight. Heath had worked from home today but tomorrow he had to go to the office and take Cookie to that dog day care. How would she manage? How would *he* manage without her around all the time?

"Okay, but something's on your mind. Is it Josie?"

With her usual laser-like precision, Jenna had zeroed in on the one subject Heath didn't want to talk about. "Why would you think that?"

"You always were a bad liar. Besides, you look even more dejected than your dog." Jenna opened a box of chocolate chip cookies and passed one to Heath. "Spill. I'm not in a rush. Greg needs time with the girls, and since I already finished setting up my classroom for school, I'm all yours."

While Jenna often dropped by unannounced, from the moment Heath had opened his door to her, he'd sensed she had another motive beyond welcoming him back to the city. Heath had to talk to someone and who else but his sister? Owing to their fractured childhood, they'd always been there for each other and now Jenna wouldn't leave until he told her the truth. "Josie and I... We aren't seeing each other anymore."

"Her decision, obviously." Jenna crunched on a cookie.

"Yeah." Heath set aside his own cookie. The store-bought brand had nothing on Josie's homemade version. "I suggested trying long-distance but her daughters have to come first and my life's in Boston." He gestured around the condo. It was cozy and comfortable but now, after Tabby Cat Hollow, it didn't feel like home.

Jenna shook her head. "Both of you can't see what's right in front of you, can you?"

"I'm not going to push Josie, if that's what you're asking. I love her but she doesn't love me so—"

"You love her?" Jenna's eyes sparkled. "Finally. Way to go, bro. Did you tell her?"

"Of course not." Not after Josie had made it clear they had no future together.

"If you love her, you have to fight for her but you're not because you're scared. You're talking about Boston and geography and logistics when they don't matter, at least not really." Jenna held up one hand just as Heath would have spoken. "I know what I'm talking about because before Greg, I used to be the same. It's natural you and me have trouble trusting people because we're always afraid they're going to leave us. It's worse for you because Danielle did leave and betray your trust. As for Josie, from the little she said to me about her marriage and losing her parents, she must have many of the same feelings."

Heath gaped at his sister. "Even if that's true…" Which it was. "I'm forty and I've never had kids. How can I be a good stepdad? At first, I kept my distance from Bella and Lottie because Josie didn't seem to want me to get too involved in their lives. Then when Drew turned up, he's nice enough but…" Heath had met lots of men like Drew. They were fun and charming and easy to like but they were too superficial, much like his dad, for Heath to consider them real friends.

"Josie was likely trying to protect her daughters. She didn't say much about Drew but he doesn't sound like the kind of guy she or the girls can count on." Jenna patted Heath's arm. "You're a fantastic uncle and from seeing you with Bella and Lottie you'd be a fine stepdad. All you'd need to do is follow Josie's lead and trust your instincts. Trust yourself and her." Jenna's expression softened. "You're a good man, and I'm proud to call you my brother. The past is gone and you still have a whole future ahead of you. Don't waste it."

"I don't plan to." Heath's thoughts spun but now it was with opportunities. "If I need city life, Boston's an easy day or weekend trip away.

I could talk to my boss and ask about working remotely more permanently, at least part of the time."

"You could also talk to Josie. Where's your phone?" Jenna moved toward the living room and Heath's desk.

"My personal phone's dead. I didn't bother plugging it in to recharge. What?" He shrugged at Jenna's disgusted expression. "You and Mom have my work number. You could still reach me in an emergency." Josie wouldn't call him so Heath hadn't wanted to talk to anyone else. "Okay." He found his phone and charger under a stack of papers on his desk and plugged it in. "Are you happy now?" He stared at the screen as it came to life and then drew in a breath.

"What is it?" Jenna leaned around him.

"Josie texted me." A tender sprig of hope bloomed in his heart.

"Well, you need to text her back. I've said my piece, so I guess the rest is up to you."

"It is." He grinned at his sister. "Thanks."

"What's family for?" Her hug was fierce, loving and protective. "I used to think there was only one kind of family, the one we didn't have as kids. But now? There's lots of families. You have to believe in them, in yourself and that you deserve happiness."

Maybe for the first time Heath did. As his sister let herself out, he sat on the sofa with Cookie and reread Josie's message.

She didn't want the money but that didn't mean she didn't want him. And he wanted to fight for her and them without messing up. What he had to say to Josie needed to be in person.

CHAPTER TWENTY-TWO

"Josie would've told us if Heath texted her back, don't you think?" Martha took quilted place mats and cutlery from the dining room sideboard and set them at each place around the table.

"It's only been a few hours." Tom followed her holding a vase with the crocheted sunflowers Martha had made a few years ago and used as a late-summer centerpiece. "The man's likely at work and they're both adults. Whatever happens now, whether it's a text or anything else, isn't our business."

"I suppose so." When Josie hurt, Martha did, as well. While she'd kept the girls and herself occupied organizing backpacks for the first day of school and making beaded friendship bracelets, part of her wanted to drive to Boston and track down Heath herself.

Yet, Tom was right. Heath and Josie had to work things out by themselves, and Martha had enough problems of her own. Tom would never be able to do heavy farmwork again and it was time he admitted it.

Her husband plunked the sunflower centerpiece on the middle of the table and sniffed the air. "Something sure smells good. Irish stew?"

She nodded. "I used your mother's recipe and we're having it with my cornbread. It's cooler today so I spent more time in the kitchen." Cooking relaxed her and as she'd chopped, measured and mixed the various ingredients, she'd kept nagging worries at bay.

"Fall's coming." Tom set a stack of plates at his place.

"And harvest…which reminds me…" Martha licked her bottom lip. Josie and the girls were in the garden picking fresh tomatoes for a salad so she and Tom had the house to themselves. "You're doing so much better with your back and the rest of your aches and pains." Her husband stood taller, his eyes were brighter and he'd even joined his friends for their regular Wednesday lunch at the Strawberry Spot two weeks running. "With all the harvest work coming up, you ever think you should keep on doing lighter chores?"

"Have you been talking to my doctor?" Tom gave her a sharp look.

"Of course not. You know I'd never—"

"I do and I'm sorry. Implying such a thing was uncalled for. I know you talk to Anne Sullivan, like I talked to Howie, but that's different." As Tom followed Martha into the kitchen, he gave her a one-armed hug. "It's not easy getting old."

"Neither's the alternative. In some ways, I'm happier now than I was at forty. I'm not saying you should retire but maybe it's time to make room in your life for other things alongside the farm. Did you call the Sullivan twins?" After all these years, she knew her husband well. If she threw out ideas, they'd percolate while they talked of other things.

Tom pulled out a kitchen chair, sat and tinkered with the broken toaster. "I did. Josie and I spoke to Colm and Connor together."

Martha took out the big mixing bowl and corn bread ingredients. "And?"

"We need to work out the details but I wager we've got a deal. I said I'd bring you in on the financials, but what those boys are figuring to offer sounds more than fair. Generous, actually."

"We've got good land. It's right they pay for the privilege of using it." Martha's hands trembled as she measured cornmeal. Could things be working out?

"Colm also said we could all make cost savings by sharing workers and equipment between our places. They're also organic certified so they can help us with our transition, and they know lots about the kind of crop rotation Josie's set to try." Tom took the cover off the toaster. "Him and Connor have got some kind of sponsorship deal with Jablonski's, too, that big farm equipment supplier an hour south of here. Influencers, Colm said they are. They promote farm life and in return they've got a whole bunch of business sponsors. Can you believe those boys have several million followers on social media?"

Martha whisked the dry corn bread ingredients together and hid a smile. Josie said all along they needed to be more active on social media but Tom had always dismissed the idea.

"Connor, he's the one who handles most of it, said if we joined forces he'd like me to record a few videos about my life in farming. He'd handle the technical stuff but we might earn money from advertising. He seems to think folks would see me as trustworthy."

"That's because you are." Martha rested her hands on the counter. "It would take time but I expect we'd even get some new milk customers from it. Given the chance, people like to know where their food comes from and we're a family farm."

"Even if I stepped back from some of the heavier work, I'd still be part of things here." Tom examined the toaster cord.

"The biggest part. Nobody could ever replace you on the farm or in our family." Had her husband worried about somehow becoming less important? "None of us want to replace you, so if that's what's troubling you, get that thought right out of your head. Josie and me want you to take things easier so you can do the most important things." And be part of their lives as long as possible.

"You know, Connor suggested I be Gramps in those videos. He said I have a 'folksy New England charm.' Can you imagine? It could be the start of a whole new job." Tom set the toaster aside. "Fixed it. Should work fine now."

Martha wiped her hands on a dish towel and went across to her husband. "Thank you." She kissed the top of his head. "And yes, I can imagine it. Folks will love you." She wagged a finger at him. "It'll be a new adventure. You might even get fan email, but no matter what, I love you, Tom, and don't forget it."

"Like I love you." He stood and wrapped his arms around her. "Always have from that day I first saw you in school wearing that pretty yellow dress. You looked like sunshine. Still do."

"Oh, go on with you." Martha rested her head against her husband's shoulder. For more than half a century, nestled into his arms had been her safe place. A happy and comforting place, too, knowing that no matter what life brought they'd cope as long as they had each other.

"I mean it." He kissed her. "I'm still not keen on moving into town but maybe it's time."

"That's a conversation for another day. Since Josie didn't get that loan, we need to wait until the farm's on a firmer financial footing before moving anywhere." Although Martha had raised the subject of a house in town months ago, in her heart she didn't want to live there any more than Tom did. She'd miss looking out over the fields and caring for her chickens and other animals. She'd also miss being so close to Josie and the girls.

One step at a time. That's what her mother always said, along with "things will work out somehow."

As she hugged Tom tighter, Martha held to that advice. She couldn't worry about the future. It was the present and her family that counted and there was nowhere else she'd rather be.

"ATTA GIRL, FIFI." Josie patted the tractor's steering wheel as they crested a low hill on the narrow two-lane road beside farm fields. They were Ryan family fields where soon the Sullivan twins would plant a crop of winter rye, but Josie was excited about their new partnership and the opportunities it could bring.

She shifted in the driver's seat, surveying the warm, early September afternoon and rolling fields fringed by trees and rugged mountains extending into the hazy distance. The ditches by the road were filled with dark purple New England asters and tall yellow goldenrod, but despite all that beauty, she couldn't settle.

Apart from a brief, verging-on-impersonal text in reply to her message, she hadn't heard anything more from Heath. Although Grams kept telling her not to lose hope, now that the girls were back at school, the only other thing Josie could think to do was to go to Boston and talk to him in person. She was the one in the wrong, so she also had to be the one to try to make things right. And if she couldn't? Well, she'd know for certain there was no place for her in his life.

She gripped the steering wheel as a sporty silver car came up behind Fifi to pass. Tourists, likely, speeding to get where they needed to go as fast as possible and oblivious to the small joys found on the journey. She squinted and half turned to wave the vehicle by and then gasped.

That car... It couldn't be. Josie shoved her sunglasses onto the top of her head. Her heart pounded as Heath beeped the horn and then slowed and pulled onto the shoulder and parked ahead of her.

Her hands trembled as she steered Fifi and stopped behind Heath's car. He now stood outside it, and from the rear seat, Cookie stuck her head out an open window.

When Josie went to scramble down from the tractor's cab, Heath was already there with both hands outstretched. "Allow me?"

Wordlessly, she took his hands, but even when she reached the ground, he didn't let go. His palms were warm and familiar, and Josie let him guide her to a path that led away from the road into a grove of old maple trees.

"Stay there and don't move. Please?" Heath ran a hand through his hair. "I have to get Cookie. Not safe to leave her in the car alone."

Josie nodded as he darted away. Seconds later, he returned with the dog, her tail wagging, body wriggling and barking and straining at the leash to greet Josie.

"Hey, Cookie." She knelt to rub the dog's ears and tried to keep her expression neutral. "What are you two doing here?" Her voice cracked and she coughed.

"Looking for you." He held out his hands again and Josie took them as she got to her feet. "I want to talk and explain."

"Me, too. I… I was going to come to Boston in a few days to see you. Your address was on that check and I wanted to apologize and tell you…" The ball of emotion rising in Josie's throat threatened to choke her.

"Tell me what?" His smile was quizzical and he took one hand away from hers to brush a flyaway curl of hair from her cheek.

"That I'm sorry and… I was wrong. I lied when I downplayed what we had this summer. It was important. It meant everything to me, but I was too scared to tell you the truth."

"What truth would that be?" His gentle hand cupped her chin. She looked up, into his eyes.

"That I care for you and…" She took a deep breath. "After Drew, I was so insecure and afraid to trust anyone. I thought I had to prove myself by being independent, but you helped me see it's okay to ask for help. Even to lean on other people when you need to. I thought you'd leave me eventually anyway so to keep myself safe I pushed you away." Her voice was thick with unshed tears but she had to keep going. "My life's complicated and you don't live here so I told myself I couldn't fall in love with you but I did and now I don't know what to do."

"Aw… Josie." Heath wrapped her in his strong arms. "I love you, too." His expression held all the love, trust and reassurance she'd ever want and need. "And love means sharing burdens and being there for each other. After Danielle cheated on me and my marriage broke up, I never thought I could trust anyone again. But then you came along and I started to imagine us building a life together. You, me and Bella and Lottie. I know they already have a dad and I don't want to take Drew's place. To be a good stepdad I'll need to learn a lot and get to know them better and—"

"You only need to be yourself." Joy rushed through Josie. "But what about Boston and your job?"

"That's why I couldn't say anything to you right away. I spoke to my boss and she's okay with me working from Strawberry Pond three days a week. I told her about you and the girls and I guess she's a romantic at heart. As for Boston?" Heath held her even closer. "It's a great city but I'd hadn't even been there a day before I realized I couldn't enjoy it without you." He paused and his blue eyes twinkled. "Say it again, won't you?"

"You mean I love you?" She teased him back. "I do, you know. With my heart, soul and everything I have to give."

"I love you just the same. We'll figure out the rest as we go." Then his mouth covered hers in a kiss that made Josie's head spin and when he lifted her off her feet, Cookie barked and ran in circles around them. "With you, I'm home."

As Josie kissed him again, she knew that while Strawberry Pond had always been home, with Heath she'd found her true home. Now and forever.

EPILOGUE

SIX WEEKS LATER on an unseasonably warm October Saturday, Heath glanced around the orchard at Tabby Cat Hollow. After having the courage to open his heart and let love and Josie in, he'd also let in lots of other things.

More family. He gave Bella and Lottie a thumbs-up where, with Tom and Martha, they hovered behind a big maple tree draped in a blaze of orange-and-red foliage.

Friends and community. Thanks to Alana, the Sullivans, Murphys and many more, the old orchard was now clear of undergrowth and well on its way to being restored to productivity. His gaze landed on the new wrought iron bench and small table between two apple trees.

"Thank you." He turned to Laura, who'd lingered to arrange toss cushions and a blanket over the back of the bench. "For everything."

She took a step back and then slid one of the cushions, shaped like a pumpkin, farther to the right. "In Strawberry Pond we look after our own. All set?"

"Yeah." Heath patted his jacket pocket. Josie would be here any minute and he wanted everything to be perfect.

"Good luck, not that you need it." Laura gave his arm an encouraging pat. "We'll all be waiting up at the house to celebrate with you."

Heath nodded. Although he'd no reason to think it wouldn't be a celebration, he'd never been more nervous in his life.

As Laura disappeared around the side of the orchard, a glint of strawberry blond hair appeared in the lane.

"Bella, Lottie?" Josie came through the open orchard gate. "I know you two are here somewhere but… Heath?" She stopped in front of him. "Have you seen the girls? Or Grams and Gramps? They insisted I change out of my barn clothes and come here for a surprise but…" Her eyes widened as she took in the bench, table and Trixie and Doc, Heath's new Morgan, tethered to a similarly new hitching post.

Muffled giggles echoed from behind Heath followed by a "shushing" sound and sharp bark.

Cookie. It had been too much to hope the dog would stay quiet. Like Josie and her daughters, Cookie had a mind of her own but Heath wouldn't have it any other way.

"What's going on?" Josie's gaze swung toward the source of the noises and then back to him.

"By working together, we've managed to put your farm on a better financial footing, right?" Heath reached for Josie's left hand and held it tight.

"Yes, of course. Without using Bea's money, either, although that milk contract finally coming through sure helped." Still, Josie stared at him. With her hair in loose waves, faded jeans, sneakers and a russet cardigan over a white T-shirt, to him she'd never looked more beautiful. "We're a good team. The best." The sun shone off her hair and between it and her clothes, she seemed to be a part of the vibrant autumn landscape.

A part of him, too, now and always. Heath dropped to one knee and took a jewelry box from his jacket pocket. "You said fall's your favorite season so I wanted to ask you here in this special place we both love. You helped me love again and you make me my best self. Will you marry me?" He opened the box.

Her mouth opened and closed as she stared at the ring, a ruby nestled between two diamonds in a rose-gold setting. "Of course I'll marry you."

"I love you so much, Josie, and I can't wait for us to spend the rest of our lives together." He slipped the ring on the fourth finger of her left hand. After talking to Grams, Heath had made sure this engagement ring was nothing like the one Josie had before. "Stella said you can come in first thing on Monday to get it sized to fit or if you don't like the ring we can—"

"It's perfect. I love it almost as much as I love you." Her eyes shone. "Let's get married as soon as we can."

"I want my mom and sister and her family here, but apart from that, yes, let's choose a date." Heath drew Josie close for a kiss.

Clapping and cheers broke out and then Bella, Lottie and Cookie joined their embrace, followed more slowly by Martha and Tom and Buster and Honey.

"What... We had an audience?" Josie put a hand to her rosy face.

"They weren't close enough to hear what I said," Heath reassured her. "But the girls and your grandparents already gave me their blessing to ask you and the four of you are kind of a package deal."

"'Cause we're a family." Lottie inserted herself between them.

"I told him you like rubies," Bella said.

"Girls." Martha gestured to her granddaughters.

"It's fine." Heath wrapped his free arm around Bella and Lottie. "I also wanted you all here because…" He glanced at Tom, who nodded. "Tabby Cat Hollow isn't big enough for all of us, but with the work I'm having done it'll be a cozy and comfortable home come winter. After Josie and I get married, what would you say about me moving into Snow Moon Hill and Tom and Martha live here at my place?"

"What a wonderful idea." Martha's pleasure was obvious. "We'd be nearby but you and Josie would have your own space and… What do you say, Tom?"

"Who do you think suggested the idea to Heath in the first place?" Tom's weathered face creased into a fond smile. "I think it sounds fine. The newlyweds need a home of their own and I'm thinking we do, too." He gave his wife a flirtatious look.

"Oh, Tom." Martha laughed and slipped her arm through his.

"Smile, everyone!"

"What?" Heath whirled around to find Fred Sinclair, the newspaper editor, holding a camera. "You're supposed to be at the house with everyone else. We don't want to be in the newspaper."

"You won't be but Cookie sure will." He bent to pat the dog, who'd run over to greet him. "She's the grand prize winner of the Pond Pets 'Fall into Fall' photo contest."

"How? I didn't enter a photo of her." With everything going on, he'd forgotten and the entry deadline had passed. Heath glanced between Josie and her family, who looked as mystified as he must.

"Anne Sullivan did." Fred adjusted something on his camera. "It was also Anne who sent me down here from the house. She figured you must've popped the question by now and although the champagne's chilling for the party, with the trees and afternoon light you've got a perfect backdrop for engagement photos. One of the happy couple alone to start and then with the family? Have to get the horses and dogs in, too."

"Sure, Fred." Josie's voice shook with laughter and she hugged Heath again. "What's this about a party?"

"I crashed the Strawberry Festival back in June and everyone was part of our first meeting, so it makes sense they're here to celebrate with us. I invited our friends and neighbors. I hope you don't mind?"

"Not at all, it's amazing and wonderful and..." She glanced back at the bench. "Later, let's slip away and watch the sunset out here, just the two of us."

Apart from when Josie had said she'd marry him, that was the best idea Heath had heard all day.

And he looked forward to sharing a lifetime of sunsets, sunrises and everything in between with her...and their family to love and cherish.

* * * * *

For more charming small-town romances from Jen Gilroy and Harlequin Heartwarming, visit www.Harlequin.com today!

Get up to 4 Free Books!

We'll send you 2 free books from each series you try PLUS a free Mystery Gift.

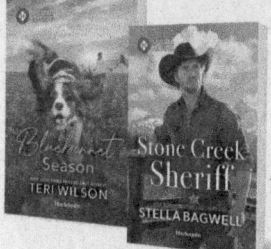

FREE Value Over $25

Both the **Harlequin® Special Edition** and **Harlequin® Heartwarming™** series feature compelling novels filled with stories of love and strength where the bonds of friendship, family and community unite.

YES! Please send me 2 FREE novels from the Harlequin Special Edition or Harlequin Heartwarming series and my FREE Gift (gift is worth about $10 retail). After receiving them, if I don't wish to receive any more books, I can return the shipping statement marked "cancel." If I don't cancel, I will receive 6 brand-new Harlequin Special Edition books every month and be billed just $6.39 each in the U.S. or $7.19 each in Canada, or 4 brand-new Harlequin Heartwarming Larger-Print books every month and be billed just $7.19 each in the U.S. or $7.99 each in Canada, a savings of 20% off the cover price. It's quite a bargain! Shipping and handling is just 50¢ per book in the U.S. and $1.25 per book in Canada.* I understand that accepting the 2 free books and gift places me under no obligation to buy anything. I can always return a shipment and cancel at any time by calling the number below. The free books and gift are mine to keep no matter what I decide.

Choose one: ☐ **Harlequin Special Edition** (235/335 BPA G36Y)   ☐ **Harlequin Heartwarming Larger-Print** (161/361 BPA G36Y)   ☐ **Or Try Both!** (235/335 & 161/361 BPA G36Z)

Name (please print)

Address   Apt. #

City   State/Province   Zip/Postal Code

Email: Please check this box ☐ if you would like to receive newsletters and promotional emails from Harlequin Enterprises ULC and its affiliates. You can unsubscribe anytime.

Mail to the Harlequin Reader Service:
IN U.S.A.: P.O. Box 1341, Buffalo, NY 14240-8531
IN CANADA: P.O. Box 603, Fort Erie, Ontario L2A 5X3

Want to explore our other series or interested in ebooks? Visit www.ReaderService.com or call 1-800-873-8635.

---

*Terms and prices subject to change without notice. Prices do not include sales taxes, which will be charged (if applicable) based on your state or country of residence. Canadian residents will be charged applicable taxes. Offer not valid in Quebec. This offer is limited to one order per household. Books received may not be as shown. Not valid for current subscribers to the Harlequin Special Edition or Harlequin Heartwarming series. All orders subject to approval. Credit or debit balances in a customer's account(s) may be offset by any other outstanding balance owed by or to the customer. Please allow 4 to 6 weeks for delivery. Offer available while quantities last.

Your Privacy—Your information is being collected by Harlequin Enterprises ULC, operating as Harlequin Reader Service. For a complete summary of the information we collect, how we use this information and to whom it is disclosed, please visit our privacy notice located at https://corporate.harlequin.com/privacy-notice. Notice to California Residents – Under California law, you have specific rights to control and access your data. For more information on these rights and how to exercise them, visit https://corporate.harlequin.com/california-privacy. For additional information for residents of other U.S. states that provide their residents with certain rights with respect to personal data, visit https://corporate.harlequin.com/other-state-residents-privacy-rights/.

HSEHW25